HITCHHIKING THROUGH FIRE

BRENT MCKNIGHT

www.aurelialeo.com

McKnight, Brent
Hitchhiking Through Fire / by Brent McKnight 1st. ed.

ISBN-13: 978-1-946024-61-9
Library of Congress Control Number: 2019938225

Editing by Lesley Sabga
Cover design by Bukovero
Book design by Inkstain Design Studio

Printed in the United States of America
First Edition:
10 9 8 7 6 5 4 3 2 1

To Melissa and the Small Dogs for putting up with my stream of continuous nonsense.

CHAPTER 1

The landscape is desolate, nothing but sand and scrub and the crumbling remains of an interstate highway stretching into the horizon. There's no green. All that lingers is a mute collection of browns and yellows. A merciless wind whips grains of sand with a sound like a woman screaming.

The decaying band of asphalt runs over the dunes, directly into the city that spreads out in a shallow valley. To the south, a band of cliffs runs parallel to the highway. A high wall, cobbled together out of whatever materials were handy, contains the miniature metropolis on all sides. Large rocks, rudimentary concrete work, and mud bricks make up the majority of the barrier, but there are boards, remnants of fences, stacks of cracked black tires, anything the inhabitants could find and put to use. An overturned charter bus forms part of the barricade. The continual blast of sand and the elements has worn off the paint of the logo, and a thick crust of dirt coats the windows. The city has a single secure entrance. Armed guards roam the top of the wall between evenly spaced medieval parapets, a watchful eye always on their surroundings.

A series of makeshift windmills of various sizes and constructions line the rim of the valley. The blades turn in the wind. Pipes snake along the ground and run into the wall of the city. Everything but these conduits has been cleared away from the grounds. Nothing else even casts a shadow. There is no place to hide, and nothing to conceal an approach. Near the wall, a rough wooden sign protrudes from the sand. Two human skulls dangle from the corner. Shreds of scalp, skin, and hair cling to the bone and sway in the wind. The sign reads "REQUIEM," the single word hand-painted in what may be blood turned black from time and exposure. More recently, someone crossed out the name and wrote, "The Turd," below.

Movement fills the streets. While the valley and the walls afford some respite from the winds, the stench of filth and sweat and garbage hangs over the city. The smell is that of too many people living in too small a space, of civilization compressed. Inside of the wall is the polar opposite of other side. A crush of humanity replaces isolated dereliction.

The people of Requiem reflect the city. Smudged and dirty and pieced together. Most dress in a similar manner; grimy patchwork clothes held together with coarse threads and squares of scavenged material. Within the walls they are safe from the winds, but many still wear goggles or glasses, pushed up onto their foreheads or hanging around their necks, and scarves to wrap around their faces should the need arise.

Like the landscape, the citizens are beaten and blanched by the elements. Many miss teeth and none of the men are clean-shaven. Their faces wear deep worn grooves, etched by the rivulets of time and worry, and they pace their confines endlessly, like caged animals on the edge of madness. Men and women alike, everyone carries a weapon. Some lug homemade shanks and crossbows. Others have rifles slung on their shoulders or pistols on their hips. A few even carry gleaming swords or rusty blades.

Near the gate, a group of taverns sells makeshift hooch. Stills smolder in the back of these businesses, churning out black trails of smoke that drift upward and dissipate. Pickpockets weave in and out of the crowd and ply their trade. Figures move behind curtained windows, engaging in illicit acts of all varieties. Any vice can be indulged. A collection of stalls, shacks, and booths form a marketplace and bazaar nearby where it's possible to barter, trade, and buy everything from foodstuffs to mechanical items to piles of unkempt clothes. Vendors hawk their wares in loud, barking voices.

Moving away from the front, rough buildings line a sprawling maze of narrow, haphazard streets. Stones fit together like a mismatched puzzle form a pavement on some, but most are simply dirt, tamped down and compacted by thousands upon thousands of aimless footsteps. There's no coherent logic to the avenues, and they shoot off from each other at odd angles or meander in long arcs. Built one on top of the other, new layers added as necessary, on the more claustrophobic streets the buildings curl over like a closing hand until there's only a splinter of sky visible.

While debauchery clearly reigns, some citizens attempt to maintain a semblance of what once constituted a normalcy, trying to remember what life was like before. Their lives form a perverse reenactment of their fading recollections of what ordinary meant. These people exist day-to-day as best as they can. They don't necessarily like the place they live, but options are few and far between, and Requiem provides a level of safety that's at a premium. Living in the belly of the beast and simply being able to live is better than the alternative.

At the center of town stands the largest structure in Requiem. A fortress of its own, with guards roaming the grounds, it sits apart from the rest of the buildings, taller than any other. An invisible hand pinched the center of town between the thumb and forefinger and drew the point to the sky. The position affords a full 360-degree view. At the apex, a man with a long-barreled rifle sits and watches with binoculars. His thick, knotted hair is tied back, a broad diagonal slash cuts across his face, and distorted black tattoos; rows of small circles, line his jaw.

Requiem is a dirge, a funeral song; a lamentation for all that humanity was, and all that still is; a celebration of the base, the ugly, and the brutal; of all that is left and the scraps that remain.

Huxley sits in the corner of a windowless tavern with his father. He is nine years old. The uneven table rocks back and forth any time either of them touches it. Two sets of dirty dishes clink as it shakes. Huxley picks at a splinter in his finger picked up from the unsanded wood, frustrated that he can see it but not get it out. He sticks his finger in his mouth and chews on the wound, tasting the dirt in the crevices of his fingerprints. In a low voice, his father tries to entertain the boy with a story. He leans toward his son, face animated, and his hands and fingers fly about, punctuating the tale. It's a story about trees and grass and animals, about things called birds, about things Huxley has never seen or experienced, about how things were before he existed. His father smiles despite the severe mood that surrounds them; the lone bastion of happiness in this otherwise miserable waste.

Huxley only half-listens. He's heard all of his father's stories many times and finds them boring. Instead of paying attention, he busies himself examining the rest of the room. Small settlements, improvised farms, isolated outposts, and the like are one thing, but he's never been anywhere that compares to Requiem. Never has he seen this many people at once, and he intends to take full advantage and explore as much as he can.

Light from improvised lamps and candles casts deep shadows over the clientele. Sun from outside throws bars of light through gaps in the wall. A woman with leathery brown skin shuffles behind the crude bar, moving back and forth in front of a collection of unlabeled brown and green glass bottles. A lone bearded man sits at the bar, hunched over a drink and a plate of food, a colorless, paste-like substance. Three men occupy a table in the middle of the room. Among these four men are approximately thirty teeth. Curious, Huxley watches everyone he can and wishes his father would be quiet and leave him to observe in peace.

A single, recessed alcove cuts into one wall. Instead of chairs, built-in benches line either side of the cracked laminate table. Two men converse in a whisper. One has a wide-brimmed hat and a long gray coat with a baggy hood. He leans forward. Huxley can only make out the outline of his profile.

Most of the boy's attention, however, falls on the other man in the booth, clad in crude black denim, held together as if by sheer will and grit. A raw wool scarf winds around his neck up to his jaw. Dark wraparound goggles, the lenses smudged and dirty, sit on the table in front of him. Obscured by a drab, colorless poncho, his arms hang at his side. A pack sits on the floor next to him, a ring of sand around the base. A bottle of water dangles from a strap on one side, a machete, caked with some sort of crusty blackened viscera, hangs on the other.

His cheeks are creased and chapped, burned by the wind and sun, and stubble that is not quite a beard rules his chin; his nose has obviously been broken and poorly reset along the way; his eyes are black, sharp, and unforgiving.

Huxley has seen all of this before. He has seen many hard men in the short span of his life, but the man's teeth capture the boy's attention. Straight and white and, as far as he can see, all in their proper place. This is a rarity, and he can't take his eyes off the stranger. An air of menace hovers over the man. His father notices the staring and nudges the boy with his foot.

"It's not polite," he says with a warning smile before he continues his story.

Huxley steals glances at the man when his father, more caught up in the tale than the boy has ever been, isn't looking.

Huxley strains to pick up bits of their conversation. All he gleans is the man's name: Bracken.

The man across from him stands up, upset, and reaches into his jacket. Bracken shakes his head then gestures downward with his eyes. The barrel of a sawed-off shotgun protrudes from his poncho. He taps the cold steel twice on the underside of the table, unconcerned that an entire bar surrounds him.

"Sit down," Bracken mouths.

None of the other patrons, attention focused on their own business, pay the situation any mind. They're not involved and they don't care to be. It's safer that way.

Bracken's companion returns to his seat, both hands flat on the tabletop, and the shotgun retreats back beneath the poncho. The whole scene settles as if nothing happened. No one noticed except for Huxley, who continues to stare. His father rambles on, uninterrupted.

Bracken finally realizes he has an audience and winks at the young boy. Caught, and unsure how to react, Huxley jumps in his seat.

"I know," his father says, nodding his head, thinking the boy responded to his words. "It does sound magical, doesn't it? But believe it or not, that is how the world used to be." He raises his right hand. "I swear."

Finished with their meal, Huxley and his father emerge from the dim interior of the tavern into the blinding mid-afternoon sun and make their way to the bazaar. The father is a tall man when standing, rail-thin beneath bulky clothes that dangle off of his frame like a wire hanger.

Lines of people stream past as the boy watches his father haggle and negotiate with a vendor for lengths of pipe, a blade for a chisel plow, and a handful of other items. The two had left the small encampment where they lived for some time, how long, Huxley was unsure. It was the latest in a line of such temporary homes, which never lasted. But his father found a place to settle, where he believes he can sink a well and where he believes crops will grow. Huxley has seen this before and remains skeptical, though he says nothing as his father lays in supplies for his latest project.

Huxley's attention wanes and he looks up at his father. The bartering engrosses the older man and Huxley wanders away from his side unnoticed; walking among the surrounding booths, taking in the sights, caught up in the current of people, drinking in as many of the sights as he can during their short stay.

A man in the crowd pays Huxley more attention than he's comfortable with. His sneer exposes thick brown teeth and his fingernails are cracked and uneven, like he chewed them. Huxley catches the man staring at him from a distance as he moves from booth to booth examining the suspicious food, piles of rags that they call clothes, and even small weapons for sale. Smells assault his nose, charred flesh, human sweat, and bodily functions he prefers not to think about.

Bracken also roams the market, striding with purpose from place to place. Huxley spies him periodically through the press of bodies, the man somehow apart from the rabble. He follows in Bracken's wake for a time, drifting along behind the stranger. Something about his face and carriage intrigues the boy. Bracken seems like someone who has stories to tell, but exciting ones, not the same bland tales Huxley's father repeats over and over again.

Huxley keeps an eye out for his unwanted admirer, but after a few moments it appears the man has lost interest and moved on to other pursuits. Nowhere to be seen, Huxley turns his awareness to other things, pushing thoughts of the man to the back of his mind.

Before long, Huxley realizes he's lost. This is a different part of the market, and in his aimless drifting he doesn't know where his father is. A moment of dread sets in and his stomach drops. He decides he can find his way back; he only has to retrace his steps, and turns to do so.

The man with the wretched teeth steps out from a dark alley and blocks Huxley's path. He grabs the boy and pulls him between two buildings before the child can react, clamping a hand over his mouth before he can scream.

"You're coming with me," the man says in a raspy voice. His clothes are rags and his voice is a menace. Huxley struggles against his grip, unable to tear free. He panics and writhes harder, kicking and throwing his small fists. A grunt accompanies every blow.

"Struggle all you want, boy, that just makes it worse for you, better for me." The man leers, exposing the full extent of his fetid smile, pressing his face close to Huxley's. Breath hot and rancid with sour meat, large black gaps fill in the space between the leftover remains of his teeth. He drags Huxley toward a low doorway. The boy kicks at the man's shins and bites at his hand.

"Hey now," the man laughs. He slaps Huxley across the face so hard his vision blurs. Tears well up, but he won't let himself cry, he won't.

With one foot through the door the man's smile withers as he hears a click and the barrel of a shotgun presses against his temple.

"Hey, Bracken," he says, releasing the boy and stepping back, his hands up in concession. "Friend of yours? Didn't mean anything by it. Just having a little fun with the kid is all." He tries to chuckle but it comes out like a croak. "Promise." He motions at the pack slung on Bracken's shoulders, wearing a nervous smile. "Going somewhere?"

Bracken says nothing, levels the gun at the frightened man's face, and shoos him away with a gesture. The thought occurs to Huxley that Bracken enjoys this sort of thing and the boy can't help but smile.

"Get out of here," Huxley says, sounding as menacing as possible.

"Okay, okay." The man turns and scuttles back into the shadows, disappearing into a doorway like an insect.

Bracken looks down at Huxley. Shaken but trying to hide it, he wipes the tears out of his eyes and terror off of his face, and sets his jaw, meeting Bracken's eyes with his best attempt at a defiant look.

Bracken smiles. His teeth clean and even. "That's the second time I've had to point this at someone today," he says says, slipping the shotgun beneath his poncho. "Come on, little dude." He turns and walks away.

"Where are we going?" Huxley asks, trying not to let his voice quiver.

Bracken pauses and looks back over his shoulder. "That's the type of thing you should have thought of before you started mixing with these ruffians."

Huxley nods and follows.

Bracken leads the way through the crowd, weaving among the people, and stops directly behind Huxley's father. He stands at the taller man's left shoulder with his hands clasped in front of him, patient. Huxley stares up, not even pretending to hide his awe. Bracken puts a fist to his mouth and clears his throat. Huxley's father, startled, spins around. When he sees who it is, he freezes and begins to stammer.

Bracken cuts him off and nods at the child. "I think you lost something."

"Oh, thank you," Huxley's father stutters. He lets out an uneasy laugh. "I didn't even notice he was gone. You need to stay close, Hux."

"Keep a closer eye on this one, he's curious about things. This isn't the safest place you'll ever come across."

"I know, I know, he's always wandering off." Bracken's presence makes him uncomfortable, and he talks in a rapid stream. "This isn't the kind of place we usually frequent, not the kind of place I would usually bring him, anyway." He pulls Huxley close. "Not that this is a horrible place, it's just a little rough around the edges. I'm sure it has a certain charm, I mean, we're trying to farm, trying to pump up water, it isn't easy, we needed some supplies, necessity dictates and all. Can't really leave him alone while I'm gone, even though we're pretty well isolated. We have a little place out north and east a ways, found what I think is a fertile stretch of land. Sheltered from the worst of the wind so the soil is still pretty good. Not many people out that far, off the high traffic routes, fewer people usually means less infected wandering around."

"Usually," Bracken says.

The father opens his mouth to continue spewing words but Bracken stops him, shaking his head. "I don't really care, man."

The vendor laughs.

"What?" Bracken growls to the grubby merchant. The dusty vendor pretends to have a coughing fit and turns away from them, his back heaving with the subterfuge. "Jackass."

Bracken gives a short nod to the boy then turns back to the father. "Just pay a little more attention next time. It'll serve you well." He turns and walks down the crowded street.

"Thank you," Huxley's father yells after him. "Thanks again."

As Bracken fades into the surrounding crowds he raises his left hand in acknowledgement of the father's words. Huxley watches after him until his is no longer distinguishable from the rest of the throng.

"You know better than that, Hux," his father says. "You can't just go running off with strangers, especially not here."

"Sorry," the boy says absently, staring at the last place he saw Bracken, kicking at the dirt beneath his oversized boots.

"Hey, what happened to your face? It's all red." He cocks his head. "Is that a handprint?"

The gates of Requiem swing inward with a grinding shriek. Those within earshot cringe for a moment; some even shiver with the sound before continuing with their business as if nothing happened. Part of the routine landscape, the sound only catches their attention in a temporary way.

Huxley and his father wait for the door to open all the way. Their vehicle is similar to a large tricycle. Homemade, metal tubes fuse together with rudimentary welds. The father sits in front, in a recumbent position, with his raised hands resting on a wide set pair of handlebars, his feet waiting on the pedals. An intricate mesh of gears connects to the underside of the contraption. Huxley sits in the back, a large square bed, fenced in on all sides by a low wall of cobbled-together lumber. He rests amidst an accumulation of mechanical parts, a large coil of dirty orange plastic piping, a few pieces of wood, and half a dozen bulging burlap sacks.

The boy rocks with the motion as his father pedals forward into a sort of airlock. Rifles protrude from slits cut in the wall, fortified positions. When they're all the way in, the door swings shut behind them. For a moment darkness swallows them. They take the brief opportunity to wrap their scarves around their noses and mouths, and to pull their goggles over their eyes.

"Any hotspots we should avoid?" Huxley's father asks the dark. "Any sightings?"

"No reports recently," a disembodied voice replies. The words echo. "Seems pretty clear lately." His father nods a wordless reply.

Another set of doors cracks open ahead of them, spilling in sunlight. Beyond the entrance the remains of the highway stretch into the blanched emptiness. Heat from the baking waste rises from the surface of the road as it snakes through the landscape. It shimmers like a dream.

They move forward along the concrete pathway. Huxley twists, watching the doors close after them, and the city recedes into the distance. A constant spray of sand whips across the asphalt like a snowstorm. It gets in Huxley's hair and stings his forehead, the only exposed skin on his body.

"Why don't you put on your hat?" his father hollers over his shoulder. The boy shakes his head, enjoying the feel of the wind on his scalp.

Once the city disappears in their wake, the view is the same in the front and the back. Road and sand and the occasional wrecked hull of a building. Boards and signs and skeletal frames protrude from the sand like the bones of long dead creatures that succumbed to the elements. Gradually, the desert reclaims the world.

They don't see another soul.

When the sun sets, they pull off of the road for the night. Leaving their conveyance near the side of the road--far enough that it will be difficult to see if anyone does pass by--they wander over a small rise searching for shelter from the wind. With the sun gone, the temperature drops to near freezing, and they set out to scavenge whatever scrap wood they can find to supplement the meager stockpile they have with them.

Wind lashes loose sand over them like sea foam spray. Huxley's father stacks the wood into a pyramid shape with dry bits of kindling in the middle, as sheltered from the wind as possible. On the seventh attempt it catches and the fire takes hold of the arid bits of lumber, climbing up the pile like something alive. He smiles at the boy, who huddles near the young flames. While the child warms his hands, his father unpacks a few supplies to make dinner.

Eating, the two sit as close to the fire as they can without burning themselves.

"Didn't I tell you to pay more attention?"

Huxley snaps around toward the source of the voice. His father does the same, and frantically unbuttons his jacket to reach for the revolver he has inside.

"Don't bother with that." At the edge of visibility, the light of the flames dance over the form of a man; heavy boots, denim pants, a rough poncho, a large pack, and the barrel of a shotgun.

"Why does no one ever listen to me?" he says and shrugs.

Huxley and his father gawk at Bracken as he walks past, muttering, and sits down on the opposite side of the fire. Huxley stares. Bracken stares back.

"You?" the father says.

"Imagine my surprise," Brackens says, nodding his head.

"What are you doing here?" Huxley asks. His father shoots him a look that tells the boy he shouldn't ask some questions.

Bracken lets out a low chuckle. "My rig broke down a ways off. The rope on my sail snapped."

"You use the wind?"

"There's a lot of it to use if you know how to put it to work for you."

"Where are you going?" Huxley asks. Again, his curiosity generates a look of disapproval from his father.

Bracken ignores the question. "If you have any lengths of rope you could part with, I'd be much obliged."

"We don't have much," the father says. "But I have some spare odds and ends in the cart. If any of them will be a help, you're more than welcome."

"Thank you." Bracken nods. "I appreciate it."

His father stands, "Hux, you stay here." The two men shake the sand off of themselves and walk in the direction of the road. Neither notices Huxley creeping behind them, eavesdropping. It's a cloudy night and Huxley has no problem keeping out of sight in the shadows.

"We're trying to farm over by . . ."

"You said that," Bracken says. He keeps his eyes trained on the dark, squinting to keep the sand out of them. "Just the two of you?"

"Yeah. That's why Huxley's with me, can't very well leave him alone while I run to town for supplies. I . . ."

"You shouldn't light a fire like that," Bracken says, interrupting. "It attracts them."

"I know I probably shouldn't," the father says. "But it seems like they keep pretty clear of this area. Close to the city it seems they sweep it pretty regular. And there isn't much to bring them around out this far."

"They aren't the only ugly things out here."

The father stops. "Did you see the fire? Is that how you found us?"

"I saw this," Bracken says, pointing at the bike.

"How did you see that? I thought it was hidden pretty well."

"Maybe I'm just that good," Bracken says. He almost smiles. Something bothers him and he scans the darkness, his hand under his poncho.

Huxley notices Bracken's attention shift and follows his eyes. He's not sure, but something is off.

"Dad," Huxley says behind them.

"I thought I told you to wait . . ." Before he can get out the words, "by the fire," a blur of motion smudges the darkness. From out of the shadows,

15

two humanoid forms move toward the child. Lurching and graceless, swift, but not entirely human. Huxley sees that even in the dark.

"Run," his father yells. He starts for them, intercepting the first figure. "No." In the spotty moonlight it looks like something that used to be a man. Tattered remnants of clothes cling to dark blue flesh, almost black with decay. Missing part of its scalp, the bare bone of the skull is dried and gritty from time in the desert. Random hunks of tissue are missing and maggots thrive in a cavity left by a bite. The creatures smell sweet with rot and are mostly naked.

Bracken draws his weapon, but Huxley and his father are in the way, between a clear shot and the attacking creatures.

The father grabs the first creature by the shoulder, his fingers digging into the tough, leathery skin. It spins, utters a guttural cry, and with rotten teeth sharpened to fine points, rips into his shoulder. He drops to the ground and takes the monster with him, grabbing its face, pushing the violent, snarling mouth away.

Huxley retreats as the second creature bears down. He loses his footing in the loose sand and falls onto his back. Crying out for his father, the boy kicks his legs in a frenzy in an involuntary, visceral reflex, an attempt to propel his small body across the dune and fend off his attacker in the same motion.

A fetid hand reaches for Huxley's leg. A snarl like a wild beast then a deafening burst as the creature's head splinters and its body jerks to the side. Bracken kicks the lifeless corpse once in the ribs for good measure and turns his attention to the creature on top of Huxley's father.

Huxley's father rolls to the side as Bracken boots the monster off of him and levels the double-barreled shotgun at its face. Smoke vomits out of the left chamber as the right spews thunder and fire. The creature, head exploded, falls backward to the sand, motionless.

An echo from the shotgun blast fades into the night and his father grunts and writhes in the sand making noises like an animal caught in a snare. Huxley runs to him and drops to his knees by his side. Bracken looms, replacing his expended shells and scanning the periphery.

"Dad, dad?" Tears stream down his face, cutting muddy swaths over his grubby cheeks.

"It'll be alright, son," his father says, trying to sit up. He shakes and convulses but sets his jaw and blinks back his own tears. Trying to sound comforting, he says, "It isn't much more than a flesh wound." Huxley's father's voice trembles despite his best efforts to control it. The words crack. "I can patch myself right up." He pulls the boy to him and kisses the top of his head. "It'll be okay."

Bracken snaps the barrel of his gun shut, steps forward, pushes the father back to the ground with one boot, and raises the barrel. His face is grim, prepared, resigned.

"Please don't kill me," Huxley's father says.

The frankness reality of the plea hits Franklin hard. It dawns on him this might be the last moment of his father's life. He wants to run and scream and cry and throw himself between the barrel of the gun and his injured father. But the weight anchors him in place. His feet won't move and his mouth opens, but no sound comes out. He feels sick and his eyes well over.

"You know as well as I do, you're already dead," Bracken says.

"Someone has to beat this. Someone has to be able to survive. No disease can kill everything it touches."

"Maybe," Bracken shakes his head. "But I've never seen it. And neither have you."

Huxley's father remains silent for a moment. His eyes search Bracken's face. Huxley wonders what he's looking for. "Take care of him," he says, meeting the cold gaze of the other man. "Please."

Bracken stands over the fallen man, gun trained on his face. Huxley watches, mouth open, unable to believe what he sees. Bracken makes motions like he's about to pull the trigger. He lurches forward a fraction of an inch and braces himself for the recoil. Huxley's father squeezes his eyes tight. Bracken's face wrinkles and creases. Furrows line his forehead.

One final time Bracken tries to pull the trigger. He can't. His eyes pull away.

"Fuck," he says under his breath as he turns and storms off. "I don't have time for this shit." He walks toward the vehicle.

Huxley clings to his father.

Loud enough for both of them to hear, Bracken yells, "Get your stuff. They hunt in packs. If there are any more of them around, we won't be alone for long."

Huxley's father nods at the boy. "You heard him. Go, grab our things." Huxley remains frozen in place, not wanting to leave his father. "Go, now. He's right. We need to hurry. I'll be fine, I promise." He kisses the top of his son's head and motions for the boy to get moving. "Go." He has to push the child to get him moving.

Huxley rushes back to their camp. His feet slip in the sand as he runs. He stuffs everything back into their single large backpack and slings it onto his shoulders. The weight almost topples him over backward and he pauses on the uneven ground to steady himself beneath the bulk of their possessions.

At that moment it occurs to him that he is alone and he scans the edge of the firelight for any movement.

Staring into the darkness before him, he tries not to think of what will happen to his father. He pushes all thoughts from his head, opting for movement over contemplation, kicks sand over what remains of the fire, and heads back toward their vehicle.

Bracken has already pushed the bicycle back onto the asphalt surface of the road and loaded Huxley's father into the back. The wounded man uses Bracken's pack to prop himself up. His body shudders and fear fills his eyes, but he smiles when he sees his son return. Huxley recognizes the forced expression.

Huxley throws the bag into the back and climbs in next to his father, pale, his face is drenched in sweat. Without a word Bracken climbs into the front seat, puts his feet on the pedals and pushes. The gears slip through the chain, once then twice.

"You have to . . ." Huxley's father motions with one hand, and leans forward. Bracken stops and turns his head halfway around.

"Never mind," the father says, waving his hand and leaning back again. He presses a rag against his wound.

Bracken fidgets with the shifters on the handlebars and in a few moments they're underway. It's slow going in the darkness but at least they move. Huxley and his father huddle together in the back, lit a vague blue in the moonlight that pokes through the clouds. His father's heart beats weak and shallow and every bump in the road causes him to grimace. He steals quick glances at his father's face, it's a set and stern as he's ever seen and that makes him afraid.

"If you have any blankets," Bracken says without turning around. His labored breaths form clouds and hang in the air. "You should wrap him up. Keep him as warm as possible. Lay him on his back and prop his feet up on one of the bags."

Huxley nods as if Bracken can see his response, digs in the bag for their blankets, and tucks them around his father. They continue forward in silence, gently rocking. Huxley leans against his father, adrenalin subsiding, and nods off.

It's light when Huxley wakes up. He lays in the bed of their vehicle, wrapped in a blanket, his hands tucked under his head as a substitute for a pillow. The rough wool scratches his cheeks and the back of his neck. He sits up like a shot and, still delirious from sleep, frantically scans for his father and Bracken.

They sit a few feet away. Bracken squats over a shallow hole filled with a small fire. He maneuvers a pan over the flames. Huxley's father huddles with a blanket over his shoulders and stares into the flames with empty eyes. When he notices Huxley's awake he gives his son a weak smile. His pale skin looks like candle wax in the sunlight. He has his shirt off under the blanket and Huxley sees all of his ribs, a sparse collection of dark hair on his belly, and a bandage taped to his shoulder.

The boy climbs out of the bed and drops to the sand.

"Morning," he says to Bracken.

"It certainly is," Bracken says, without looking up. Something sizzles in the pan.

Huxley sits by his father and leans on him. The older man puts his arm around his son. The motion takes quite a bit of effort; his muscles are stiff and movement is painful. He grimaces with the effort. From beneath the bandage, deep blue fingers spread out, reaching across his body. Rearranging the fabric of the blanket, he hides the tendrils. Huxley tries not to stare, tries not to cry.

They sit on a high patch of ground. The wind is severe but their perch affords them a full view of their surroundings. Huxley doesn't see the road anywhere. Every few minutes Bracken stands up and makes a thorough scan of the desert around them. Every few minutes Bracken stares hard at Huxley's father. Huxley stares back.

Huxley's father reaches into the pocket on the leg of his pants, removes a small pair of black binoculars, and hands them to the boy.

"Here," he says. "If you want to have a look around."

Huxley stays silent, unable to figure out what to say. All of the words that occur to him are pointless. He wants to ask his father if he is going to die, he wants to beg and plead with him not to leave him alone. He wants to ask Bracken things, but can't think of what questions to ask. Nothing he can say will change anything and the words all shrivel and die in his mind long before his tongue can begin to form them.

Silent, he takes the binoculars and puts them up to his eyes, adjusts the focus, and looks over the arid landscape. The countryside is neither familiar or unfamiliar to him. It could be anywhere he has ever seen in his short life; it could very well be any place he has ever been. The whole world is sun bleached and empty. Nothing moves. Nothing lives. Despite a few long rolls in the earth, the land is flat.

Bracken hands Huxley the pan, the handle wrapped in a scrap of fabric. "Eat." He doesn't extend the offer to his father, and his father doesn't ask.

While Huxley chews and swallows, his father leans over and heaves three times into the sand. He quickly covers it, though Huxley notices a deep crimson mixed in with the bile that makes him nervous.

"Sorry about that," he says. He leans down and puts his forehead against Huxley's. It's so hot it's almost painful to touch. Huxley feels a slight vibration running through his father, a low-level tremor. His father closes his eyes and pulls the blanket tight around his shoulders.

Even with his father fading and flickering, Huxley can't help but stare at Bracken. In the harsh, brilliant sunlight, his face somehow seems shadowed and heavy. The way he watches Huxley's father, the way he methodically inspects the surrounding terrain, he looks like a man who needs to be on the move, who has someplace he needs to be.

"Your eyes," Bracken says. His head is down, bent over filling in the hole from the fire, and he looks up through his eyebrows. "Your eyes are bloodshot."

Huxley's father coughs into his fist and spits to one side. "It's moving fast, isn't it?"

Bracken nods. "Can you move? I need to be on my way."

"I don't know. Hey Hux, could you go get me my coat? It's sitting on top of our bag."

Huxley gets up and retrieves his father's jacket. Thick and heavy, an extra weight swings in the breast pocket. Bracken and Huxley's father talk while he's away, their lips move, but can't make out the words. They don't notice when he's back in earshot. Their voices remain flat and calm, like they're talking about mundane trivia, and Huxley knows their words are a mere formality.

"Someone has to live through this," his father says. His words carry a plea.

"Maybe," Bracken nods. He stares into the distance. "Maybe. But we both know it isn't going to be you. You're already close to the final stages." Bracken looks at Huxley and chucks his chin.

"Thanks, Hux," his father says, taking the jacket from the boy. He lets the blanket slide off of his shoulders onto the sand. All of his skin is a pale shade of blue, darker the closer it gets to the wound. Labored breaths rattle deep in his chest and the whites of his eyes are red where the blood vessels have burst. It's the worst thing Huxley has ever seen.

"You know what needs to be done," Bracken says. He stands and walks away, making a show of searching the empty landscape for any threats.

"Hey, buddy," he says. "I suppose you know I'm not doing so hot, huh?" Huxley nods. "I don't know how much longer I have."

"Your eyes?" Huxley points at his father's face, a tear of blood leaks from the corner of his eye. He wipes his cheek and sees the stains on his fingertips. He stares at them like he can't believe what he sees, coughs weakly three times, and though it's barely more than a light exhale, he laughs once.

Bracken comes over. Silent, eyebrows arched in a question.

Huxley's father nods. Careful not to get any blood on his son, he kisses Huxley on the forehead. "I love you, Hux, don't ever forget that."

Huxley can only stare.

"I need you to go over there," he says, pointing toward the vehicle.

Huxley begins to head toward where he is instructed, but stops. He turns to watch. Neither of the men seem to notice him.

Huxley's father reaches into his jacket and pulls out his silver revolver. His breathing is heavy now, his shoulders and chest heave with each breath as he stares at the gun in his hand and tries not to sob. He pulls back the hammer, crushes his eyes closed, and puts the barrel up to his temple. A grimace tears at his face and he clenches his jaw, grinding his teeth. He pulls the gun away from his head and vomits into the sand. Quickly he puts gun under his chin and contorts his face. The silver handgun quivers below his jaw, the barrel pressed hard into the flesh.

He opens his eyes, tosses the gun on the ground, and looks at it glinting in the sunlight.

"I can't, I can't, I can't," he says under his breath. He looks up at Bracken and shakes his head. "I can't. I just can't. Help me. Please."

Bracken steps forward and raises his shotgun. He hesitates for a split second.

"Thank you."

Bracken pulls the trigger and his gun spews thunder and fire. He looks at the body, his expression unchanged. He picks up the revolver and walks past Huxley. He stops, steps back, and puts the gun in Huxley's hands without looking at him. "This is yours now. Be careful with it," he says, and walks away.

"You," the boy stammers. "You killed him."

Bracken stops. "He wouldn't have been your father much longer. In a few hours he would have killed you." He walks over to the vehicle and roots around in his bag.

Huxley kneels beside the bloody mess. His eyes burn, but no tears come. He stands silent. Shock takes over for the time being and pushes grief to the side. Grains of sand cling to the sticky red bits of meat and to the ashen lumps of brain. Blood soaks into the sand. The wind screams its hollow scream over the top of the boy.

He is alone. Truly, utterly alone.

He doesn't remember his mother. She died when he was too young to know her. Whenever he asked about her, her life, how she died, his father got a far-away look in his eyes as if he was watching something Huxley couldn't see, and changed the subject in his jovial way.

They never stayed in one place or with other people for long. When they did, Huxley's father kept them mostly to themselves, leaving when things looked like they were going bad, both with people and infected. It was people more often than monsters.

Even if there is someone out there waiting for him, who might take him in, Huxley has no idea where they are or how to find them.

He stares at the corpse with a blank expression on his face, trying to connect the lifeless body to his father, but he can't. The two things are separate, distinct.

Bracken returns with a small olive-green shovel. He kneels next to the body and digs a shallow grave in the sand. Huxley watches the hole grow deeper and deeper with each scoop. When Bracken finishes a sheen of sweat covers his face and he looks at Huxley.

"You need to say your good-byes and we need to get moving."

Huxley says nothing. Bracken's words are muffled and come from far away and Huxley can only think he's dreaming as the world around him melts and warps and blurs.

Bracken slides the body into the grave and quickly covers it with sand and dirt. He stands and brushes himself off. Huxley stares at the mound, at the remaining globs of blood sticking to the sand in clumps.

"There was nothing else we could have done," Bracken says. "He knew that." He walks back to the bicycle, stows his shovel, and stands with one hand on the bed. "We need to move. We've been here too long as it is. I need to be someplace and I've wasted enough of my time on you people already."

Huxley remains frozen in place.

"Come on, kid, let's get a move on."

He sighs.

"Fine," he yells. "I don't need this. You want to stay out here and die along with him, be my guest. Have a nice life, kid."

Bracken climbs into the front seat, adjusts himself, and pedals forward. Less than a hundred meters away he stops. It looks like he's arguing with himself.

Something snaps to life inside of Huxley and he moves. He stands, tucks the revolver into the inside of his jacket, and runs across the sand. Struggling to keep his balance, he falls twice. When he reaches Bracken, he climbs into the back. Bracken starts to pedal even before Huxley sits down. Huxley's knees give out and he drops down onto his backside, breathing heavy from the sprint.

Wind sweeps the sun-scorched earth. The bumper of an automobile protrudes from the dirt. It's as if a lingering echo pursues Bracken across the dunes.

The boy only knows that he now has nowhere else to go, nothing to go back to.

CHAPTER 2

Huxley rides in the back of the cart as they cruise over the desert floor. He wraps his face in his scarf, puts his goggles over his eyes, and turns inward. The monotonous landscape slips past and he's unsure if they travel north or south or east or west. Direction means little at this point; in fact, he keeps his eyes closed most of the time.

The feel of the ground beneath them isn't asphalt. He can tell the difference. They're not on a road. This much he does know.

Bracken continues on like a man possessed. His legs push the pedals that turn the gears that power the wheels. Neither traveler utters a syllable. Huxley only hears the wind whipping past his ears, the churn of wheels, and the crunch of tires over the dirt.

He stares blankly at Bracken's feet as they propel them forward as the day crept into evening and night. Only once did his father let Huxley try to pedal. On a bright, cool afternoon they stopped to eat and Huxley pleaded with his father to let him drive for a while, as he called it. This always made his father smile, though Huxley never knew why.

After much consideration, his father nodded and said, "Why not?" with a shrug.

Huxley leaped up from where he sat cross-legged on the ground and ran to the front seat, giggling the whole way. Standing with his hands tucked into his pockets and a curious look on his face, his father watched as Huxley hoisted his small body into the seat.

When he leaned against the cracked synthetic leather, liberated from the ruins of a car, his legs stuck straight out, and it was his father's turn to laugh. Huxley gave him a mock glare, then scooted forward until his legs bent over the edge. Reaching up, he grasped the handlebars, one end in each hand, but even stretching he couldn't touch the pedals with his feet. He looked at his father for help.

His father shook his head, crossed his arms, and said, "You can figure it out for yourself, I believe in you."

Huxley turned back to his problem and with a stroke of inspiration, inched forward until he teetered on the edge of the seat. He kicked his legs once, then twice, and the third time, making sure he kept a firm grip on the handlebars, he thrust the lower part of his body forward off of the seat and reached out with his toes.

The soles of his shoes made solid contact with pedals and between that and his hold on the handlebars, he supported himself. He cast another quick look at his father and pressed all of his weight into the top pedal. With the pressure the crank lurched forward and the front wheel spun free in the dirt.

The jump caught Huxley off guard and he almost let go. Steadying himself, he tried again, deliberate and with an even amount of force. Again, the wheel spun, but after skidding for a second it caught and the vehicle crept forward.

Huxley kicked again and again, lurching forward a few feet at a time. Once in motion, it was easier to continue and each stroke moved him farther and farther with less and less effort. He tried to turn, but was only able to skew the path a few degrees to the left. His father walked alongside as Huxley pedaled.

After a short while, the boy's arms began to burn. He lowered himself, let go of the handlebars, and rested his shoulders against the edge of the seat behind him, keeping his feet on the pedals. The corner bit into his back, but the discomfort was mild. The effort made him breathe hard and he looked up at his father standing next to him, gazing down on him with a smile.

"Hey, Kid," Bracken says over his shoulder.

Huxley remains silent, still thinking of his father's approving smile.

"Come on, kid." Bracken tries again. "Talk to me. Say something. I'm going to take care of you. Promise." He waits a moment. "You're not going to go all mental on me, are you?"

Finally Huxley responds, his head bowed, and his chin pressed down against his chest. "I don't want to talk." He says each word like a separate sentence. His voice surprises him. Rough and weary, he sounds much older.

They don't stop for anything until after dark, when they come to a halt at a seemingly random point, next to an outcrop of fissured rock at the bottom of an incline. When they pause, Huxley wipes away the tears and pretends nothing is wrong.

A chill surrounds them, the sky is empty of clouds, and in the cold,

Bracken steams with the cost of his efforts. He watches the distance with his shotgun held ready in his hands.

"Wait here," he says to Huxley. "I have to go get something." He walks away without looking back, sniffs the air, and listens. All of his senses search for threats.

Huxley watches Bracken slowly pick his way around a number of boulders. Cautious to create as little noise as possible, he drops to the ground and follows the footprints in the moonlight. When he sees the shadow outline ahead of him, Huxley slows his own pace to match. Bracken and his shadow proceed through a winding path between boulders. Huxley contemplates turning back but wants to know where Bracken is going. And he wants to be with someone, not left alone, waiting in the night with the thoughts of his father dead on the ground.

He skulks around a boulder and spies Bracken, paused at the edge of a wide swatch of open space. Beyond him, in the center of the exposed area, Huxley sees a compound, small but well-fortified. The walls are part sturdy mud bricks, while the rest is pieced together with stray bits of wood, everything from old boards to dry tree trunks. Rows of sharpened sticks line the rim and the tops of the trees have been carved into irregular points. Torches illuminate the emptiness. Shadows flicker on the sand and boulders. It looks like a miniature version of Requiem.

Bracken waits suspended at the very edge of the light, hunching over. He looks like part of the rock. Huxley creeps up behind him until he can reach out and touch the dingy poncho draped over his shoulders. Bracken pivots and levels the barrel of his shotgun just above the top of Huxley's head.

"What the fuck are you doing here?" Bracken says. His voice comes out a whispered hiss. "I thought I told you to wait back at, whatever that thing is." He looks the child up and down.

"You're not my dad," Huxley mutters.

Bracken laughs. "Tough little guy. Good thing you're not taller." He turns his attention back to the stronghold. "Did anyone ever tell you you're not very good at following directions?"

"Okay," he continues. "I don't have time to hold your hand and walk you back, so you're just going to have to come with me. Stay close, there are mines all over up there." He looks at Huxley. "Do you know what mines are?" Huxley nods. "Then you know what they can do?" Again, Huxley nods. "Follow me, step exactly where I step." He pauses. "Unless I blow up. Then don't step there."

Bracken stands and strides forward into the light. He walks in a deliberate pattern, measuring his steps. Behind him Huxley follows exactly. His small boots step only into the middle of Bracken's tracks. He hops from footprint to footprint.

Bracken turns to look at him. He laughs an uneasy laugh. "See, it isn't so difficult, is it?"

Huxley sees shadows of movement from inside. Someone notices their approach. They near the door in the center of the wall and a thin hatch slides open. A rifle protrudes from the slit and the grizzled visage of a man examines Bracken and the boy. Huxley shifts from foot to foot and keeps his head down. Bracken raises his arms, palms up, and shrugs, impatient at being kept waiting.

"Two of you then?" the man asks. A yellowish foam clings to the corners of his mouth, and the hairs of his ragged mustache curl inward over his lips.

Bracken stares him down. His gaze unnerves the guard, who glances at unseen compatriots on his side of the wall. "Infected? Bitten?"

Bracken turns his head to one side and spits. He scarcely notices the weapon hovering inches from his face.

"Did you see any infected or signs of them in the area?"

Bracken waits. "No." There's finality in his voice. "You know who I am, Hutch, and you know why I'm here."

"You're late."

"I am well aware of that. But problems do arise out here, don't they? Now why don't you let me in and go tell the lady of the house that I'm here, like a good little lackey."

Hutch is not used to being spoken to in this manner and Huxley sees the wounded pride on his face. The man thinks about taking some sort of action but reconsiders and relents. Whatever consequences he envisions don't appeal to him and he retracts the rifle, sliding the window shut. A moment later the door swings open. Three men with guns cover the area beyond the open door as Bracken enters. Huxley scuttles in behind him.

Within the walls a collection of small structures spreads, randomly spaced throughout the compound, some fashioned out of wood, while others from rough mud bricks, listing to one side. Light spills out of cracks in the unsealed walls and pipes and tubes run in and out of the buildings through poorly cut holes. Huxley wouldn't be surprised if any or all of them collapsed at that very moment.

A handful of people dart about and a woman stands in a doorway. Thick dreadlocks protrude from her scalp, a heavy layer of soot covers her face, and she watches the newcomers in silence. She stares at Huxley, who stares back; her jaw works a mouthful of something, and for a moment Huxley thinks she's speaking to him. The woman spits into the dirt, breaks eye contact, and enters the shanty, pulling the door closed behind her.

In the center of the compound sits a structure larger than the others, low to the ground but long. From the appearance, Huxley assumes it's the main building. Even in the darkness he can tell it's by far the most solid of all the ramshackle structures. Bracken heads for the door without waiting for any of the men to say a word. Huxley sticks close to him, knowing it's in his best interest.

Bracken enters without knocking or announcing his presence. Huxley scans the interior as he follows. Inside looks surprisingly like a home. There's a single main room with furniture; a couch, two chairs, and a desk. Heavy and close, the air smells lived in. In the corner, a man sits at a kitchen table. He stares at the intruders with round, wet eyes, neither moving nor speaking. A dark woman stands in the middle of the room, waiting, her hands clasped before her, an expectant look on her face.

"Hello there, Bracken," she says. Her nose pressed flat against her face, her nostrils flare with each breath, and her eyes sit wide apart. Huxley is sure she can look in multiple directions at once. Her body thick, she pants through her mouth rather than breathing comfortably. When she smiles, her gums present a shocking pink with patches of black and her teeth jut out at odd angles.

"Lexi," Bracken says. Then he nods at the man at the table. "Weird Grady."

"You're late," Lexi says, still smiling.

"So I've been told. I . . ."

"I don't really care. I'm not the one who has to explain myself to Elwood, now am I?"

Bracken shakes his head and sneers. "You most certainly are not."

"What's with the kid?" she asks. Huxley hovers behind Bracken, close to his poncho. "I didn't know that was your style."

"Followed me home. Can't seem to shake him."

"Want to sell him?"

"Sometimes." Bracken nods with a smile.

"We can always use some extra hands around here. Give you a good price. Fair market value and all."

Huxley freezes. He thinks Bracken is joking, knows he's joking, but for a quick instant, fears his companion might actually sell him.

"Enough pleasantries," Bracken interrupts. "I believe you have something for me and I would like to be on my way as soon as possible. As you pointed out, I'm a bit behind schedule."

"Direct. As always. That's why I like you." Lexi indicates that Bracken should follow her through a door in the back of the room.

He turns to Huxley and says, "Stay here with Weird Grady."

Huxley opens his mouth, about to ask why he's called Weird Grady, but he eyes the man and decides that he's not completely sure he wants to know the answer, suspecting the origin of the name is something awful. Instead he starts to ask why he has to stay here, but Bracken cuts him off before the words form.

"Because I told you to," Bracken says in a low growl, then turns and follows Lexi.

Through the door, bottles and vials and tubs full of liquids and powders of various colors line the walls of the room. A pot sits on a thick table next to a mortar and pestle. Copper tubes snake from one container to the next in an elaborate tangle.

When the door shuts, Huxley stands there, unsure what to do with his hands. He laces his fingers together in front of him, but decides that position feels wrong; he lets them hang by his sides, but his fingers feel restless and exposed; he shoves his hands first into the pockets of his pants, then the pockets of his coat, pretending to look for something. Weird Grady watches the show, his own hands rest on the tabletop, an absent, crooked grin on his lips. His eyes are the same shape as Lexi's, wide and wet, but his teeth are sharp and straight.

Huxley edges over to the wall and stares at Weird Grady. He finds a certain security having a wall at his back, knowing no one or nothing can sneak up from behind. His gaze darts back to the door and he watches it as if his eyes can draw Bracken from the mysterious confines of the room. Beneath the layers of his clothes, his heart races and his skin breaks out in a cold sweat.

Raised voices come from the other side of the door, followed by the dull sound of something colliding with human flesh. Weird Grady pushes back from the table and stands as Bracken throws open the door. It swings wide behind him and bounces against the wall. Huxley doesn't see Lexi but knows she's back there someplace.

"Don't ever try to run a con on me again," Bracken says without turning around. He heads straight for the door. In his hand, he has a small package wrapped in rough fabric and tied with raw twine, which he tucks into his poncho as he walks. "Sit the fuck down, Grady."

As tense as the room has become, the sight of Bracken calms Huxley, despite the anger scratched into his face, and he's glad to hurry out the door.

Bracken strides directly to the main gate and stops in front of the guards. The armed men hold their ground and glare. Most members of the crew have visible scars; one man is missing an eye and the lone woman only has one hand, the stump at the end of her left arm wrapped in a dirty bandage. These are not people to trifle with.

Hutch, the grizzled gatekeeper, takes a long step forward and stops, barely a foot from Bracken, blocking the way out. The man looks past them toward the building they just left. Lexi stands in the doorway glaring, evil in her eyes. Huxley tries not to imagine what is about to happen, only to fail, and the scenarios he thinks up are not good.

With a speed that catches Huxley by surprise, Bracken grabs the front of Hutch's jacket, twists, throws him over his hip to the ground and hits the fallen man in the face with the butt of his palm. Bracken steps over the body writing on the ground, opens the door by himself, and walks through. Unconcerned, he proceeds without glancing back. Huxley hurries after him.

Behind them, the door remains open for a moment. The armed guards, dumbstruck and frozen, watch the figures recede into the night. Muffled confusion erupts as all the guards begin to speak at once. Lexi's sharp voice cuts through all of the others, they fall silent, and someone finally closes the door, sealing the wall.

Bracken's pace is casual but purposeful. Huxley stays close to his heels, turning back every other step to look for the swarm of armed nightmares he expects to momentarily burst through the doors. Against his expectations, no one comes.

So focused on the possibilities of what's behind them, when Bracken stops short, Huxley collides with his hip, bounces back, and tumbles to the ground his face inches from the ground. Scrambling to get to his feet, Bracken grabs him by the back of the neck and holds him still.

He bends down until his face nearly touches Huxley's.

"Remember what I said about mines?"

Huxley nods as much as he can, his neck caught in the older man's iron grip.

Bracken reaches out a few inches in front of Huxley's face, gently brushes the top off of what appears to be a small mound of sand, and blows the remaining grains off of a black metal cylinder. He releases his grip on the boy and stands up.

Huxley remains frozen in place, rigid, his hands back, hovering off of the ground as he stares down the mine right in front of his nose.

"I don't usually say things I don't mean," Bracken says, turning to walk away.

Inch by inch, Huxley slithers away from the mine, until he feels safe enough to push himself upright. His heart beats like a snare drum in his ears, his breath quick and shallow. He swallows hard and moves on, careful to step only in Bracken's footprints, acutely aware of every grain of sand beneath his feet and what it might hide.

Bracken stops again. His eyes scan the edge of the light. Huxley shuffles up behind him, trying to see what he sees. Bracken raises his gun. Huxley edges even closer, until the tip of his nose touches the rough fabric of Bracken's poncho and the musty smell of it fills his nostrils.

Finally his eyes find purchase. Something's wrong with the shadows.

Spots are a deeper black than the surrounding night. It dawns on him that he's looking at a crouching figure and that another paces at the brink of the darkness. Two of them, they approach, moving laterally as they advance. One, that used to be a man, is completely nude. His left forearm, broken, dangles at an angle that makes Huxley's stomach churn, but the fingers still wriggle and grasp. The second was once a woman. Her clothes cling to her in tatters and a large section of her scalp is gone, torn off, exposing the muscle and tissue beneath. Dried gore covers both of their chins and each lets out a low hiss.

Bracken levels his gun and backs up. His body stands between Huxley and the infected and he pushes the boy away. Huxley creeps backward, eyes flicking back and forth between the creatures and Bracken, still as a slab of stone. Inside his chest, Huxley's heart pounds against his ribs, and the tips of his fingers tingle and quiver. With great effort he swallows. The panic is physical within him, he's sure he is about to die, to join his father, and only the thought of the surrounding minefield keeps him from sprinting into the darkness.

"What do I . . ." he starts.

Without turning around, Bracken cuts the question short with a sharp wave. He indicates for Huxley to stay still. "Stay behind me."

Huxley shrieks as a blur, a third, unnoticed creature, leaps out of the shadows and tackles Bracken to the ground. He lands on his back, grabs its throat, and squeezes. The monster lets out a roar and paws madly at him.

Bracken shifts, pins one of the creature's arms under his body, and clamps the other in his armpit to avoid being bitten. Fingers around his attacker's windpipe, he digs into the deep blue flesh with a grunt. Working his other hand free, he clubs the side of the monster's skull with the butt of his shotgun. The sound of the moist impact makes Huxley cringe. Once, twice Bracken brings the gun down like a club, and with the third blow he rolls over on top of creature, jams the barrel underneath its chin, turns his head away, and pulls the trigger.

With the roar of the gun the creature's head explodes into the sand and it ceases to struggle.

At the surprise attack, the attackers at the periphery unleash screams that make Huxley's blood run cold, and bolt toward the action. The man takes three steps toward the boy before his legs explode. A hidden mine shreds the lower half of his body. A wave of sand and toes and viscera erupts. An acrid smell, the smell of charred flesh, coats the inside of Huxley's nose and he almost retches. The woman dives on top of Bracken just as he stands and turns to face her. Again, he falls to his back, wrestling with his assailant.

Huxley backs away and cowers until the screams of a fourth infected make him twist around. Outstretched hands reach for him and he trips on his own feet, falling to the ground. The creature looms over him, his legs flail, trying to beat the monster back and scoot himself away at the same time.

A sharp crack comes from the direction of the compound and the infected's head whips to one side and bounces off its shoulder. The body goes limp, falls to its knees, and slumps forward to the ground, lifeless. Huxley turns his head and sees the silhouette of a person standing on top of the fortress wall, holding a long rifle.

Bracken pins the woman's arms against her body. Keeping her mouth away so she can't bite him, he forces her jaw shut and wrenches her head backward as hard as he can. What is left of her hair, stringy and coated with filth, dangles into his mouth, and it hides both of their faces from Huxley's view. In the struggle and shadows and flickering torchlight he can barely tell what's going on.

With a final, guttural, barely human roar, Bracken forces himself up, holding his attacker at arm's length. Pushing her back, he scans the surrounding ground. She tears one arm free and swipes at him. He ducks the blow, reestablishes his grip, and braces his feet. With a furious twist, he throws the creature over his hip and dives face down in the opposite direction, covering his head with his hands as he hits the dirt.

Time slows as Huxley watches the creature tumble through the air, arms and legs akimbo. Her limbs splay out as she hits the ground and her head whips back. Huxley has just enough time to duck and cover as the back of her skull collides with the top of the exposed mine he almost stepped on.

Another roar, and another cascade of dirt and other things.

He peeks through his fingers. The creature's head is gone, all that remains is a smoldering hole; the upper portion of her body is torn and fragmented. Sharp ends of shattered bone stick through the dehydrated flesh, a shock of white and clean compared to the filth and dirt of the exterior.

Bracken rises and scours the fringes for any more potential attackers. The only movement is the shredded torso of the infected that stepped on the first mine. It twitches and writhes, lurching in the dirt. The arms reach for its prey, trying to drag itself forward, and the mouth churns and bites and cries and hisses.

Bracken looks at Huxley, shakes off the sand, walks over to the torso, and shoots it in the head. Silence returns as the echo fades away. He breaks open the barrel of his gun, removes the spent shells, places them in his pocket, and replaces them in the chamber with fresh ammunition. Huxley remains on the ground, shivering in place.

Bracken looks back at the compound, raises his hand to them in a salute, nods, and continues on his way.

Huxley stares after him, gulping air, his fingers quake and he balls them into fist to stop. He reclaims his feet and follows, careful to mimic Bracken's path exactly. At the cart, Bracken rummages around in Huxley's bag. He sees the boy and drops the pack.

"Why did we come here?" Huxley asks.

"I'm on the clock, kid," Bracken replies. "Had to pick something up."

"For who?"

"Not someone you want to keep waiting or disappoint."

Huxley nods as if he understands.

Even as they roll away in the night, Huxley watches the emptiness spool out behind them, waiting for something to appear. Nothing comes. And he waits, alone with the thoughts in his head, not sure which he is more afraid of, the monsters in the darkness, or the people, or if there is much of a difference.

"Where are we going?" Huxley asks.

"We're headed back to the Turd," Bracken says.

"What's "the Turd?""

"Just a little nickname I'm trying out for Requiem. I always thought that was a stupid name to begin with, and it's a basically a giant piece of shit, so . . ."

Despite himself, Huxley smiles in the darkness.

"Where did it come from?" Huxley asks. "I knew it was there, I heard people talk about it, but my father never told me anything about it."

"Where did Requiem come from? That's a kind of a long story," Bracken says. He looks back at Huxley and shrugs, turning his eyes forward again. "But I guess we've got time, don't we?"

This isn't the kind of question you respond to, so Huxley remains silent, and after a moment Bracken continues talking. His voice is different, with less of an edge to his words, and he sounds far away.

"The world wasn't always like . . . this," he begins. "But you probably know that, don't you? You're too young to have lived it, but there was a time before the infection, before there were monsters, before people like Elwood would slit your throat for a pair of socks."

"Who's Elwood?" Huxley says.

"He's a jackass with a messiah complex who insists on wearing white robes in a world made almost exclusively of dirt. Requiem is his baby, he runs the whole thing. Hopefully you'll never have the pleasure of meeting him. He used to be some sort of small-time crime boss in Seattle. That used to be a city."

He pauses. "See, even before the infection hit, the world had gone to shit. The weather changed, it stopped raining almost entirely. Believe it or not, you used to be able to grow food almost anywhere. Even what passed for a barren wasteland had something that would grow there. Maybe you didn't want to eat it, but it grew."

"But eventually everything dried up and blew away," Huxley says.

"Right?"

"Pretty much," Bracken says. "Some people stayed and tried to hang on, but eventually most people gave up and moved to the cities. There's nothing I can compare them to that would make you understand what they were like. They were huge, hundreds or thousands of times the size of Requiem. They were already crowded to begin with, and when everyone abandoned the middle of the country and headed for the coasts, where things were at least a little better, it got even worse.

"Somewhere along the line, Elwood and his ilk got the bright idea that they could rob all of these people streaming toward the cities. They were easy targets, they had everything they owned in the world, and Elwood took it, took whatever he wanted."

"That's horrible," Huxley says. The word seems lacking, but he can't come up with anything more powerful.

"Like I said, he's a piece of shit." Bracken nods. "They cruised around the highways looking for people without any hope left and . . ." He shrugs and trails off. "The news called them Winnebago Pirates, made it sound funny, almost glamorous. Requiem was a little town in what used to be Utah, west of Salt Lake City, that had kind of blown away in the dust. So he took it over and used it as a base, as a place to stash all their loot after raids. After a while it became its own little scumbag village."

"People just let it happen?"

Bracken nods. "They didn't have any money, so no one cared."

He continues. "Then, ten years ago, at least that's how long the people who've kept count say it's been, a particularly nasty little disease reared its ugly little head. It's some kind of virus, not that that means much to you.

It spreads fast, through blood and saliva. Starts as a vicious fever that starves your body of oxygen and eventually kills you, or most of you. It keeps a small part of your brain alive, the part driven by the most basic, survival instincts. Basically, all that's left is the desire to consume and feed and spread. But you've seen that part."

The images of the infected tearing into his father invades Huxley's mind. A violent shiver runs through his body.

Bracken looks back. "Sorry." He has an awkward look on his face, like he's unsure how to comfort another person.

He takes a deep breath and keeps talking, like he doesn't know what else to do. Huxley tries to focus on the words and squeeze his own thoughts out of his head.

"The cities were so crowded," Bracken says. "People stacked on top of one another, the virus just ripped through almost the entire population." He shakes his head. "But Requiem, it was already removed from other people, and fairly insular, so when the plague hit, they were able to cobble together some walls and fortify the town against the infected.

"Actually, this is version 2.0. The second try. At first, they backed up against the cliff that sits to the south of where town is now, thinking it would be a good natural barrier against the infected. And it was, at least until the monsters started chucking themselves off of the cliff and landing inside the walls. Broken legs don't bother them, and even half-crippled, they can still bite."

"They jumped off of the cliff?" Huxley says. He's aware how disinterested he sounds.

Bracken turns. "They don't have the same self-preservation instincts that we do. All they want is to feed and spread their disease, they don't really care how." He shakes his head. "So they moved town out into the middle of the emptiness.

"With the walls, Requiem was safe. Well, safe from infected at least. People are another story. But desperation makes people do things they normally wouldn't. Some folks think being safe from one threat is better than being safe from nothing. It became a kind of weigh station, a place survivors could stop and barter and find things they needed as they made their way to wherever it was they were headed.

"More and more stayed, and Elwood realized that what he had was his own little kingdom where he could rule with absolute power. And being a total psychopath, that idea appealed to him. Over the years its grown. He sends out groups to scavenge anything they can find as far a food and building materials and anything else that's useful. The roaming hordes of infected have thinned out some, and he has enough muscle that he can man a few farms where things still grow and provide protection. Whatever they coax out of the ground comes directly to him. There's not much in the way of livestock, infected like to eat them as well, I once saw one eating rats."

"Is that where we were?" Huxley asks. "Lexi's is a farm?"

"Sort of," Bracken says. "Some people look at her like a witch or a shaman or some nonsense. That's why Elwood keeps her around. Partly. Mostly, though, she makes drugs, which people seem to enjoy.

"Now Elwood fancies himself as some sort of savior politician. He stages fights and death matches to entertain his masses. I guess he's never heard of the Romans. Believe it or not, living on the edge, living with imminent death, tends to wind most people up. Everyone gets so crazy, they don't have any other way to get a release, so Elwood gives them a spectacle. And they love him for it. It gives him and his goons even more power."

Huxley looks at the back of Bracken's head. He thinks about his father's reaction the first time they encountered Bracken, the obvious fear and wariness. "You're one of his goons, aren't you?"

Bracken's head bobs in the darkness, but Huxley can't tell if it's a nod or simply a byproduct of their movement as he pedals along. Bracken blows a stream of air between his lips. When he speaks, he speaks slowly, as if he is picking his words carefully. "I'm definitely a goon, though I prefer to think of myself as independent contractor."

Huxley is confused.

"I worked for him," Bracken says. He corrects himself. "I've done work for him, but I don't work for him. I'm not one of those mindless assholes who dress all in black and tattoo their faces." He shakes his head and talks to himself. "It's like a fucking football team."

Huxley begins to feel frightened, wondering for the first time who this man really is, and what he plans to do with him. "If he's so bad, why did you help him?"

"Listen, kid, we all lost. We all lost a lot. Hell, we all lost everything. I came out here to . . . I had my reasons for coming out here. After a while, all I cared about was surviving, and I did, I do, bad things to achieve that goal. Not a lot of job options these days for someone with my limited skill set."

Huxley stays quiet for a moment. "Why are you helping me?"

Bracken remains silent and keeps pedaling forward into the darkness. Huxley sits back in the bed and watches the back of his head, trying to figure out what's going on inside.

They don't stop. Huxley forgets to eat. Instead of asking Bracken to stop pedaling and pull over, he stands and pisses into their wake. He stays awake and watches the sun break into the sky, bathing everything in red, and he squints against the light.

Eventually their path crosses the lost highway, or at least a lost highway. Bracken maneuvers the vehicle onto the disintegrating asphalt, swerving around gaping potholes. On the solid surface, his pedaling turns even and rhythmic. They follow the black strip directly into the new sun. Instead of putting on his goggles, Huxley closes his eyes and feels the warmth creep into his forehead, nose, and cheeks.

"Where is this farm of yours?" Bracken asks. "I've got one more stop to make, then I'll drop you off with your people."

Huxley keeps his eyes closed. "I don't have any people. It was just the two of us. Dad didn't want to live in town anymore, places like Requiem, or even with anyone else. He said we could be free out here." Tears start to form behind his eyelids and he clamps them down, forces them back. "That no one would notice us, that no one would bother us."

"Freedom is one way to look at it. If you know what you're getting into." After a minute of silence, he says, "So you don't have any place to go." It was somewhere between a question and a statement.

"I have an uncle in San Francisco," Huxley says.

Bracken doesn't say anything. He considers the name. "That's a bit out of the way, isn't it?"

Huxley opens his eyes and stares at the back of his head. "You did kill my father."

"True." Bracken nods. "Still, I'd rather not go back there. I'll see what I can do."

Bracken slows and stops as they crest the ridge of the shallow valley where Requiem sits. Sweat coats his forehead and face. He breathes deep and regular. Huxley examines him as he watches the town below, not wanting to go forward, convincing himself to proceed. He inhales, holds it in, and exhales.

When they do continue, their advance is gradual. Confusion seeps into Huxley. For someone who said he needed to be somewhere, Bracken takes his time about getting there, savoring every moment outside of the walls. They stop in front of the gate and he dismounts, grabbing his pack.

"Get your stuff," he says to the boy.

Huxley grabs his bag, everything he owns in the world, and jumps to the ground.

With the butt of his fist, Bracken pounds on the gate. A dull thud sounds within the walls that falls silent without an echo. Impatient, he bangs on the metal again.

"I know you saw us," he says in a half-yell. "You see everyone."

Huxley lingers a good distance behind, intimidated at being watched. Bracken cocks his leg back to kick the door, but before he can swing, it creaks open.

He steps back and stands with his hands folded in front of him; his head tilts forward, and he watches. Walking into the airlock, he passes a man with a grubby eye patch and a cracked black leather vest, scarcely acknowledging his existence. Huxley scoots in behind him as the doors close, looking at the handful of blurry tattoos along the man's jaw.

"Almost given up on you," the man says. "You're late."

"Everybody seems very concerned with my business," Bracken says without looking at his inquisitor.

"Where'd you get the kid?"

Bracken turns and glares at the man as the outer doors clang shut. The sun blocked out, darkness envelops them. He stares until the man waves his hand in the air. The inner doors grind open and the guard turns away.

"Not my problem," he says.

"No," Bracken says, stepping through the door. "It isn't."

Like a shadow, Huxley sticks to Bracken, who walks ahead, deliberate and with a purpose. The sea of people parts around them. No one panhandles from Bracken, no one attempts to sell him anything or entice him into a tavern. Not a single hand stretches out to him. Pickpockets don't push their luck. Those who do bump him mumble frightened apologies and move along without making eye contact. They leave him alone and let him go about his way unfettered, even those who tower over him.

Recognizing he is not someone to mess with right now, they leave him be. At the same time, they all cast quick glances when they think it will go unnoticed, and they watch him pass by with a small boy in tow. The attention puzzles Huxley. He's not used to seeing other children, but is he really such an anomaly? Or is it his company?

The crowded, close-pressed blocks give way to less teeming streets. Foot traffic thins out and the buildings appear to be homes and things other than bars or brothels. Bracken makes a move left down an even less populated side street. Their path leads them through a snaking maze of lanes each one more claustrophobic than the last. The walls press in. Buildings curl over until only a splinter of sky is visible. Even in the daylight the street is shrouded in shadows. There's little to no space between the structures, walls butt up against each other, every square inch of space employed, rickety staircases lead to upper floors.

The further they get from the gates of Requiem, the fewer people they see on the street. There are doors set into thick mud and concrete walls, but few windows at ground level. Shards of broken glass, clear, green, brown, are cemented along top of the barriers.

They are the only people on the street when Bracken stops in front of a wrought iron gate. Metal bars run diagonally, crisscrossing in front of a sheet of heavy mesh welded to the sturdy frame. The top and bottom are jagged, cut like saw teeth. Past the gate, a thick door made out of a solid slab of wood blocks the way.

Bracken pounds on the door with the butt of his fist and waits with his arms crossed. Huxley watches but can't read his face; he isn't anxious or angry, frustrated or upset. Nothing happens. He pounds again, longer and harder this time. The clang of the gate echoes off of the walls around them and the walls inside, making Huxley even more acutely aware of how alone they are. It's an odd sensation going from being nearly crushed by people to being on an empty street.

Bracken tries one more time and the first hints of impatience stew in his eyes.

Finally Huxley hears the sound of locks and bolts moving inside, and the door behind the gate opens. A woman stands behind the metal barrier with a hunting rifle planted on her hip, pointing the barrel at the center of Bracken's chest. If he notices the weapon, neither its presence or aim bothers him.

Almost as tall as Bracken, the woman wears thick denim overalls over a sleeveless white t-shirt marred by stains and sweat, grease and dirt. Blue veins run beneath the taut skin of her well-muscled arms. She wears her hair short and a black smudge cuts across her cheek.

She eyes Bracken with a surprised recognition, takes half a step back, knits her brow, and turns her head a few degrees. Her posture becomes newly guarded.

"What are you doing here?" she asks.

"It's good to see you too, Haley." He pauses then adds, "You look well."

This makes her tighten up even more. Her jaw clenches and the muscles in her neck twist into ropes. "I'll ask you again, why are you here?"

"I got something for you," Bracken says, his arms still crossed.

"We don't want or need anything you have." She moves to shut the door.

"You don't take in strays anymore?"

She stops, her hand on the edge of the door. With the gun still trained on Bracken, she peers around him and notices the boy standing in his shadow. He puts his hand on Huxley's shoulder, positions the boy in front of him, and shrugs.

"Say hello, Huxley," Bracken says.

The boy squeaks out a small, "Hello."

"How the hell did a thug like you wind up with a child?" Haley says.

"He followed me home," Bracken says. "For the life of me I can't shake him." They look at each other for a moment in silence. "He doesn't have anywhere to go, and this," he gestures around them, "is somewhere."

Haley peeks to either side, trying to see the street without getting too close to the gate. "You alone?" Bracken nods. "Alright." She opens the door just long enough for them to slip in then she slams it shut. Next she shuts and bolts the inner door, securing two grave deadbolts, plus three sets of metal bars and brackets—one on the top, one on the bottom, and a third in the middle, over the knob.

The walls reach up into the sky, nearly twenty feet tall, and because there's no roof where they stand, they can see light clouds drift past high in the atmosphere like a moving picture in a frame.

Haley walks past them.

"She's good people," Bracken says to Huxley. "She hates my guts, but she's good people." He looks at her retreating form. "Hell, I'd think less of her if she didn't hate me."

"I heard that," she says, not turning around.

"And you know it's true."

The walls are bare concrete. Scraps of metal, wood, stacks of cinder blocks, and other building supplies occupy the corners along with improvised tools and a welding apparatus. A layer of dirt and sand covers the ground. The air smells like dust and wood and metal. Haley leads them under a ceiling made of the same dim material, into a concrete rectangle, then out again into an open space, a courtyard.

"This looks like a warehouse I worked in when I was a kid," Bracken says, examining the walls.

They stop at the base of a stairwell, also welded metal, but less utilitarian, almost decorative, that leads to a second story. Above that there's a third floor. Haley waves at a man with a rifle positioned on the roof and he disappears from view. A door with a padlock sits to their left.

Haley's face softens as she crouches in front of the boy. The look takes some effort, but she shoots a wicked sideways glance at Bracken. Whatever he did to her, it must have been bad.

Looking back at Huxley, she affects a soothing voice and says, "Huxley, is it?"

He nods.

"I'm Haley." She reaches out her hand. He reluctantly reaches out his and shakes it loosely. "It's nice to meet you. I'm glad you're here. How old are you?"

"Nine," he mumbles, without looking her in the eye.

"We have some other boys and girls here about your age. They'd love to meet you, too. I'll introduce you in a minute, but first I want to talk to Bracken, okay?"

"Why can't I go with him?" Huxley asks.

Haley stands without responding to the question and pulls Bracken a few steps away. In a low tone, thinking they're out of earshot, she asks, "Who did you have to kill to get him?"

Bracken looks past her at Huxley. "His father."

"Of course. I'm amazed you felt guilty enough to do something about it."

"Not like that. Stumbled across them outside. Dad wasn't exactly what I would call cautious and got himself bit."

"But they didn't get the boy?"

"No," Bracken shakes his head. "It was only two strays. I stuck with them until he was about to turn. He couldn't do what he needed to do . . . so I did."

"That's what you're good at." She spits her words like weapons.

"The kid saw everything. The bite. The deterioration. The end."

"Jesus."

"A lot of ugly."

"Mother?"

He shakes his head.

"Relatives?"

"Nope. At least nowhere practical."

She considers the boy with her arms crossed. "I would've guessed you'd just leave him out there. You're not the foster parent type."

"Hey, I was almost as surprised as you." Bracken laughs and looks up at her. "I wasn't always a bastard."

"That's news to me. But I guess we were all real people once upon a time."

"In a galaxy far, far away." He smiles. It's awkward and he stops "So, you got room for one more?"

Haley sighs. "We'll make room." She looks him directly in the eyes. "That's what we do. That's all of the stuff he has with him?"

"All he grabbed."

Haley nods.

Bracken walks over to Huxley and crouches down in front of him. "Hey kid, you're going to stay here, okay?"

"I don't want to stay here." Huxley eyes the man in front of him, searching his face for something. "Why can't I go with you?"

"Why the hell do you want to go with me?" Bracken snaps. His face softens and he forces a laugh. "That's not a good idea, kid. I've got to go deal with some bad people. Not the place for a nice boy like you. To be honest, I'm late for something and probably in a fair bit of trouble because of all this running around."

"That's what you had to do at Lexi's . . ."

"No no no no," Bracken interrupts in a quiet voice. "You don't need to be throwing around people's names like that." He glances back at Haley. "No one needs to know that you were ever there. That's our little secret." He looks at the ground and itches his chin, searching for something to say. "You'll be safe here. They'll take good care of you. It's not a good place for you out there."

Huxley looks at Bracken, the two on the same level for the first time.

"One more thing," Bracken says. He shrugs off his backpack, opens the main compartment, and rummages around through a collection of clothes, food, and other unidentifiable parcels. The contents jumble together in no particular order and it takes him a moment to find what he is looking for. With an air of triumph, he removes a slim rectangular box wrapped in cellophane and a crinkled tube. He extends the gifts to Huxley. "Here."

"What is that?"

Bracken looks at the boy. "It's a toothbrush." He gestures with the toothbrush one more time. "Go ahead, take it. I have a stockpile. You wouldn't believe what I have to go through to find these, let alone toothpaste. This tube is the most valuable thing I own." He laughs and glances over his shoulder at Haley.

"What do you do with them?"

"Seriously?" Bracken scrunches up his face. "You don't know what this is for?"

Huxley shakes his head.

"Bunch of savages in this town." Bracken sighs and shakes his head, muttering to himself, "No wonder I like it better out there." He looks at Haley again and raises the toothbrush. "Will you show him what to do with this?" She nods.

Bracken stands. His knees crack. He puts and hand on Huxley's head and musses the boy's hair.

"See you around," Huxley says.

Bracken shakes his head. "I seriously doubt that." Turning to go, he nods at Haley. Huxley stands still and watches them as Haley walks Bracken to the door, unfastens the locks, and releases him out into the street.

CHAPTER 3

The second Bracken steps out the door, Haley slams the iron gate behind him, shuts the heavy wooden door, and sets the deadbolts. She leans into the metal bars and throws all of her weight behind her shoulders to get the stubborn rods to slip into place. Once satisfied the door is secure, she turns and walks toward Huxley. Her boots echo and bounce off of the concrete walls. With her final step she slides up next him, the thick waffle soles grate along the ground, rasping across the layer of silt and dirt.

"How did you wind up with him?" Haley asks.

Huxley gazes up at her in silence.

"Did he hurt you?"

Huxley continues to stare. Haley puts her hand on his shoulder and urges him up the stairs one at a time.

Huxley stops at the top. "Why can't I go with him?"

"Like he said, you don't belong in the places he goes," Haley says. Her hand still on his shoulder she looks back at the door. "No one belongs in the places he goes. Not even him."

The door at the top of the stairs looks nothing like the outer doors. Instead of heavy wood and metal reinforcements that serve a purely functional purpose, it's more elaborately crafted and ornamental. The wood couldn't endure a single well-placed kick. The lock in the knob and the deadbolt are more for show than protection. Four panes of frosted glass are set into the wood. Huxley sees colors and rough shapes through the windows, but the edges blur and blend into a mess of indistinct blobs.

Haley opens the door and ushers Huxley inside. Compared to the outside, the interior isn't what he expects. The walls are painted warm colors— yellows, oranges, and light blues. A bulky, handmade table and eight chairs occupy the center of the room. In one corner a wood-burning stove with a large iron cooking surface sits, a black pipe that runs into the ceiling. Tall cupboards line the walls and an open door leads to a pantry with shelves of food. Dark brown glazed tiles make up the floor. Tin cutouts of sacred hearts and crosses adorn the walls. A sickly potted plant stands in another corner next to a rickety shelf piled with a collection of sorry looking, dog-eared books, many without covers and with spines so creased the names have all but disappeared. There's a couch with mismatched cushions, patched together out of random scraps of fabric. Stairs in the far corner lead both up and down. It's a warm space, cozy, like an embrace.

"This is our main room," Haley says. The hand on his shoulder rotates him, giving him a panoramic view of the space. Huxley clutches the toothbrush in his fist. "And the kitchen. This is where we make all the meals. Everybody eats together. Everybody pitches in. Once you get settled and figure out what you like, we'll give you some regular chores."

"And through here is where you'll be staying." Haley guides Huxley through a door into a long, thin room. His body follows her influence automatically. The walls are a deep maroon. Windowless, light filters in from two openings overhead. Rows of bunk beds, also handmade, line the walls. A small girl with light red hair lies on her stomach, reading a book on a top bunk, and a smaller boy sits on a chair in the corner.

"This is Freya and Gwili," Haley says. To the other children she says, "This is Huxley, he's going to be staying with us from now on." She pats the bunk below Freya. "You can have this bed. The others are all out right now, but I'll introduce you when they get back. I'll leave you to settle in. I have some things to do, but if you need me, these two know where I'll be. Okay?" She looks down at him and nods. "Don't worry, you're safe."

Haley leaves the room. Huxley stands rooted to one spot. Without setting down his pack or lying down, he watches the other children in silence. Gwili has short arms and legs. His pants are rolled up into thick cuffs. The contrast makes his body seem disproportionately long. Most of his right ear is missing. The other two children stare back at the newcomer.

"What's that?" Gwili says, indicating Huxley's hands.

"A toothbrush."

"What's that?"

"I don't know." He shakes his head. "You have weird names."

"So do you," Freya says. No one continues the conversation, and she and Gwili turn back to what they were doing.

Huxley rests on his back in the dark, staring at the bottom of the top bunk, fully clothed, down to his boots. The mattress is made of hay packed into a rough fabric container. He uses his pack as a pillow and listens to the breathing of the dozen other children sleeping around him. His own breaths come deep and measured. His stomach gurgles. Someone snores at the other end of the room. His father snored and the thought makes the breath catch in his lungs before he can push it to the side. No one moves anywhere in the rest of the house. The collection of adults that was out there before has gone to bed. Huxley waits even longer to be sure, to be sure everyone is really asleep.

There's no sound. There hasn't been for some time. Huxley sits up. He waits. No one notices. No one stirs. He swivels around and puts his feet on the floor. Again he waits. Again no one notices. He stands and pauses. With every new movement he waits as long as it takes until he's comfortable and certain no one else is aware of his actions.

Slowly he lifts his bag off of the bed. The contents settle against the coarse canvas. Inside, the pan and pot clank together. Huxley grimaces and squeezes his eyes shut, waiting for someone to confront him. When no one wakes, he removes his canteen and holds it in one hand so it won't bounce against the rest of the pack. He backs toward the door, reaches behind him, twists the knob, and cringes with apprehension as the internal metal workings click together. The sound is barely audible to, but it's like a cacophony in his ears.

When no one stirs, he opens the door a crack and peers through. Confirming the emptiness of the outer room, he slips out, as light on his feet as he can be, and eases the door shut in his wake.

He heads straight toward the pantry, opens the mouth of his pack, and crams in as much food as possible. The score consists of glass jars full of homemade preserves, a few random cans without labels, and dried grains and beans. Stuffing the containers into his bag, Huxley notices a small package among his possessions wrapped in heavy oilcloth and bound with twine, something he hasn't seen before. He touches it then immediately pushes it from his mind. It must be something his father picked up along their travels. There will be time to examine it later, when he's out of this place.

After filling his bag, he looks for somewhere to fill his water bottle. On a counter rests a black cauldron. He picks up one of the dense wooden chairs and carries it over. It's heavy and has to set it down twice. The weight is awkward and it tips back in his arms. One leg cracks against the stone wall and the sound reverberates off of the others. Again, Huxley flinches, sure someone has been alerted to his doings. But no one comes.

He exhales, thankful for sound sleepers, positions the chair at the counter, and climbs up. The cistern is full of water and he submerges his canteen, holding it underwater until no more bubbles escape. He brings it to his lips and drinks deeply. The brackish water tastes like earth. When his thirst is satisfied, he submerges the vessel again, fills it, and secures the cap.

Glancing around for anything else that might be of use, he gently hoists his pack onto his shoulders and heads for the exit. With the same caution, Huxley sneaks through the door with the glass inlay. Deliberate, measured, he pauses as the top of the metal stairs, breathes deep, and listens for any indication inside that he has been discovered.

He takes a quick mental stock and briefly considers what awaits him out there in the streets. The only plan he has is to leave and find Bracken. Even though this place is safe and secure, and he's welcome here, that plan is all he has. It's too quiet here; there's nothing to keep his mind from running rampant. At least outside he's too busy to dwell. A shiver sprints through his body and he pushes the image of his father, dead on the ground with a hole in his face, from his thoughts.

His head relatively clear, Huxley takes a cursory step down. It is not a full step. The sole of his shoe rests on the step below, but the bulk of his weight remains on the upper foot.

He transfers all of his weight to his front foot and grasps the railing to keep from falling head first down the stairs as a shriek of twisting metal invades the night air. But it isn't his step. This has nothing to do with him. The sound comes from someone forcibly removing the front gate from its home in the wall.

The sound rouses the people inside. He retreats back through the door, no longer concerned with silence, and bolts up the stairs to the roof. The roof is a flat slab of concrete peopled only by a mismatched table and two vinyl chairs. From his vantage point he can see the front door as the sounds of confused people mustering fill the space beneath him.

A final cry of rending metal signals the gate has given way. One solid thud then another against the dense wood of the front door. A third impact sounds and the door gives up the ghost and bursts inward. Dark outlines of half a dozen men flow through the open door and fan out into the shadows cast by the moonlight. One final figure enters after the first sortie, his gait slow and casual compared to the others.

Spurts of gunfire originate from below. The vibrations travel through Huxley, from the floor up through his legs. His body jerks involuntarily, as if it has been shot. He backs away from the edge and moves to the corner of the building. The roof next door looms eight feet above him. He searches frantically for a way off the roof, but it's three floors to the ground with nothing to climb down.

"Find him," a man yells below. His voice, raspy and deep, carries power and authority behind it.

Huxley drags a chair over to the base of the wall. With all the power he can muster he heaves his bag at the lip. It catches and dangles for a second. He thinks it will stay. Instead, the pack crashes to the ground. With the gunshots and screaming and commotion, no one takes any notice. He tries again, this time the bag clears the edge and remains on the neighboring roof.

He hears Haley yell, followed by the dull thud of flesh on flesh impact, and a man groaning. Who's here? What they are after? He suspects it involves him, that it has something to do with Bracken, he can't imagine why else anyone might bother with this place. Whatever they want, he knows that he needs to go, quick.

He backs up, breathing fast and heavy, checks over his shoulder, and sees movement in the stairwell behind him. This is his only chance. Adrenaline courses through his brain and limbs and he sprints at the waiting chair and launches his little body with all of his might at the roof above.

The moment happens in slow motion. It feels like it takes years. It feels almost like he has the time to pause and rest. The chair clatters to the ground and skids across the roof with the force of the jump and the sense of soaring takes over.

His small body slams against the wall and time jerks back to normal in an instant as his fingers claw with the mad fury of instinct, barely catching on the lip. The muscles in his shoulders stretch and start to give, the joints almost pop from the sockets, but he won't let go, he can't let go. Churning his legs, the toes of his oversized boots grate against the concrete and leave scuff marks. Little by little he gains a solid grip and hoists himself up and over and onto the hard, dusty surface of the roof next door.

Panting, but unable to rest, he pops up into a crouch and grabs his pack. He stays low and scuttles across the roof. Behind him the clamor dies down. The initial uproar has become a mess of men yelling, children crying, and the sporadic pop of a gun.

The raspy voice yells, "Will someone please kill that bitch."

Huxley comes to the edge and waits, but no one stirs. He sees no movement and hears no sounds beneath him. The far side of the new roof drops down to the next. He tosses his bag over the lip, unconcerned with making noise, lowers himself as far as he can, releases his grasp, and falls the rest of the way down.

In a similar manner he scurries across the adjoining rooftops. Where he has to, he leaps small gaps from one to another.

The last building ends in a sheer wall that drops more than two stories to the ground below. Huxley looks around for anything to dangle himself from, a pipe, a rope, a ladder, anything.

He finds nothing.

He crouches, about to jump, shakes his head, and backs away. Too far. He hears a gunshot behind him, and he moves forward and crouches again. He can't.

"Fuck," he says under his breath, without truly comprehending the gravity of the word. He only knows that it's what adults say in extreme circumstances, what his father said in dire moments.

A hand touches his shoulder and Huxley spins in terror, fists flying, and almost topples backward off of the roof. He balances on one foot and flails his arms in attempt to reestablish his balance. The weight of his pack slowly pulls him over, past the point of no return, and he tumbles.

Haley grabs the straps of his pack just as Huxley passes beyond her grasp. She pulls him up and throws him to the floor and crouches next to him. Blood streams down her face from a gash at her hairline and her breathing verges on hyperventilation. She presses her hand to her ribs and every move makes her grimace.

"Which one . . ." she whispers as she inspects Huxley's face. "It's you. I didn't think anyone else made it out." Her eyes fall on his bag and a question she doesn't ask forms in her eyes. There's no time for specifics right now. On the rooftops behind them come voices.

"Who . . .?" Huxley asks.

"I don't know." Haley shakes her head.

"What . . .?"

"That either," she cuts him off. "Quick." She pulls the straps off of his shoulders, checks over the edge, and throws his bag over the side. She looks again, longer this time, judging distance, and motions Huxley over. A pistol sticks out of her waistband.

"Come on." She offers her hand. "I'll lower you as far as I can, but you'll have to drop the rest of the way."

He grabs her hand with both of his and scoots over the edge. His stomach jumps into his throat as he drops, weightless for a split second before Haley catches him with a grunt. He dangles, his legs kicking, as she lowers him. She leans out from the building, extending and stretching as far as she can without toppling over herself. The distance remains dizzying.

"This is as far as I can get you," she says through clenched teeth. "You have to let go."

Huxley looks at the ground below him then back up at Haley.

"Drop. Be quiet. Run. Hide."

Huxley looks down again. His legs kick automatically, looking for an invisible purchase.

"We don't have time for this." She shakes her head. "I'll keep them off, but you have to let go. Now."

One last desperate look up, their eyes meet, and Huxley let's go. The brief feeling of flight returns, coupled with the sensation of plummeting like a rock.

His feet hit the ground and sink in. His knees buckle and his legs give way. He falls to his back and lands on his bag. A pot or a pan in the pack digs into his ribs and forces the air from his lungs. Rolling onto his face, he coughs into the dirt and tries to regain his breath. Bruised, shaking, and terrified, but generally unhurt.

He scrambles to his feet still searching for air, grabs his pack, and runs, slinging the weight over his shoulders as he goes, lungs heaving. He runs around and corner, pauses, and looks back at the roof. Only his fingers and one eye creep around the edge of the building.

Haley's silhouette stands out black against the deep blue of the night sky. She raises her arm and sinks into a crouch. There's nothing for her to hide behind, no cover at all. Huxley watches, stuck in place. She has to do something. She has to jump, to follow him, to get away. She can't just stay there. The drop is huge, but a broken leg is better than dead. She has to, she has to get away.

Huxley watches and waits and breathes. His fingers clutch the corner. The skin on his hands stretches tight, his knuckles white. He rests his forehead against the cool stone in front of him, his knees shake and the shuddering movement reverberates until his entire body quivers.

Haley's arm pulls to one side and the end of the shadow explodes in a flash. Bursts of red and muddy, indistinct yells answer from in front of her. Her hand flashes again. More unseen gunshots sound.

Her shoulder jerks back like it's connected to a string. Her hand flashes one more time. A volley of bullets answers. Her outline crumples to the ground, out of sight. The echoes of the gunshots die away. The night is quiet. Silence hangs in the air. The surrounding homes remain still and dark. No one else seems bothered by the commotion.

Huxley stands frozen in place. Haley is dead and it's his fault. Death follows him everywhere. His eyes squeeze back tears. Voices on the roof break the temporary hush and shadowy figures glide back and forth. All he's aware of is his heartbeat in his ears and the leaden ball at the bottom of his stomach. His fingers tremble and he pulls back, heaves forward, and retches into the sand, throwing up a stomach full of bile and gritty water.

He runs. He runs until his legs can't run anymore. He runs, looking for a place to hide, a place to stay.

CHAPTER 4

uxley runs. With no specific place in mind, he just runs. There's nowhere for him to go. No one to run to. Only one acquaintance remains in the world, Bracken, and he's unsure of where to even begin looking for him. All he has to go on are Haley's words, that the places Bracken goes are places no one should go. He isn't sure what that means, aside from dangerous places, places that scare him, places his father ushered him past quickly, told him not to look, and to avoid eye contact. He doesn't know where those places are, or what they are, but they are a place to start.

Bracken has to help Huxley. He killed his father, he owes him that much at least. If he doesn't care, why did he save him in the first place? Why did he bring him to Haley instead of leaving him to die in the desert or selling him at Lexi's? He will help him, the boy is sure of it, he knows it, even if he can't explain why.

Moving just to move, he finds a small hole, a gap between the base of a building and the ground. Looking around, he sees that the street is empty. No one walks around this late. The wall is solid, made of rock with no windows, so no one inside can see him. He scoots over, hunches down in the shadows, checks one more time, and scoops away the dirt until he can force his small body through the opening. Behind him he fills in the hole, trying to make it look undisturbed.

Underneath the building is dark, the floor above made of wood. There are no sounds of people, no footsteps, no voices. He twists around until he faces the entrance to his crawlspace. He places his bag between himself and the hole in case some curious passerby or other happens to stick a head in. He peers over the pack and watches. His breathing feels perilously loud. Every nerve ending tingles, every muscle fiber in his small body stands ready and poised for movement.

He tries not to think about Haley. He tries not to think about his father. He tries not to think of the cries of the other children, of the gunshots, of the last man through the door and how he casually strolled in. The more the tries not to think of these things, the more they occupy the forefront of his mind. His body quakes, whether from cold or fear or adrenaline, he can't tell. He simply shakes; lying there, alone, afraid, and stuffed into the underside of a house.

A thought occurs to Huxley and he crawls toward the mouth of his bag, digging until he finds what he's looking for. Pulling his hand back, his fingers grasp his father's revolver. Holding the weapon in his hand, before his face, it gives him a sense of weight, of reassurance. Greasy fingerprints smudge the chrome skin. Everything inside and around him quiets down as his eyes roam over the firearm.

For hours, he stares at the mouth of the hole. For hours, he waits for something to happen, for someone to come, his grip tight on his gun. Nothing happens. No one comes. Outside, the darkness fades. Light creeps into the night. Before long the black becomes gray. Above him life stirs within the house. Muffled voices and three distinct sets of footsteps. One is light and measured. One sounds like a scuttle. One heavy and solid, and with each footfall the floorboards creak and dust drops from above. The motes catch in the slivers of morning sun that shine through the cracks. Huxley tries not to breath in the dust. He tries not to sneeze and give himself away.

Beyond his hiding place, the city comes to life. Feet pass by the opening, though no one pays it any mind. Shoes and boots flash past but none of them stop or even linger. The feeling changes from terrified anticipation, waiting to be discovered in his hole, to a sense of being trapped. He lies perfectly still, watching, his heartbeat quickening, his breathing shallow, trying to figure a way to escape without drawing attention.

Where can he go if he leaves? People seem to know Bracken. People are aware of who he is. Would it be as simple as asking someone? The bartender at the restaurant knew him, the first day they saw him. Or the vendor at the market. Huxley shivers as he remembers the man grabbing him out of the alley. He shakes it off and tries to think of what Bracken would do in this situation.

He has no idea. Bracken exists so far outside the realm of his perception that Huxley can't even conceive how his life works. Which is why Huxley needs Bracken. He can't survive on his own out there, and he certainly can't survive here alone. Bracken can. Huxley needs someone to teach him, someone to protect him. Bracken killed Huxley's father, he owes him for that.

He waits, face down in the dirt, beneath a building. The day progresses without touching him as he envisions an army hunting him, searching every home and building, digging to find him, stabbing into the dirt with long bayonets. It feels like they're right there, lurking at the periphery, waiting for him to make the first move. For the entire morning he doesn't eat, he doesn't piss, and he doesn't cough. He keeps his breathing as minimal as possible.

He is cold and he is alone.

Huxley watches through the hole as the light of the day begins to fade. Night hasn't fallen yet, but the sun hangs low enough that all of Requiem sits in shadow. He can't stay still much longer. His muscles and limbs need to move, to feel blood pump through them, to know they're still alive.

The bowels of the house close in around him. The confines of his hiding space crush in over the top of him. Heavy with dust and dirt, every breath fills his lungs until it feels like he's breathing through a sand dune. A layer of grime coats his nostrils and the passages feel clogged with mud or cement. The weight, the pressure, it's all too much to take.

His fingers move first, drumming, picking at the seams of his bag, unable to remain static. But the rest of his body doesn't linger far behind. Finally, he reaches the breaking point and scuttles on this belly toward the opening, bag in tow, cutting a groove in the dirt. Reckless, without even looking first, he bursts out through the barrier he made and onto the street. Cool, light air fills his lungs and he coughs and spits out a mouthful of grit.

A lone man stands on the corner. He shoots Huxley a curious glance then turns back to what he's doing, as if it's completely normal to see a small child dig his way out from beneath a building. Huxley realizes he still has the gun in his hand and quickly tucks it into his pocket, nothing out of the ordinary.

Huxley clears his nostrils, shoulders his pack, and heads away from the man. For the first few blocks he walks with a purpose, head down, shoulders forward, and his steps coming in rapid succession. He stops when it dawns on him, he's not en route to any specific place and he still has no idea how to begin his search for Bracken.

But he keeps moving forward, even though he's unsure where. His pace slows, but he continues on. Turning another corner, he sees a stream of people, all moving in the same direction. Individuals walking alone, pairs and threes and fours, and even what look like families and groups traveling together make up the crowd.

Huxley approaches the flow and merges with them. His stride shortens. He proceeds, slower than the crowd, and people course around him on both sides. Even though he moves with them, he moves on his own, separate. No one pays him any extra attention and he drifts along with the current. The pack moves ahead toward the farthest edge of Requiem.

In the near dark, Huxley splinters off from the group and hides behind the corner of a building. The street dead ends in a doorway and forms a bottleneck. Gaping and black, the door opens wide enough for three people to enter side by side. The crowd piles up and people enter and descend into the earth. Inch by inch he backs away, sensing something sinister about the gateway. A sour smell emanates from within and taints the surrounding air, and a low-level rumbling static noise comes from the opening. It seems to him that the people are jumping directly into the fiery bowels of the desert.

His heart beats faster. Haley's voice sounds in his head. There are some places where people shouldn't go. There are places where no one should go. And those are the places where Bracken goes. He stares at the door, at the passageway into the first circle of hell. Bracken would go here, which is why Huxley needs to.

His fingers quiver and his knees stiffen as he takes one step forward. He stops and retreats. Another false start follows. He eyes the crowd, still snaking into the door. On the third try, he finally leaves behind safe anchor of the wall and rejoins the mob. As he nears the entrance, a wide frame made of heavy wooden beams, he wants to turn and run. Every survival instinct tells him to flee, to turn tail and find someplace safe and dark and empty. With great effort he ignores the rational thoughts and moves forward, step by step, toward looming oblivion.

The crowd catches him and surges, breaking against the wall like a wave, thickening as is spreads. Dozens, maybe hundreds of people wait to seep through the door, pushing and jockeying for position. Bodies jostle and press Huxley and he sways back and forth, unable to move on his own even if he tries. Thoroughly part of the swarm, the gaping maw of the doorway swallows him down along with the others.

The light fades at his back and the passageway grows darker and darker with every downward step. An almost physical stench hits his nose, the bitter, musky smell of people squeezed against one another. The atmosphere changes and the air grows moist and heavy with breath and perspiration. Huxley begins to sweat. At his height, there's even less illumination. The collar of his shirt feels newly tight around his throat and he tugs at it to no avail. Darkness and bodies compress around him and the space constricts more and more. The walls sweat. He reaches out and touches them and moisture sticks to his fingers. He wipes it on his pants, somehow comforted by the coolness of the stone. Hands in his pockets, the solid form of the gun reassures him and calms his mind.

A dull hum emanates from ahead. The boy nearly falls in the faint light. He catches himself on a stair. He can hear the steps of those around him, but their sounds mix with the increasing reverberation. It builds into waves that crash over the top of him. Dim fingers of light cling to the walls and the noise becomes the voice of a crowd.

Through a passageway, they emerge into the ruins of a massive underground parking structure. The central part of the building has caved in, leaving a yawning chasm that rises up five stories. The rubble has been cleared out and the structure serves as a de facto arena. People crowd each tier. Those near the edge teeter on the verge of toppling, but still, people jockey and elbow, trying to get the best seat in the house. Above them all, the roof opens up to let in the night sky.

Huxley knows that whatever he's about to witness can't be good.

On each level cars intermingle with the crowd and gray concrete columns, four on each plane. Their headlamps provide light. Huxley has seen cars before, but not like this. He's seen wreckage, skeletons stripped like the bones of a dead animal. He's seen bumpers protruding from sand dunes, rims without tires, and chassis stripped bare. He's seen bits and pieces and ruins. A handful of times he's encountered a truck that ran and had chunks of jagged metal welded to its frame, enough to recognize the rumble of engines beneath the noise of the mob.

These are not those cars. Pristine, paint without scratches, windows intact; chrome and gleam and completely foreign to the world that the boy knows. Huxley wonders where so many cars could possibly have come from.

The voice of the crowd, raw and thirsty for blood, calls him back from his reverie.

The smell of sweat mixes with sand, blood, smoke, urine, exhaust, and bodies piled on top of each other.

Stuck in the throng, pushed against the legs and hips of the crowd, unable to see what everyone else sees, Huxley looks for a way to a higher floor.

In one corner he locates a stairwell. Shadowy forms and faces etched with deep furrows, weighed down with leaden eyes, line the walls around the entrance. Slumping against the concrete, the owners nod off. Fingers of light flicker over them. Hands pass bottles of murky liquid and what appear to be lit cigarettes from one to another. Their voices slur and mumble.

Huxley peers into the stairwell, full of more of the same. Limp, lifeless bodies adorn the steps. Again, every instinct tells him not to go in, but there's no other way to get a better vantage point, and again, he denies his initial impulses. As quickly as he can, he ducks into the dark passageway. The outline of a woman kneels in front of man, his head lolling back against the wall.

Climbing, Huxley hops over strewn out limbs and cadaverous bodies, vague and indistinct in the dark. A few notice him and hands and moans reach out. One man laying on the ground, a wide, unnatural grin on his face, catches Huxley by the cuff of his pants. Huxley starts to pull out the gun, but the man is intoxicated, his fingers weak. The grip can't hold and the boy hurries upward, two stairs at a time.

Lower than the rest of the crowd, barely waist level to many, Huxley wriggles and squirms his way through the bodies until he stands at the edge of the second tier. Bent rebar protrudes from the crumbling concrete edges. Growing impatient, the crowd noise increases.

Below him, the roaring horde, almost deafening, surrounds three sides of an elevated square enclosed by substantial fencing. All of the light focuses here; this is the stage, whatever the planned spectacle, it will happen here. The fourth side butts up against a wall with a reinforced steel door dead in the center.

A lone man stands in the cage, a sturdy club in one hand, a crude shield of wood strapped to the opposite forearm. Black and red paint smear his chest and his muscles pulse under his skin.

The crowd seethes around Huxley and he steadies himself, adjusting his footing so he doesn't tumble over the edge. The energy is palpable, a physical force that crackles around him. He wants to scan the crowd for Bracken, but the sound and the spectacle draw his attention toward the stage.

A bolt in the center of the steel door twists and two thick metal rods draw inward. The heavy slab opens and hands force an infected through the opening.

It used to be human; it used to be a man. Now it's naked, a ravenous monster. Flesh a mixture of blue and grey and green, its genitals have been hacked off in one last attempt at humiliation, and it has no eyes. The crowd roars, not so much a snarl or a cheer as an avalanche, as a force of nature that swallows everything in its path.

The creature pauses and cocks its head in an attempt to orient itself. Without a catch in its motion it spins and attacks the armed man. With an easy motion he dodges to the left and brings the club down on the creature's ribs as it rushes by. It impacts the fence, bounces back, and attacks again. Again the man parries and crushes a knee with the club. The blows slow the creature, but only vaguely. Pain is something it no longer feels; it has only impulse and drive, and that impulse is to attack and that drive is to feed.

Its stride isn't as smooth, but the decline in the speed of attack is negligible. It comes and comes and comes at the man, arms outstretched, a horrible wail from its mouth. Relentless, only death will stop this beast. The man evades and deflects and counters with exaggerated flourishes. A grin appears on his lips as the damage mounts and the monster breaks down by degrees. He feels victory close at hand and plays to the crowd.

This pride is his downfall.

He knocks the beast to the ground then turns to the crowd to bow his head ever so slightly. The beast takes the opportunity to leap up and jump on him. Broken teeth sink into the flesh of his neck, and fingers with bones protruding from the tips dig into his clavicle. He screams and falls to his back. In desperation he flails and bellows, kicks and screams and swears. He pries at the creature's hands and beats at its head with his fists. When the head and skull are little more than a gelatinous lump, he finally pushes the monster off and finishes the job with the reclaimed club.

Panting, he stands over the carcass, drops the weapon, and touches his wound. Huxley sees the fear and panic as the realization sets in, and his own stomach drops. The steel door opens and four armed men emerge, surrounding the victor.

"No," he yells. "No, no, you can't take me."

He puts up his hands and attempts to fight them off. The guards are wary now he's been bitten. Wearing thick gloves and coats with heavy sleeves, one guard keeps him at bay while two others get behind him to restrain his flailing arms. After a brief struggle, they subdue him and drag him through the door kicking and cursing and sobbing.

The crowd reaches full boil. People pile on top of one another, pumping their fists into the air and howling. The mob tastes the blood and screams for more, about to devour itself.

To one side of the stage, elevated, relaxing in a soft, cushioned seat, a man clad in white robes sits and claps his hands. He looks more solid than the rest of the crowd, not fat, but noticeably well fed in comparison with the skeleton people that surround Huxley. While others waste away, he alone remains stout. His black and gray hair is meticulous, as are the folds of his immaculate white robes. Though he cheers and laughs with the others, he's separate from the mob in distance and rank. Fortified thugs border him on all sides. He occupies the lone seat of privilege, somehow untouched by the filth and grime around him.

Huxley thinks back to what Bracken told him about the man in charge of Requiem; this must be Elwood, it has to be.

Elwood stands and raises his hands, palms toward the sky. The crowd grows silent and still. In the cage behind him, two men drag away the dead body of the infected. It leaves a trail of brown slime behind.

"Friends," the man says. His voice booms and echoes as the stadium grows strangely quiet. The grin on his face is so wide Huxley can see his teeth. He loves this. "I hope you're enjoying yourself as much as I am. This is indeed quite a spectacle to behold. Now more than ever we need something to take our minds away from the horrors and realities of our daily existence.

"As I am sure you are all aware, these games, this . . . sport, is nothing new. We gather regularly for such events. As we should; we are long suffering and in need of release. Our world is hard. Our world is dangerous." He shakes his head. "Our world is not a pretty place."

"Hell no it isn't," a lone voice yells in response.

"But tonight." Elwood smiles and holds up one finger. His words are careful and calculated. "Tonight, my dear friends, my family. Tonight, we have something truly special planned for your entertainment. A man known to many of you. I daresay, a man known to every single man and woman in this audience tonight. This man that you all know, has volunteered to fight in this arena. To fight. For you, for your entertainment, for your pleasure, for your approval. Show him your love and let's give a rowdy Requiem welcome to our very own, Bracken."

He executes a sweeping turn, robes flowing, as a quartet of armed guards thrust Bracken through the door into the ring. A man with a head full of black dreadlocks, tattoos on his face, and a black vest, supervises.

Huxley sinks. He hoped to find Bracken here, but as part of the crowd, not a participant in this mayhem. This is bad. If something happens to him in the cage, Huxley runs out of options. And this isn't something Bracken chose on his own, this is a punishment and isn't supposed to go in his favor.

It hits him how much he needs Bracken, how much he needs this near-stranger to survive. He has nowhere to go, no one else in this world, and even if there is someone out there waiting, there's no way to get anywhere on his own. If Bracken dies, he dies. He exhales as his body tightens with the realization.

At the mention of Bracken's name and his abrupt appearance, the crowd erupts like never before. Deafening, the noise hurts Huxley's ears, and he loses his balance as the throng seethes and sways and lurches. He almost grabs onto a man behind him to prevent tumbling over the edge, but thinking better of inviting the attention of a stranger, he pushes back from the brink until he feels comfortable, he won't pitch forward.

Above him, on the top rung, two men are not so lucky, and topple over the edge, flailing and screaming to the ground below. Their bodies splay out on the pavement, bent and broken. One's leg spasms and kicks for a moment, but then he lies still and unmoving.

This only adds fuel to the fire, inciting the crowd still further and further into mayhem and chaos. A fight erupts on the lower level. A man and a woman attack another man. Instead of stepping in and preventing the attack, the surrounding crowd allows it to continue until the second man is on the ground. Other members of the mass join the fracas, kicking and stomping the fallen man until he, too, stops moving and lies dead on the ground.

Bracken stands alone in the cage. He scans the crowd. Huxley isn't sure, but he thinks Bracken's gaze stops and rests on him for a brief second. Bracken's chest inflates and deflates. His shoulders rise and fall with each deep, labored breath. Shirtless, the knuckles of his left hand are taut and white and his fingers wrap around a short length of pipe.

Even from his vantage point Huxley can see that Bracken is injured. His torso lists to the right and the grimace on his face tightens every time his lungs expand and contract. Somewhere inside of his body his ribs are broken, or at least bruised and cracked enough to hobble him.

Elwood turns from the crowd to face Bracken. The two men glare at each other. Bracken wears a look of blood and pain and vengeance, so deep that even from this distance Huxley sees it. He hopes he is never on the receiving end of such a look. Bracken twists his head to the left and then the right, cracking his neck while his hand absently taps the end of the pipe against the meat of his thigh in no particular rhythm.

Just as the crowd seems about to completely turn on itself, just as it is coming to the brink of explosion, Elwood nods to someone unseen, and once again the bolt in the center of the door turns and the door opens inward.

Guards herd four infected out into the arena. Heavy chains bind them, but the guards hold them at length with long poles attached to the shackles around their necks. The guards glance back and forth at each other until one steps forward to unleash the ghouls.

One creature, immediately upon release, turns on the nearest captor, and clamps down on the guard's neck, twisting and tearing with its jaws. Blood spews from the guard's throat and he tries to scream, but all that comes is a gurgle. The others swarm and beat the fiend back with the butts of their rifles. Once free, they drag their fallen comrade back out of the ring and the door slams shut.

Over the roar of the crowd, Huxley thinks he hears the sound of a single gunshot on the other side of the door. Maybe he imagines it.

The infected turn and freeze, taking in the madness around them. These are not the same as the creatures in the earlier fights. These have not been mutilated or handicapped. The blue of their skin is lighter; they have eyes and arms, fingers and teeth; there is little to no muscle deterioration; their movement is full and as agile as they can be.

They're fresh. Huxley shivers at the prospect of where such recent creatures come from.

Quickly, their attention turns to Bracken, the closest, most available prey. He spins his length of pipe once, and positions his back to the fence, keeping the creatures in front of him. Huxley swallows as the infected fan out, trying to encircle Bracken. They creep toward him, moving laterally the entire time. The infected on the far-right darts toward Bracken with a quick step, swiping at him with one hand. In a blur, Bracken counters with a blow from his pipe and crushes the bones in the back of the creature's hand.

Huxley's muscles tighten, his stomach knots, and his breathing quickens as the action begins. "Come on, come on, come on," he mutters, feeling almost like he's the one fighting. His survival hangs in the balance.

Hands grab Bracken from behind and he spins with an elbow that catches the infected in the temple. He steps back and brings the pipe down on its skull. It drops to its knees and Bracken crushes its skull with two more blows that come in a downward X pattern. The once human form slumps to the ground and Bracken raises the pipe at his three remaining attackers, positioning his body so nothing can get slip in and attack him from the blind side again.

One darts in. Bracken dodges to his left, brings the pipe down on its jaw with a crack, and quickly steps out of range. The creature's chin juts out at a different angle, dislocated or broken. The damage looks painful to Huxley, but it doesn't slow the creature down, or impact it at all. Instead of crying out, it only hisses in anger.

Bracken sweeps to his left. He leaps forward, bringing the pipe down twice, once to the left and the right, and lands a blow on either side of the nearest creature's clavicle. It shrieks and retreats out of harm's way. Fragments of crushed bone stick through its skin.

Focusing all of his attention on the enemies before him, Bracken takes a step backward, trips, and falls over the corpse of the first creature he killed. He regains his feet, but two of the infected take the opportunity to attack.

Bracken lunges into the assault, flailing the pipe like a madman. For a moment they turn into a blur of thrashing limbs, snarls, and screams. Huxley can't distinguish between Bracken's howls and those of the infected. Blows land with dull thuds as he hammers first one then the other. He steps back, rotates, and kicks one in the sternum, sending it toppling backward to the ground.

The crowd fumes and churns. If it were a single entity it would froth at the mouth. The cacophony crush Huxley's eardrums. Beneath his feet, the very structure of the parking garage quakes. Chunks of concrete crack and fall off of the edges of the crumbled structure and fall on the people below, but no one pays any attention to the collapse.

Fury overcomes Bracken. Ignoring his injuries, he picks up the corpse at his feet and heaves it at the others. The flying corpse knocks one to the ground, landing on top of the one that's already there before it can rise.

Bracken rushes the only one left standing. The monster meets him. His momentum and velocity are too much, and they fall to the ground, Bracken on top. He clutches the creature's jaw with one hand and the back of its head with the other. It claws at him, but with a mad, primal scream, Bracken jerks, wrenching its head, snapping its neck. The sound carries over the intensity of the crowd.

The creature's legs kick twice, twitch, and go limp.

Bracken falls upon the other two that struggle to get up from beneath the corpse. Pipe in hand, he hacks and chops and kicks and stomps their skulls. He keeps swinging until long after they quit moving, until long after their craniums become a pair of viscous lumps of flesh that only roughly resemble the people they once were.

When he ceases his onslaught, he stands, body glistening with sweat and gore. Huxley sees Bracken quickly check himself to make sure that there are no open wounds for the infection to come through. Bracken's chest heaves, he takes one step back, tosses the pipe to the ground, and turns to the crowd. His face is sinister and dark, drunk with rage. He looks more like a monster than the man he is. Clenching his jaw tight, he stares down Elwood, who sits atop his elevated throne looking mildly amused.

The robed man mouths words toward Bracken, but Huxley is too far away to get any idea of their meaning, and gives cursory round of applause for the benefit of the spectators.

Neither man looks away. Guards emerge from the steel door and, wearing heavy, cumbersome gloves, grab Bracken by his shoulders, and drag him backward out of the stadium. Even then he maintains the shared look until he's deep within the passageway and the door clangs shut in front of him.

Huxley watches Bracken until the door blocks him from view. Below his perch, Elwood stands, turns to the crowd, and bows with a flourish, accepting their cheers and appreciation for himself. His robes and hair flap with the gesture. With that, he makes his exit. Guards at his side, he slips from his podium and vanishes around the side of the cage. The disappearance takes Huxley by surprise, until he surmises that there must be some sort of concealed escape route at the base of his throne.

With the Elwood's departure, the crowd roars one final time. The noise subsides to a murmur and the people remain in place, unsure of what to do next. Everyone looks to everyone else for a hint or clue. A few turn to shuffle away, elbowing a path through the press of flesh. Gradually, the rest follow suit. The energy goes out in the blink of an eye. The feeling of celebration, debauchery, and frenzy dissipates. Inebriated men and women lean against the walls as they hobble toward the exits, barely able to stand or move at all.

Like when Huxley entered, a bottleneck forms. Faces that only moments before were animated and screaming for blood now hang heavy with wrinkles, heading back to the weight of reality. The creases and shadows look so much deeper. Tension and leftover bloodlust hang over the pack. Bodies bump one another. Shoves are exchanged, elbows thrown, curses muttered. Huxley waits for an eruption of violence like he witnessed earlier. The scene lingers on the brink of hostility, but never quite reaches the point of no return. Too spent to fight any further, everyone simply moves toward home.

Using his size to his advantage, Huxley scurries between the legs of the ambling crowd. He ignores the protestations of the people he knocks into with his pack, hurrying on toward his goal. One inebriate takes a half-hearted swing at the back of the boy's head before muttering something unintelligible to no one in particular and continuing on along his way.

Huxley elbows his way down the stairs. Once on the bottom level, he changes direction and swims against the flowing tide of spectators. The bodies of the man they stomped to death, along with the two that fell from the top floor, lay on the floor where they landed. No one pays them any mind. The spectators step over the corpses like a fallen branch or some other obstacle lying in the street, a minor annoyance. The bodies remain, to be dealt with later. Huxley pauses and stares at them, broken, limbs splayed out at uncomfortable angles, marionettes with the strings cut. There's not as much blood as he expected. At least, Huxley hopes, someone will eventually come for them.

He hides in the darkest corner he can find and waits for the crowd to clear out completely. Above him unseen men take the cars away until he's left alone in the dark and the silence, only the moon and stars overhead for light.

Making sure no one sees him, that there is no one to see him, Huxley creeps up to the stage and looks for the door Elwood used to escape. He finds footprints that go directly into the concrete wall. In the moonlight he sees that the gray of the panel in front of him is a slightly different shade than its surroundings. This must be a door, but the wall feels sturdy and has no give, nor any echo from within that betrays hollowness.

He pushes against it with his shoulder.

Nothing moves.

He pushes again.

Nothing.

Again and again he tries. He throws himself against the wall. He bounces off and falls to the ground. He pushes with his legs until the muscles burn and shake. Tears of frustration come and drip down his face. They cut canyon lines down his cheeks, through the caked-on dirt and dust. He punches the wall until his knuckles bleed. He kicks and kicks and kicks, grunting and cursing with every blow.

He falls to the ground in a limp pile, his head in his hands, sobbing.

On the ground, in the dirt, back to the wall, Huxley sits with his head bowed. His chest and shoulders heave with silent sobs, and he slaps the ground with open palms. The sound echoes in the empty space. Small clouds of dust burst into the air and settle on his clothes, adding to the grit already there.

He crouches in the blue shadows for what feels like forever. The only light comes in from the patch of stars overhead, shining through the gaping hole in the top of the parking garage. The darkness surrounds him, sinister and full of demons. In every corner, every gloom-shrouded space, he sees movement, ghosts and monsters, some *thing*, some creature, coming for him. What frightens him even more is the idea that whatever lurks in the periphery is no monster at all, but a person, a human.

The darkness encroaches; it encloses and penetrates him. His entire body trembles and shakes with a cold like he's never felt before. Hopeless and lost; alone and afraid; desolate.

He can't. He can't do this. He can't be this way. He can't be afraid. He can't crack. He's alone. Nothing will change that. He can't curl up in a corner and wait to die. He can't quit or give up. His father wouldn't. They failed so many times trying to farm. They moved from place to place to place, hoping the next spot would be better, but it never was. Every time they started anew, they failed as miserably as before. There were a number of false starts and wells that brought up nothing and rows of seeds that never sprouted, never took root, and never amounted to anything.

They failed so many times. But his father saw other people who somehow managed to make something grow, to make new life out of nothing but hope and determination. His father never quit. Bracken wouldn't quit. Bracken would laugh at him and call him some vulgar name if he tried to give up, or just stare at him like he didn't know what he was looking at. Bracken would probably leave Huxley sitting there and walk away. In his mind, Huxley has created an image of Bracken as some sort of heroic figure, someone who can help him, and Bracken won't tolerate quitters and cry babies.

Huxley pushes the shadows and monsters and vicious men away, back into the darkness, back into a deep corner of his skull where they can't bother him. He coughs. He snorts back the snot that leaks out of his nose. He blinks back the new tears and wipes the ones that have already come on his sleeves. This is the last time he'll cry. This is the last time he'll let himself be that weak little boy.

He pushes himself up against the wall, wipes his nose one final time, and begins his search for a way to open the door anew.

He throws his small body against the door and bounces off like a pebble. Getting a running start, he rams his shoulder into the stone, repeatedly, until it throbs and pulses with pain. He kicks and punches and yells and curses as much as he knows how.

Dust flies up around him like he's caught in a diminutive tornado. Grains of sand and dirt catch in the cold light. They stick to inside of his nostrils and he sneezes. Sound reflects off of the hard surfaces surrounding him.

"Bless you," he says into the darkness. He stands there as the echo dies. It seems to take longer than it should. His mind plays tricks, still seeing movement in the shadows, but he shoves such ideas from his head and focuses on the task at hand. Arms at his sides, tiny shoulders heaving, he stands, his small lungs burning and gulping air.

Doubt forms in Huxley's mind as he glares at the wall, willing it to move, to do anything. Maybe this isn't even a door. Maybe he only thought he saw the man disappear through this section of the wall. Maybe he just lost him in the crowd. It's possible. There was so much going on, so much commotion, and so many bodies moving in every direction keeping track of any single one would have been almost impossible. Was that it? Was that all it was? Did he simply think he saw something he didn't actually see?

He crosses his arms and tries to calm down and remember exactly what he saw. After the man in white bowed to the crowd, he climbed down from his pedestal, walked directly to where Huxley now stands, and disappeared. He didn't mix with the crowd. The bodyguards saw that no one touched him. Huxley swears that's how it happened, his mind convinced he saw a door open right in this very spot. There must be a door right here, there's no other option.

He stomps back and forth, wracking his brain for anything else, trying to recapture any other details he might have missed. Nothing comes to him. He balls up his fists and pounds his thighs as he strides, muttering to himself.

"Fuck," he screams into the night. "Fuck. Fuck. Fuck." The reverberations of his voice reflect off of the walls, layer over each other, and fade into the night as a whispering chorus of small voices.

He stops his mad pacing and puts his hands on the cage. His fingers grip the pieced together chain link and rattles the metal into a sonic storm, stops, and shakes it again.

He lets his head sag between his outstretched arms, unsure of what to do. He thinks about turning around and searching for another entrance, but has no idea where to start. His fingers squeeze together the links of the fence.

His shoulder tightens up and throbs. With his right foot, he kicks at the base of the cage, patched together from random pieces of wood. He picks at splinters in the supports, tearing strips off of the wooden slabs. Nails shriek as he pulls boards away from other boards. The wood cracks and fractures under the pressure of his little muscles. He wants to tear the whole thing down. Grabbing the end of a post with both hands, he pulls. His back tenses and he rocks back, bending the board repeatedly until it snaps off in his hands.

He stands, clutching the board in one hand, like a weapon he used to kill an infected. Written across his small face is all of the anger and frustration of his young life—the starts, the stops, the failures, his father, dead in a hole somewhere in the desert. He raises the board and slams it again and again against the base of the cage.

Another board, a piece of the structure that seems out of place, like an extra scrap nailed in the corner for good measure, moves, and Huxley stops. He stares it down. Was it an optical illusion? A trick played on his eyes in the dark? Thin and square, the board has no obvious practical function. Huxley's club clatters to the ground as his fingers release and he reaches for the surplus wood.

Splinters dig into the flesh of his hand. The board feels loose under his grasp. He resets his fingers into a tighter grip, his knuckles white, and draws it toward him. The end moves in a smooth, even arc, connected to something he can't see in the darkness.

This is a lever, a release.

Huxley hears a pop, then a grind as the panel in front of him twists.

This is a door.

Anchored in the middle, the door spins around a central point. He gawks for a moment then springs into action, clawing at the front edge of the door, trying to pull it further open, but his fingers find no purchase and slip away on the smooth surface. He moves to the other end and pushes with all of the strength his small frame can muster.

The door moves, halting at first. But once he gets it going, it swings easily until the gate sticks out perpendicular to the wall.

Huxley stands and pants, staring into a gaping black entrance at something that he can't see, which is even darker. He has no idea where the passageway leads, or what it hides.

He steps forward into the unknown.

CHAPTER 5

The air hangs thick and stale in the passageway. It smells stagnant, like a crowded room with no windows. The odor of bodies lingers, like ghosts. Dust, sweat, something sour, and an animal scent he can't place, bombard Huxley's olfactory senses and he wrinkles his nose.

He closes the door behind him so he can't go back, so he has to go forward. A deep, meaty sounding clack indicates that it's secure, and the last of his light, the leftover remains from the night sky, disappears. Complete darkness surrounds and swallows him. He breathes it in and listens, hoping his eyes will pick up on some faint glimmer from somewhere, something he can't see yet, but that his eyes will register.

He waits, but there's nothing for his eyes adjust to. The pure, inky black remains the same after a minute as after five then ten and fifteen. No sound trips his eardrums. He floats in the murk, senseless. Which way is up, forward, backward? He feels like he's falling. Fear overtakes his body again and he regrets the decision to shut the door. His heart beats faster, his breaths come quicker, and imagined shapes and movement swim in the empty void before him. Dizziness engulfs him, his head spins, and sweat leeches out of his skin.

There's no time for this. He squeezes his eyes shut, takes a breath, and swallows his terror and fright. He gulps it down and buries it deep. When he opens his eyes, though he knows it's no lighter, it's somehow less dark than before.

His left hand reaches out until the tips of his index and middle fingers touch the rough concrete of the wall. This grounds him, gives him something solid and real to cling to, and he stabilizes. After a few deep breaths the dizziness abates. He still can't see, but he has something to feel, something to anchor him to the physical world.

A few more minutes pass as Huxley regains himself. His first step reaches forward, slow and exploratory. With the weight of the pack on his shoulders, and no visual cues, he wobbles, his balance is precarious. He probes with his toes outstretched and waits to transfer any weight from his back foot to his front until absolutely certain that solid ground waits before him; he doesn't want to take that fact for granted. Moving his body forward, his fingertips drag and scrape against the cement wall, and in the compresses space silence, that miniscule sound looms large.

Another step follows, as cautious and vigilant as the first. In this manner he steals forward, foot by deliberate foot. After one hundred steps he loses count and can't decide if he lost count or simply stopped paying attention. Steady, his pace doesn't quicken, and he creeps on and on until he comes to a gap in the wall.

When he reaches his hand around the corner and into the emptiness, as wary as with his steps, his fingers fall on a recessed door. He gropes around and finds a handle. Locked, he jiggles it once, with barely any force, and waits, listening for the sound of movement in the room beyond the barrier. With his eyes closed, despite the darkness, he waits, muscles tense and ready for fight or flight.

No sound comes. He jostles the handle more convincingly, with a metallic rattle that echoes through the dungeon. Still he hears no indication of life behind the door. He tries, but is unable to coerce open the gate by force or ingenuity.

Finally, he decides this task is futile and continues his gradual quest forward. Occasionally, he finds other doors at irregular intervals along the wall, all secured in a similar fashion, and none betray signs of life from the other side.

The wall ends. He reaches his hand around the corner, expecting to find another door. Instead, he extends the entire length of his arm only to find that the wall continues into the darkness far beyond his reach.

At this crossroads he stops.

With his hand resting on the corner, he stares straight ahead into the blackness as if he'll be able to see if he concentrates hard enough. He turns to the left, stares into an identical blankness and sniffs, hoping perhaps his nose can provide some hint of which way to go. Squeezing his eyes shut, he concentrates on his ears, searching for any miniscule sonic wave that might possibly vibrate one of the membranes or tiny bones that register sound. There's nothing, nothing to indicate he even exists, nothing to connect him to the concrete world, and he hovers in place like a bad dream.

Huxley pushes all of the air out of his lungs in one long exhale, raises his arms, and, waving his hands, searching for anything solid to touch, steps forward. Vertigo returns in a rush and with each halting stride, his body lists and leans, wobbling over his knees. The feeling of floating loose in space washes over him again, like he came unmoored from reality. Pausing with each step to reestablish balance, he advances at a snail's pace, even slower and more cautious than before.

Step after step. Inch by inch. Until he fears he foolishly abandoned his anchor and wandered blindly into an empty void from which there's no return. Panic builds in his limbs and stomach. His muscles tighten and his fingers tingle. He fights the impulse to spin and flee back the way he came. At the same time, he fights the desire to run forward. Reckless, that urge will only lead to the loss of the minimal orientation he does have. He knows this and settles himself, strengthening his resolve.

He stops and breathes, calming his rapid heartbeat. Five more steps. Five more steps then he'll turn around.

He moves forward again. And again. On the third step, the back of his left hand makes contact with concrete. A shudder of relief runs through the length of his body as the top layer of skin scrapes off two of his knuckles. The brief pain is like a welcome embrace and he smiles to himself in the darkness, sinking into the joy of the sensation of touching something solid.

He hugs the wall, pressing his face against the cool surface, exhales, and continues.

Just as he has no spatial reference points, Huxley has nothing to measure the time that flows over him. He has no idea how many minutes or hours pass. They simply dissipate into the surrounding ether. He encounters more gaps in the walls, and when his path meets a solid wall that blocks his way, he makes the choice to go left. There's no reason, he doesn't base this decision on any tangible information. Left is only one of two equally indefinite options. His head swims and he feels like he's been wandering down here in the darkness for months.

In this manner he moves forward in the empty maze, choosing new directions when barriers demand, until he makes so many turns, he loses all sense of where is and where he's been. The network of passages keeps going and he tries not to consider the possibility he's been travelling in circles and will never find his way to the surface. Such thoughts make his heartbeat quicken and his lungs go into overdrive. He does his best to block such fears and concerns from his mind and focuses on continuing forward.

Forward is all there is. Forward is all he has. Forward is Bracken and escape and survival. Behind him there's only death and the final memories of his father clinging to life. With each step he takes, he attempts to outrun that ghost lurking over his shoulder whispering doubt into his ear. He takes a deep breath, swallows, steels himself, and continues.

He comes to another break in the wall and stops. Out of habit he peers around the corner, expecting nothing but ink black. But he furrows his brow. Something's different, the darkness is less complete. His mind must be playing tricks on him, but there appears to be the faintest, single wave of light coming from in front of him. So pale, so frail it doesn't even cast real shadows, he can't be certain if it is real or if it's an invention of his fractured mind.

Watching, he blinks his eyes. Then he rubs them with the butt of his hands and stares some more. He does this and waits until he's absolutely sure what he sees is real and not illusion, hallucination, or imagination. He can see the walls, the ground, and his own hands before his eyes.

He skulks around the corner, keeping tight to the wall like a shadow, and shuffles toward the source of the light. The illumination, seemingly less than that of a single candle, dribbles out of an opening in the distance, originating in another of the branching arms of the subterranean maze. Huxley comes to the brink and peeks around the corner. The view is more of the same; a long, empty passage with shadowy doorways with more mysterious roads branching off.

A more intense light pours from the mouth of the nearest opening and he sees faint indications of movement. Ghost silhouettes play in the glow. As he creeps near, he hears the sounds of voices. Again, he sneaks up to the edge and peeks beyond the lip of the wall. In the split-second glimpse, he sees two men standing watch outside of a closed door.

He steals another look, longer this time. Both men carry rifles. One holds an oil lantern down at his waist, casting shadows up across their faces. Dressed in dusty black clothes, heavy boots cling to their feet. One has a sleeveless denim jacket with a row of chrome studs along the collar and smudged homemade tattoos on his arms. Both faces sport deep withered creases, but the one with his back to the door looks older and he maintains a rigid posture. The one facing him sways on his feet, his face red and wearing a wide, intoxicated smile. Huxley ducks back and strains to listen to the middle of their conversation.

"C'mon man," the younger voice says. The words have a round, filed-down sound. "I'm fine. Sure, I had a couple of drinks, but it's a party. The whole town is partying tonight, that shit was epic."

"I like to party after the fights as much as anybody," the older guard says. His voice sounds like shifting gravel in his throat. Huxley imagines him shaking his head. "But not when I got a job to do. This is serious. This guy is dangerous."

"Seriously, I'm fine. I take this shit serious, so serious. There isn't any reason I can't do this. You've been here for hours, now it's my turns. He's chained to a fucking wall for fuck's sake. He's not going anywhere. Fuck, I'm not even gonna go in there. I'm just gonna stand right here and do my job."

It must be Bracken. They only took him away. Who else would they guard? Who else needs to be chained to a wall? Huxley's heart rate jumps and he feels hope first time in forever. He presses his forehead against the cool wall, closes his eyes, and focuses all of his attention on the voices around the corner.

"Fine," the older voice says. "I'm sick of arguing."

"That's right. Get out of here. Go join the party. Go find something with boobs and a fuck hole."

The older guard laughs to himself, despite himself. "Fucking maniac. Just don't let Cyrus catch you slipping or I'm just as fucked as you for handing this over to a drunk." His words are pleasant and familiar, but a sharp, serious edge lurks just beneath the surface.

"Man, fuck him. That old bastard isn't shit. Everyone's so scared of him for no fucking reason at all."

The older guard laughs. "You keep thinking that way, see where it gets you." The sound of footsteps moves away, and his voice grows quieter until it is muddy. "Just watch yourself, young blood."

It has to be Bracken. Has to be.

Huxley risks another glance. The new guard leans his against the wall, watching the direction that the older guard went. His head lolls forward, his neck bounces gently, and he hums a tuneless melody to himself. With a groan, he slides his back down the wall with a slow grind until he sits on the ground. The rifle against his shoulder, his elbows rest on his knees, and he examines the back of his hand until his attention wanes. He leans his head back and closes his eyes.

Huxley pulls back and listens and waits. Bracken has to be in there.

Before long, the guard's hum dies, and Huxley hears the deep-throated rattle of snoring. Peeking around the corner, he sees the guard sitting on the ground, slumped against the wall, clutching his rifle to his cheek. The lamp sits on the ground, sputtering in the dust, casting shadows that waver along the hallway. He listens to the sawing of his snores, waiting even though the guard appears sound asleep.

Convincing himself into motion, Huxley takes a single step around the corner and pauses, watching the guard's face for any sign that he may wake up. He sees no indications, and takes another step. A shorter one this time. Huxley clutches the revolver in his pocket, the grip is cold against his palm.

With each successive step, the interruption decreases, until Huxley gingerly takes regular steps, taking great care to keep his pack and possessions from jingling and jangling, and finds himself halfway up the hallway. He holds his breath for as long as he can in order to cut down on the noise he produces.

He stops again, cocking his head to the side and crouching down. His eyes fixate on the space between the small of the guard's back and the wall. A heavy ring of keys dangles from the guard's belt.

Huxley slows his approach, painfully aware of the sound of every spec and grain of dirt grinding beneath his feet. He glances at the door, made of dense, rugged wood. He reaches out and touches the surface without taking his eyes off of the guard. It feels solid beneath his fingers, reinforced with a pair of heavy metal bands and the top and bottom. A large black lock holds the door shut. He thinks to himself that the lock is comically oversized and for a moment he almost chuckles.

Collecting himself, he continues to creep up on the sleeping guard.

All he hears are his own footsteps and his breathing and his heartbeat. They echo and reflect off of the walls and grow into a cacophony that threatens to overwhelm him. He crouches and reaches out toward the keys. The sound grows until it overpowers him like a wave and he has to pause. For a moment he almost turns and retreats. His fingers hang in the air, quaking, pointing to the guard's belt. The muscles in his shoulder are stiff from slamming into the wall. Snores grow and rattle in the guard's sinuses, and even from a distance Huxley smells his breath, sour and thick and foul.

He inhales as deeply as his lungs allow. Slowly pushing the air out, he reaches his hand behind the guard, eyes to the man's face, looking for any sign of stirring. The keys are far enough under his body Huxley's face almost touches the guard's. His own hot breath reflects off of the grown man's cheek as his fingers touch the keys. The guard's brow twitches.

Huxley's heart stops for two beats as he imagines the guard sitting bolt upright and seizing him by the neck. Phantom fingers dig into Huxley's throat, choking off his airflow as his vision fades into black. The guard's face, twisted mass of rage, teeth looming over Huxley's body, squeezing the life out of the boy, taking great pleasure in the act.

Pulling himself back, the weight of the pistol in his pocket reassures him, and Huxley refocuses his eyes and squeezes the arm of the carabiner that holds the keys. A grimace crosses his face as he works the clasp gently back and forth. The lip catches on the cracked leather belt. He works it loose time and again, but it seems to catch anew each time. It takes every bit of restraint he can muster not to simply yank it free.

Along the bridge of his nose, he feels a bead of sweat form. Once the drop reaches critical mass, it begins a slow descent. When it reaches the tip, it dangles, and Huxley attempts to blow it back up his face, scowling as the drip remains in place. He tilts his head back just as the drop breaks free, and it slides harmlessly down and over his lips. The salt taste coats the tip of his tongue and he goes back to work on the key ring. Gradually, the clip slips free and the weight of the keys falls into the palm of his hand. Gently bouncing the mass in his grasp he smiles a nervous smile.

For a second, Huxley looms over the guard. He pulls back and, not turning, steps to the door, trying the first of a dozen keys in the lock. His fingers shake so much that it takes repeated attempts to separate a single key from the rest and see if it fits. The third key slips in, but will not turn. The seventh and eighth do the same. Key number ten slides easily into the jagged crease with a light click and immediately Huxley knows that the tumblers and pins will line up and turn.

He twists the key and the shackle pops out of body of the lock with an audible clack. Careful to avoid scraping metal against metal, always watching the guard, he removes the lock and sets it on the ground. As vigilant as possible, he releases the latch on the door, and sets himself to push it open.

What if it isn't Bracken in there? What if it is someone else? What if whoever it is raises an alarm? Potential catastrophes swirl and circle in front of him and he freezes. He considers walking away, taking the guard's lamp and weapon and trying to find his way back, or at least some other way out of these catacombs. But where is there to go? What is there to go back to?

Forward or backward are his choices. Those are the two directions.

Forward. He chooses forward. He has to choose forward. Through the door. That's the only option, the only real choice that he has.

He leans his shoulder against the slab of a door, wincing from the pain of the bruised flesh, and edges it inward. The wood groans in the frame and Huxley shivers. Again he presses his weight into the door. Again a small, shrill scream accompanies the slight movement. The guard twitches and the pattern of his snoring shifts. His head rolls forward, and he sounds like he's choking. To be so lucky.

Huxley checks his movement and waits. With one final application of pressure, the door clears the inside edge of the frame and swings free.

Pausing, he listens for any sound from within, watching the guard for any signs that he may wake up. The black-clad body slumps limp and still against the wall and only the snores indicate life. Behind the door is a silent open space. No light comes from inside.

Taking a deep breath, Huxley pushes the door all the way open. The hinges release a miniscule shriek of metal on metal. A rectangle of illumination burns into the darkness and falls across the form of a man, shirtless, wet and shivering, his hands chained over his head to the wall behind him. His head hangs forward between his shoulders and his eyes, open, watch the door with an intense hatred.

It's Bracken.

Huxley stands in the doorway, his shadow stretching out before him.

When the man's eyes fall on the boy, the look on his face, the revulsion and anger, changes to confusion then recognition and bewilderment.

His mouth tries to form words, but fails. Huxley raises a finger to his lips.

"What the hell are you doing here?" Bracken mouths in less than a whisper. "Where did you come from?"

Huxley remains still.

Bracken shakes his head and says, loud enough to be heard, "You shouldn't have come here."

Huxley holds up the ring of keys.

Bracken smiles. "Good boy." With his head he motions Huxley over. They look at his shackles. At the same time, they both realize the boy won't be able to reach the locks. Bracken can't bring his arms down far enough and there's nothing for Huxley to stand on.

Bracken laughs quietly.

"I have an idea," he whispers, raising his leg until his thigh is parallel with the ground. "Climb on. Take the backpack off first."

Huxley nods, slides off is pack, then turns and hoists himself up until he sits on Bracken's leg. He picks a key and reaches for the lock.

"Not that one," Bracken says, his face twists with the effort of holding Huxley's weight and the pain from his injured ribs.

Hurrying, Huxley picks the next key on the ring. Bracken shakes his head. "Three more that way."

Huxley pinches a key between two fingers, holds it up and looks at Bracken with his eyebrows up. Bracken nods. Huxley continues to look at him with a question on his face.

"Believe it or not," Bracken whispers. "I've been in this situation before."

Huxley reaches up, inserts the key, and opens the lock. Bracken drops him back to the ground and pulls his wrist free, shaking his fingers and making a fist, trying to get the circulation back into his hand. Huxley freezes and watches the open door.

Bracken takes the keys and frees his other hand.

"I thought I was going to have to teach you to pick locks like Magnum."

Huxley looks at him. "What?"

"Yeah. Right," he says. "Guards?"

Huxley holds up one finger, "Just one."

"How did you get by?"

"Quietly," Huxley says.

Bracken smiles and stifles a laugh then crouches and moves toward the door. At the opening, he stops, places his right hand on the frame, and peeks around the edge. Pulling back, he stands up straight and steps casually around the corner. Huxley hurries after him.

Bracken stands over the sleeping guard, examining him with his eyes. He nudges the guard with the toe of his boot and gets no response. He tries again. The third time he winds up and kicks the man in the ribs.

The guard lurches awake and looks up at Bracken. "Wha . . .? Who . . .?" His drunken eyes recognize Bracken, and he mutters, "Oh shit."

Bracken's torso jerks forward and his fist drives into the guard's face, once, twice, three and four times, until he stops moving. Blood trickles from his nose and his body slumps against the wall. Huxley flinches with each punch, but keeps watching with morbid fascination.

A small part of him revels in the violent act.

Bracken drags the unconscious man into the room. "Grab his gun and his light," he says over his shoulder. Huxley scurries to collect the dust coated bolt-action rifle and light source. In the lamplight he sees the word "Bird" tattooed in simple letters in the middle of Bracken's chest, over his heart.

Bracken peels the man's clothes off to replace his own bloody, soaked garments. He searches his new pockets for anything useful, coming back with a handful of bullets and a dust-covered multi-tool. Hoisting the limp guard, he pins the body against the wall with his own weight, lifts one arm, and clamps it in the shackle on the wall. Stepping back, the weight of the limp body dangles awkwardly from the wrist.

He looks at Huxley and says, "The other one?"

Huxley nods.

Bracken shrugs and says, "I like the way you think," and cuffs the other hand. He stands back, crosses his arms, and examines his handiwork with an air of pride. "There, that looks more comfortable."

He stops, turns to Huxley, and looks at the boy. Shaking his head, he says, "I don't know where you came from, or how the hell you found this place, but you shouldn't have come here. This isn't safe for you. I can take care of myself. You, you're not equipped to deal with this shit." He breaks off and walks past the boy. At Huxley's shoulder he pauses and takes the rifle. Looking down, he puts his hand on Huxley's shoulder and squeezes lightly. Huxley winces under the grip.

"Thanks."

The boy smiles.

"Let's go," Bracken says over his shoulder. "Get your bag."

Huxley scurries after him, hoisting his bag onto his shoulder, and raising the lantern above his head with his left arm. Bracken walks into the darkness and takes an immediate right, the rifle held loosely in his hands, his gait causal and easy, like he knows exactly where he's going.

The light from the lamp reaches ahead of them, casting a long shadow where Bracken's body blocks the rays. He doesn't pause before going around corners. He doesn't stop at intersections and deliberate for minutes about which avenue to take. He moves forward with confidence and certainty. Huxley follows, bouncing from side to side, peering ahead into the darkness, and trying to discern some reason for their path. Nothing presents itself, no obvious end in sight, but Bracken appears to have a goal, so he continues to follow along.

"Where are we going?" Huxley finally asks.

Bracken doesn't respond.

A few minutes pass.

"How do you know where you're going?"

Bracken stops, gazing into the distance. "Been down here before, kid. Going to get you out of here. Bad things happen down here."

"Bad things happen everywhere."

"That is certainly true." He nods and turns toward Huxley. "But this place has seen more than its fair share." He turns back and starts forward again. "Even compared to the rest of this fucked up world."

Again, Huxley loses track of time. Thankful that he no longer has to make every decision on his own, he automatically trails behind Bracken for what could be minutes or hours. Now that he has found Bracken, he plans follow the man as long as possible, to learn as much as he can.

"Why did you do that back there?" Huxley asks quietly as they walk.

"Fight."

"Didn't exactly have a choice." Bracken keeps his eyes ahead and his voice low.

"No, I mean, why…at all."

Bracken shakes his head. "It's spectacle. It keeps people occupied, entertained. If people are busy watching that, it's easier to get away with things you don't want them to see. It's another way Elwood keeps control. He gives them just enough to look forward to and distract them."

Huxley opens his mouth but Bracken puts up a finger for silence. Their path takes a perpendicular corner, Bracken raises his hand and indicates for Huxley to stop. He motions for the boy to give him the lamp, which he takes and blows out.

Huxley fears their only source of light is gone, until his eyes adjust and pick up traces of illumination coming from around the corner ahead. In front of him, Bracken crouches down and raises the rifle to his shoulder, ready, and creeps toward the bend. With the palm of his hand he tells Huxley to stay put, but the boy ignores him and keeps close behind.

Bracken pauses at the brink and closes his eyes. Huxley strains to listen for anything. Bracken opens his eyes and takes a rapid step around the corner, low, bracing himself, sweeping in front of him with the barrel of the gun. He moves forward, out of Huxley's line of sight, and the boy scampers after.

Another elbow in the hallway, and Bracken repeats the drill at the next corner, stepping and sweeping and moving forward.

When Huxley follows, he sees the passageway open up into a large room. Bracken stands at the mouth of the corridor, rifle up, senses alert, looking and listening, and, Huxley thinks, maybe even trying to smell any threat. Sensing no signs of immediate danger, Bracken relaxes, letting the rifle barrel list toward the ground.

The main body of the room stretches out longer than it is wide. A single lantern burns on the wall and indicates that someone has been here recently. More open gaps in the wall indicate routes out of the room. The light dances and flickers and reflects off of the immaculate skins of two rows of cars lined up parallel to each other. Each row faces the other at an angle.

Bracken stands with the gun in his hands and a slight smile on his face as he takes it all in.

"Aren't they pretty?" he says, more to himself than to Huxley.

Huxley has seen cars before. A few. A handful of times. They were few and far between, and all utilitarian in nature. Rough and corroded, they were primarily for transport. Fuel was precious and exceedingly rare, so their use was sparse and limited to times of absolute necessity. Every last one was pieced together from any spare parts that were still functional and not corrupted by time or invaded by sand. They were patchwork creations, jerry-rigged, a collage of random, improvised mechanics. He has never ridden in one, and never given them much attention.

Huxley has seen cars before, but he has never seen anything like collection of vehicles in front of him. These are pristine. He's never seen anything so clean in his life, so smooth and free of scratches. Brilliant greens and reds and blues and blacks glisten under the primal light of the burning oil. There are no dents, no rust, no jagged welded edges or seams crisscrossing the body like surgical scars. These look like nothing he has ever seen in his short life, nothing his mind has a previous frame of reference for. Not even a speck of dust on any of them.

He runs his hands along the sleek bodies; his fingers glide down ribbons of chrome trim. They sparkle like alien creatures. These are truly artifacts from another world.

Bracken drifts down between the rows, bouncing from side to side, examining them. There are twenty-two, eleven in each column. It occurs to Huxley that he's seen these before, these cars provided the illumination at Bracken's fight.

Bracken stops in front of a black car at the end of the left row. He stands and looks at it, a mean-spirited smile on his face, nodding to himself.

"What's this?" Huxley says, sidling up to his side.

"What's this?" Bracken shakes his head. "This? Kid, this is a thing of beauty."

Huxley looks at it, trying to see what Bracken sees, then looks up at the man, pinching his brows together, searching for any clue as to what he means.

"This, my boy, is a '68 Chevy Nova SS." He speaks to himself more than Huxley. "Big block V8. Rock Crusher four-speed. This is a man machine. American muscle at its finest." He looks at Huxley. "You have no idea what I'm talking about, do you?"

Huxley shakes his head.

"Didn't think so. Elwood calls her Maggie."

"Is Elwood that turd in the white robes?"

"You saw that dick?"

Huxley nods.

"Yeah, that's Elwood." Bracken waves his hand above his head. "Like I told you, he's a piece of shit. And this," he reaches out and touches the skin of the car with reverence. "This may be the only thing in the world that he loves. Or, at least as close as he can come to love." He nods to himself and smiles. "And this is how we're going to get out of here."

"Won't that just make him mad?"

Bracken laughs. "Oh, buddy, he's already plenty mad at me. This is just going to be funny."

"Why is he so mad at you?" Huxley asks.

"I was supposed to pick up a package from that witch out there, Lexi." Bracken nods. "I did pick up a package, but I was late. Ran into some hang ups along the way." He glances at Huxley.

It dawns on the boy that he is the reason for Bracken's delay, he and his father. He pictures his father, shivering and near the end, but pushes the image away.

"Something valuable?" he asks.

Bracken shrugs. "To him."

"You never delivered it, did you?"

Bracken shakes his head. "Didn't have the chance. His goon squad grabbed me and, well, you saw how that ended up."

He opens the car door and looks as the gauges on the dashboard.

"Why don't you make yourself useful," he says. He motions to the other cars, "Go through all of these and see if there's anything we can use. Tools. Weapons. Food. Containers. Anything. You're a smart kid. You know what I'm talking about. Be quick about it, though, I don't want to hang around here any longer than we have to."

The faint smell of gasoline and grease mixed with the ever-present aroma of dust and dirt hangs over the room as Huxley checks through all of the vehicles. He swipes his hands under all of the seats, digs into every side pocket, and opens every glove box and console he can find. If he can open a trunk he does, but all he finds are a couple of spare tires and chrome lug wrenches.

While he searches, he sees Bracken's legs stick out from Maggie's driver side door. Wedged underneath the steering wheel, when he's close enough, Huxley hears him muttering about red wires and green wires.

Bracken sits up in the bucket seat when he notices Huxley standing by the door. The leather and springs creak beneath him. "You got some creep to you. I didn't even notice you were there. That everything?"

Huxley shrugs and nods, indicating his meager haul.

"Toss it all in back, it certainly won't hurt anything." He puts his hand on the boy's head as he stands. "No buckets, hoses? Containers of any sort?"

Huxley shakes his head.

Bracken considers the situation a moment. He clicks his tongue absently. "Well, okay then." Crouching down in front of the boy he brings himself to Huxley's level and locks eyes, a serious expression on his face. "You did good. You did a good job. And right now, we're about to get the hell out of here. That sound like a good idea?"

Huxley nods without breaking eye contact. "That's the best idea I've ever heard."

"I thought it might be. What I need you to do is wait here. Right here." He points to the ground. "Just for a couple of minutes. Got that?"

Again the boy nods.

Bracken stands, looks over his shoulder at the passageway at the far end of the room, and picks up the rifle from where it leans against the fender of the car. In his clothes he looks like one of the guards and Huxley has to remind himself he isn't. Bracken looks back at Huxley. "I'll be right back."

Bracken walks to the outer edge of the tunnel. At the brink he raises the rifle to his shoulder, crouches, and continues to move forward. From behind Maggie's open door, Huxley watches him until he's out of sight up and around the curve, then he continues to watch the empty space left behind.

Silence fills the air around him and he becomes aware of every sound his body makes; his breath, his heartbeat, and the dull rumble as his stomach tightens on itself. He hopes Bracken returns before the owner of the burning lamp. The quiet gets heavy and time takes forever to pass. He cranes his neck, hoping to hear some sound, focuses his eyes hoping to see some movement. Despite the chill of being underground, beads of sweat force through his skin.

Finally, his ears pick up a noise. Vague and dampened, it quickly matures into the unmistakable sounds of a scuffle. He recognizes the dull thud of flesh pounding into flesh, of knuckles on cheekbones, and something solid against a skull. Grunts and ambiguous visceral growls come from the darkness, and as quickly as they began, they stop and the silence returns, flowing at him from the tunnel like an icy breath of air.

Fortunately, the silence doesn't last long this time. A loud grinding of rock on rock and dim shrieks of twisting wood come from the tunnel. Huxley isn't sure if he should stay put or turn and run in the opposite direction, and he weighs the pros and cons. Before he establishes any sound argument either way, the outline of a human figure strolls casually into view; Bracken, the hunting rifle against his shoulder. Another rifle, black and more sinister, dangles across his chest, and the butt of a pistol sticks out of his belt. He carries two plastic jugs of water and wears different clothes.

A thick black jacket covers his arms and chest, a scarf hangs around his neck, and a pair of goggles sit backward on his head.

His jaw works something and he hands Huxley half of a sandwich as he arrives at the car.

"Here, you need their lunch more than they do." Bracken unshoulders the rifle and looks at Huxley. "Do you know how to shoot this?"

Huxley nods. "My father showed me how."

Bracken hands the weapon over. "This is yours then." He pats the assault rifle. "I'll keep this HK, it's in better shape, and more my style." The weapon's skin shines black and cold, clean and free of grit. He sights it against the far wall. "Those Germans do make a fine firearm." He pauses and thinks and says, "I wonder if there even is a Germany anymore?"

He snaps out of his momentary reverie and chucks his chin at the passenger side door. "Get in. Unless you have some burning desire to stay here, we're getting the fuck out of Dodge, but quick. I just made a bunch of racket."

Huxley scurries to the other side of the car and opens the door. He slips his pack from his shoulder, passing the gun from one hand to the other in order to free his arms then, depositing the bag on the floorboards, climbs in and pulls the door shut behind him. He slides down along the leather, and uses his bag to as a brace to push his body upright so he can see out the window.

Jumpy, he glances around, behind them where they entered the room, toward the exit, and into every corner. At any moment he expects a throng of armed men to emerge and come after them.

"We should go," Huxley says. He clutches his rifle. "We should go now."

"Momentarily, young fella." Bracken winks. "Momentarily."

Bracken climbs in, the gun still slung across his belly, and reaches underneath the steering column, grabbing a handful of loose wires. Huxley watches without understanding as he selects and twists various ends together.

"First time in a car?" Bracken asks, looking up.

Huxley nods. A smile actually breaks through his lips.

"Exciting, huh?"

Bracken makes one last movement with the wires and car roars to life beneath them. The snarl of the engine rattles Huxley's insides and toes and he can't suppress a nervous smile.

"Nice," Bracken says. He shuts his own door. "I also found this." He tosses a pink plastic lighter to Huxley. "Probably come in handy sooner or later."

Huxley flicks the wheel of the lighter and the brief spark lights up the interior of the car for a fraction of a second and his eyes have to readjust. Bracken slams the car into gear, pops the clutch, and the car lurches forward toward the tunnel. With a hint of a gleam in his eye, he pilots the car through the mouth of the passage that curves up and away. Huxley grips the edge of the seat as the force of their velocity pushes him against the door.

In front of them, a portal opens up into the night. The heavy doors have been dragged open, two bodies piled to one side. As the car bursts through the threshold, Huxley turns and looks at the fallen men.

"Did you kill them?" he asks.

"Right now, me killing them is the least of their worries," Bracken says. He shifts, keeping his eyes glued to the windshield. "Might have been a favor if I had, when they wake up, they're in a world of hurt."

Bracken rolls down the window halfway. A cool fresh breeze rushes in and forces out the lingering subterranean air; crisp and light replaces stagnant and heavy. Huxley breathes deeply through his nose. The sharp air tingles in his nostrils and lungs. Mimicking Bracken, he rolls down his own window and sticks his face out into the night.

He turns and peers through the rear window. It looks like they drove straight out of a sheer cliff. Behind the car, he sees the outline of Requiem in the distance. Mostly it's a black rectangle even blacker than night. Stars hover in the sky above. From this vantage point, it looks peaceful and calm, but he knows the churning and tumult that lurks inside the wall.

Perched on his seat, he watches the city recede into the distance and fade into the remnants of the night. They're going faster than the boy has ever travelled before, faster than he ever thought possible.

Bracken clamps his jaw and remains silent. Huxley shifts in his seat, inching his back closer to the door. The engine rumbles in the darkness. Outside the wind whips past the car. Huxley examines Bracken's face. In the night he can't tell if it is sadness or rage written across his features.

Huxley breaks the silence. "So, Requiem is just the worst of everything?"

"Pretty much," Bracken says. "Not entirely. Not everyone is like Elwood and his posse. People are mostly just hardened by what the world's become. Everyone is to some degree. A few people try to hang onto the old ways. Try to keep things normal, normal like it used to be anyway. Now normal is something else entirely. It's amazing what you can get used to.

"A few people try to make the world a better place, at least as much as they can."

"Like Haley?" Huxley asks. "She takes care of people, right?"

"Yeah, like Haley." Bracken nods. His fingers tighten on the steering wheel. "What . . . Back there . . ." After a few false starts, he gives up, and mutters, "Later." He hunches forward, and Huxley can tell he's done talking. They sit in silence for a time.

Huxley examines Bracken, trying to decide if it's safe to ask one more question.

Bracken notices Huxley's gaze. His features soften a degree, and he says, anticipating the question, "You're wondering where we're going."

Huxley nods.

"You got people in San Francisco, right?"

Huxley nods again, almost hypnotized by the momentum of the car.

"Then I guess we're going to San Francisco." Under his breath he says, "Go west, young man, go west."

Huxley sits in his seat in the darkness. The rifle leans across his body, the barrel rests against the glass. He rubs the wood of the stock under his hands. Calluses on his palm rasp quietly against the wood grain. He tries not to think of his father teaching him how to line the front sight up with the back, how to draw in a breath and hold it, how to pull the trigger back smooth instead of yanking or jerking. He tries not to think of these things and fails; he tries to squeeze the tears back, but fails in this as well. Only a few get through and he's careful to keep them to himself. They're his and his alone. Bracken doesn't need to know, they're Huxley's weights to keep and carry.

Huxley collects himself to keep his voice steady, and asks, "If we're going to San Francisco, why are we going south?"

Bracken looks at the boy and chuckles. "You can navigate?"

"My dad taught me." He tries to hide the tremor in his voice, hoping it passes unnoticed.

"Well, color me impressed," Bracken says. This phrase confuses Huxley and he waits for Bracken to continue. "If we go the quickest route, the most direct route, there are more people. More people on the road, and there are strips and slivers of land that are still fertile, so there are more farms and outposts and whatnot. And in our present circumstances, people present an unacceptable risk. The fewer eyes that see us, the better. We'll stay south for as long as we can, get as far as we can on this tank of gas. Then we walk. Through the mountains we don't have much choice, but farther south there's nothing. It's like the wasteland of the wasteland."

"Why is it so bad down there?"

Bracken shakes his head. "Drier, flatter, windier, just generally uglier."

"Won't it be more dangerous?" Huxley asks.

Bracken laughs and smiles, nodding his head without a word. The silence troubles Huxley, and he leans back into his seat, watching the empty darkness through the windshield.

Huxley sits and wonders about San Francisco. He knows it's supposed to be big, but Requiem is the biggest place he's ever been, ever seen with his own eyes. Will Bracken deliver him like a package, drop him off again like he did at Haley's and leave? Furrowing his brow, he tries not to think about what happened to her.

Bracken leaves the headlights off, steering by the light of the moon and the stars. Hard-baked earth and the remains of a freeway speed past beneath them. Outside, the wind whips sand. The landscape looks even more desolate and lonely in the blue light of darkness. The emptiness expands forever in every direction. Nothing good awaits them in this wasteland.

The car plows south and west, shrinking into the dark.

Somewhere, in the rocking of car, the constant grumble of the engine, the tumult of memory, and the feeling of being safe, even for a moment, for the first time in what feels like years, sleep finally overtakes Huxley, and his body slumps easily against Bracken's arm.

CHAPTER 6

The sun rises in the distance, clawing over the horizon line to spill over the thirsty landscape. Long shadows stretch as light falls over the severe browns and yellows. Dark patches spot the terrain, indicating the presence of clouds passing overhead high in the atmosphere. Wind shrieks and howls, whipping grains of sand and tearing at the naked scrub and bones of long dead plants.

Even through a layer of dust and grit, the high-gloss black paint of the car stands in direct contrast to the surrounding dull tones. It rests in the basin between a convergence of dunes, gleaming in the early morning light. The driver's side door hangs open. Bracken sits atop a mound of earth, the rifle across his lap. He squints against the wind and the sun that comes from the same direction they did, like it's following them. Soon it will overtake them and they will follow. Oh, to move that quickly.

He watches the point where the earth meets the sky. There's no movement but the wind. There's nothing to see and only the sound of the screaming stream of air that snakes past his ears. Behind him the boy, Huxley, still sleeps in the car, on the passenger's side, his little legs drawn up beneath him on the smooth leather bucket seats, his arms wrapped around the bolt-action rifle like a security blanket. The wooden stock offers something concrete and solid for him to hang onto in this world of chaos and uncertainty.

For a moment, for this moment, everything remains still and calm. The threats of being this exposed, of being on the run, of being pursued, dwell far off in the distance, and for the moment, Bracken simply sits. But at the perimeter of his thoughts the need to continue moving forward looms. The danger is real, the peril imminent, no matter how distant and obscure it might seem right now.

Bracken takes a drink from the jug of water at his feet and stands.

The car shifts under his weight as he sits behind the wheel. Huxley jolts awake with the motion of the vehicle. Instinctively, he pushes his back against the door and moves to point the rifle at Bracken. The older man grabs the barrel and gently raises it up toward the roof.

"Careful there, Hoss," he says. "Remember, that's the end you point at whatever you want to die."

Huxley blinks rapidly, clearing the sleep from his eyes. He recognizes Bracken and his initial confusion dissipates. Squinting in the morning sun, he relaxes and starts to inhale slow, even breaths.

"Sorry I startled you," Bracken says.

Huxley starts to ask where they are, but a yawn interrupts his words and he covers his gaping mouth with his hand.

"We aren't really much of anywhere," Bracken says, in answer to the unasked question. He looks around at the hills of sand around them. "This is just where the tank hit empty."

Huxley wipes the corner of his eyes. "We should have brought more gas, huh? Isn't that what makes cars go?"

Bracken nods. "Would have if we could have. There wasn't anything to carry it in."

Huxley sits silent for a moment and takes in the scene around them. "Won't they find the car?"

Bracken chews his lip. "In a perfect world, no. But this world is far from perfect, isn't it?" He stretches and winces, and touches his ribs with light fingers. "We're pretty far off of the road, or anything that passes for a road, so we've got that going for us, which is nice. When the car died I pushed it in here," he indicates the mounds of sand. "This spot is pretty sheltered, and there isn't any high ground close by, so unless they happen right upon this exact corner of the desert right here, it'll be difficult to find." He looks at the boy. "Plus we're going to bury it."

Huxley furrows his brow and looks at him, thinking about how long it will take to dig a hole big enough to conceal an entire car. "Bury it?"

"In a manner of speaking. But that can wait until after breakfast."

Outside, Bracken digs into Huxley's bag and removes two unlabeled cans. Before he closes the mouth of the pack, he notes the contents, Huxley sees him count the cans and jars. The silver metal and glass containers gleam in the sunlight. Huxley angles his to catch the rays and bounces them around the tires and hubcaps of the car. Bracken rolls his between the palms of his hands and watches the boy. He pulls the multi-tool he took from the guard out of his pocket, motions for the boy to give him his can, pries open the lid, and hands the peach slices in heavy syrup back to Huxley with a nod. Opening his can reveals whole black beans.

They stay silent as they consume their respective meals.

Huxley finishes first, tipping his can to get every last drop. Bracken reaches out the hand that holds his can, still partially full. He gestures for the boy to take it. They lock eyes and after a moment Huxley tosses the empty away and grabs the beans from Bracken and digs in.

Bracken returns to the car to pack up their meager belongings, a ghost of a smile on his lips.

He makes a pile of everything they have between them, which amounts to little more than Huxley's worn pack and the jugs of water pilfered from the guards. He keeps a hold of the rifle.

The two examine the sparse collection and Huxley can't help but think of the ground they are going to attempt to cover. The prospect feels heavy and empty and endless. Desolate and void of anything, save danger and risk. Monsters wait for them, both literal and figurative. Who knows how many infected roam the wastes? And the people they may encounter aren't any better.

And Elwood will come hard after them, of that Huxley is certain. He won't stand the slight of their escape and the theft of his beloved car. Then there's whatever was in the package Bracken never delivered. Beyond any human, or formerly human threats, starvation, dehydration, and mishaps and catastrophes of every kind hang like black clouds. Their belongings personify the imminent danger, the thin line between life and death, between the end and whatever survival means.

Huxley pushes his thoughts from his head as Bracken speaks.

"You ready to dig?" he asks.

Huxley looks at him with confusion.

He laughs a little. "Okay, we're not going to bury it for real." He bends down, cups his hands, and tosses a scoop of dirt onto the hood of the car. He stops and looks at Huxley. The glint of recognition appears in his eyes.

"If we cover it with dirt . . ." Huxley says.

Bracken nods as he throws another handful onto the car. "We don't want to leave anything that will reflect. Hopefully from a distance it'll just look like a pile of dirt. Might as well make is as hard as we can for them to follow us."

The two stoop to the work and before long a layer of dirt coats the car. Bracken stops, lifts the butt of his gun, and smashes out the driver's side window. Huxley takes a cue from him and scoots to the other side, raising his rifle. He brings the stock down against the glass. It bounces back and he immediately swings again. On the second try the glass shatters inward. A wide smile crosses his face as they break out the rest of the windows. Bracken kicks off the chrome rearview mirror and makes sure to bury it completely.

Finished, the two stand next to each other admiring their handiwork.

"This might have been a huge waste of time," Bracken says. "This might not accomplish a damned thing, and that's as good as it's going to get, which isn't much. But you know what?" He looks down at Huxley. "I thoroughly enjoyed that."

Huxley nods and smiles, inhaling deep gulps of air, a smile on his face.

Bracken crosses his arms and takes one last look at the dirt-covered car. "Well, that's enough of that. "We need to move while we still can."

They don't see a single sign of life. Nothing but barren emptiness envelops them as they trudge into the heart of the desert. The only sounds the cries of the wind and the soles of their boots stamping into the earth in rhythm. All joy from the destruction of the car has evaporated. Neither of Bracken nor Huxley talk. They simply take one step after another in an endless procession.

Bracken keeps his head bent forward against the elements, scanning their surroundings in every direction. Constantly at attention, he checks the horizon in all directions, examining every hill, giving every mound, roll, and dip in the terrain wide berth. Anything that could hide an infected or where Elwood could lay a trap. He pulls the collar of his coat up to covers as much of his face as possible. Stubble sticks through the skin of his jaw like the points of staples and grate against the rough denim. He wears his rifle slung across the front of his body, his hand on pistol grip, finger in the trigger guard, ready, his other hand cradling the barrel. On his shoulders he carries the pack full of their collected supplies and belongings.

Huxley trails behind Bracken. He carries his rifle up against his shoulder, like a toy soldier marching in formation. He fixes his gaze firmly on Bracken's feet and does his best to step in the tracks that appear in front of him, stretching his legs to reach, like a game. Despite the fact that he's well aware of the potential dangers around them, and despite the fact that his mind occasionally drifts into scenarios where both he and Bracken die in horrific fashion, thoughts that give him momentary chills, the boy feels safe. Watching Bracken tromp along in front of him, he almost relaxes.

They trudge forward through the day, Bracken on the lookout for trouble. He searches for any signs of people approaching in the distance and for any of the telltale indications of roaming infected. It seems like nothing has ever existed here in this place, like they're trekking across some wild, uninhabited, forlorn world deep in space.

"You probably don't know what it would mean if I said the words 'Clint' and 'Eastwood,' would you?" Bracken says over his shoulder without taking his eyes away from the horizon.

"No," Huxley answers without breaking stride. He does look up at the back of Bracken's head. Sand has burrowed down in between the strands of dark hair, giving it the appearance of patches of gray, like watching Bracken age in fast-forward. He half expects the man's face to show the signs of advanced years, worn and furrowed.

Bracken shakes his head and continues forward.

Night chases them across the desert. Both Huxley and Bracken keep their faces wrapped and their heads covered as they walk into the face of the setting sun. The coverings protect them from the wind and heat, and when the darkness overtakes them, they serve as a barrier against the accompanying cold. Finally, Bracken finds a suitable place to camp, explaining that the position is hidden from view, easily defensible, and readily abandoned at the drop of a hat if necessary. Huxley takes note.

Bracken sits on a rock, takes a swig of water from one of their plastic jugs, and passes it to Huxley. In the blue light of the evening, Huxley sits opposite Bracken, shivering despite the blanket around his shoulders. After so much walking, the cold sets in and his muscles tighten. His fingers feel thick and clumsy, he flexes them to ward off stiffness, and he feels the drop in temperature in his joints, especially his knees and his ankles. But he won't complain, he knows Bracken is cold too, so he sits there alone in his own head with his thoughts.

Bracken watches Huxley for a time, furrows his brow, whispers a single word to himself, and stands up.

"Wait here," he says, and walks past the boy. Huxley looks after him, only a little curious about where he went.

When Bracken returns a few moments later he carries a collection of sticks and twigs beneath one arm. The fingers of his other hand still fidget with the trigger of his gun.

"This is everything I could find within a reasonable distance that'll burn," he says, dumping his collection in a pile on the ground. The largest pieces are little more than stray branches and twigs. Silently, Huxley reaches out and starts to arrange the wood in a strategic manner.

"You still have that lighter I gave you?" he asks.

Huxley pulls the pink plastic cigarette lighter from his front pocket and holds it out to Bracken, who chucks his chin at the pile. "You build it, you light it."

Huxley reaches toward the top of the small wooden pyramid. He thinks better of his action, and picks out a small, brittle twig. With a flick of his thumb, he lights the lighter, and touches off the end of the stick. The flame bites in and climbs. Cupping one hand around the new flame to keep it from going out, he gently pokes the burning end into the base of the woodpile.

"You have to light it from the bottom, so the flames can climb up," he says, mostly talking to himself. "Or else it will go out."

It takes a second for the flame to catch on a small shoot near the bottom. At first the light from the flame is weak and barely alive, but the fire grows and hungrily consumes the fuel. The flames crackle and come to life, climbing like he said it would, until it illuminates a small circle between them.

Bracken takes the pot from the bag and dumps the contents of a can into it. He sets the container in the middle of the fire, pulling his hand back quickly from the heat. With a large spoon he stirs the mixture, careful not to burn himself. When the contents of the pot bubble and sputter, he pulls it out of the flames using his scarf as an oven mitt, and hands it to Huxley. The boy wraps the pot in the excess end of his blanket and sets it in his lap. He huddles over and around the warmth provided and eats, blowing on each mouthful so he doesn't scald the inside of his mouth.

The metal of the spoon scrapes against the metal of the pot. The burning wood snaps in the fire. Huxley barely chews each steaming mouthful before swallowing, feeling the warmth travel down the length of his throat and settle in the bottom of his stomach. It heats him from the inside out.

"I don't like this," Bracken says, indicating the flames. "A fire is a giveaway to anyone following us. Or a beacon if there's anything stalking around out there." He pauses and exhales, rubbing his chin between his hands. "But we're hidden pretty well, and it's dark enough that it should be hard to see the smoke." He talks mostly to himself. "I haven't seen any signs of infected or Elwood, so . . ." He trails off, watching the edge of the circle where the darkness meets the light. "Still, that fire is what got your father . . ." He stops himself.

At the mention of his father Huxley flinches almost like he has been hit. He scowls at Bracken and clenches his jaw. Bracken's features soften for a brief moment and Huxley thinks he gets a quick glimpse behind the toughened exterior.

"Just don't get used to it," Bracken says.

"Then why risk it tonight?" Huxley asks.

"Because you're cold."

Huxley shovels food into his mouth and mutters, "I'll be cold tomorrow," to himself.

Bracken seems older in the light of the fire. The flames cast shadows across his cheeks and brow, and lines not visible in the harsh light of day appear. Though his face stays still, the light of the flames creates an illusion of movement, dancing and scampering over his features. The shadows blend with the smudges of dirt on his skin and leave thumbprints of darkness.

"You've been to San Francisco before, haven't you?" Huxley says, breaking the silence.

"What?" The question takes Bracken by surprise and his gaze snaps back toward Huxley. He considers the question for some time, as if the answer takes him someplace far away. Finally, he nods. "Yeah. I've been to San Francisco."

He looks to leave it at that, but Huxley presses.

"What's it like?" His voice is small. He hunches over, turning in on himself.

"Honestly," Bracken shakes his head. "I don't know anymore. It's been . . . well, it's been a while." He laughs once, but his face quickly changes back to severity, and he sits in silence again.

After a moment he starts to talk. "When this," he indicates everything around them. "When all of this first started, that's where we lived. That's where *I* lived." He looks at the boy.

"I don't know what you know and what you don't. If you know anything about what it was like before. I don't even know how to describe it to you. Where do you start when there's nothing left of it, when there's

128

nothing to compare it to?"

He laughs again. Not a gesture of mirth or amusement, but a sad reflex. "I guess it was like the Turd back there. That's probably the closest thing you've ever seen anyway. But that's like," he holds out his hands, palm up, looking at his outstretched fingers as if they contained something besides empty space. "Have you ever seen an apple or an orange?"

"Just old pictures." Huxley shakes his head.

"I didn't think so. It's like comparing two things that have absolutely no relation to each other." He pauses and rubs the tips of his middle fingers with the tips of his thumbs. "Everything was fucked up already, the dust bowl and migrations and squatters and the repression and . . . And when the infection hit, it spread like, well, like it was already everywhere. There were so many people in such little space, and there was no time to prepare. No time to plan or strategize. It was like you closed your eyes for a second and by the time you opened them again you were in some sort of nightmare warzone." Again he trails off. Huxley watches, waiting.

"San Francisco did better than most places, the city proper anyway. It's on a peninsula, that's land that sticks out into the ocean, into a lot of water." He gestures with his hands trying to demonstrate the concept. "So there was only one real way in, and we managed to block that off with a big wall. It was basically a giant line of trash, but it did the trick. While we were fighting off the swarm of infected on the outside, we had to worry about infection spreading inside, too. I don't even know how many thousands of people died, or changed over, but we managed to keep out. Sort of.

"A few other places managed to hold out. For a while anyway. Seattle did okay. They had water on either side, so they were able to pinch it off at the ends. For a little bit there was some boat traffic along the coast, but that fell off. LA held out for a minute, but they got overrun pretty quick. A few islands here and there. Manhattan held out for a good bit, but we lost contact with the rest of the east coast right away. I don't even know if there is an Asia anymore. A couple of boats took off that way, but no one ever heard from them again. Who even knows about Europe? I guess there are more pressing concerns than having pen pals."

Bracken stops talking, but his mouth still hangs open. It's like the man hasn't spoken in years, like his own voice sounds heavy and foreign to him.

"But I left all that a long time ago," he continues. "There," he breathes in deeply and winces at the pain in his ribs. "There wasn't anything left there for me anymore." He stops and stares into the fire. It looks like his body is too heavy and the creases in his face are deeper than Huxley has ever seen.

"Your dad," Bracken says, looking up at the boy. "He didn't tell you any of this? Anything about what happened?"

Huxley shakes his head. "I asked a few times, but he always told me that I didn't need to know about that. He said I wouldn't believe it anyway, that it was better for me not to dwell on the bad things, things that happened before I was even born." He pauses. "I stopped asking after a while."

There's so much Huxley doesn't know. About the world, about the way things were, about the way things are. He hunches forward and watches the flames, thinking of his father and feels a twinge of anger.

His father wanted to protect him, to shelter him from the ugliness. He understands this. But he's too often helpless as a result. His father always put a happy spin on everything. They weren't in danger, they moved like it was an adventure. People didn't die, they simply weren't there anymore. Huxley didn't need to know how to scrape and fight and survive. But now he does need those skills. He's here, relying on someone else instead of doing for himself.

This anger leads to guilt. His father died, died trying to save him. Died saving him. It gets difficult to breathe and he coughs once into his fist.

The fire continues to burn and crackle, the flames devouring the dry fuel like a starving creature. Over time it dies down until all that remains is a small collection of embers glowing in the darkness. Bracken's face fades into shadows as the light expires, his expression far off and distant. Huxley pulls his knees to his chest and hugs his legs. The blanket sits on his shoulders as he wonders what is going on inside of Bracken's head. What things has he seen that Huxley will never know and can only guess at?

When all that's of the fire is nothing but a single red dot in the night, something in Bracken finally breaks loose and he looks up at Huxley. The boy doesn't know how to read the face he can barely see. It looks like he wants to ask a question but isn't sure what to ask, or how.

"What," Bracken begins. "What happened, back there? At the orphanarium?" He rubs his jaw and looks away. "What happened to Haley?" His eyes are round and almost wet when he looks up and meets Huxley's gaze.

Huxley blinks and for the first time really considers everything that took place after Bracken left him, everything moved so fast that he hasn't had the opportunity to think about it.

He starts talking, his voice small and barely audible over the sound of the wind. The words drift out of his mouth as he starts from the beginning, from the moment the door shut and Haley locked Bracken out. Huxley looks into the darkness, at nothing specific, as he speaks, though he occasionally glances at Bracken.

The older man leans forward and angles one ear toward the boy. He clenches his jaw and breathes deep and slow, focusing to hear every word. When Huxley gets to the part about Haley, he sits back, clenches his fists, and stuffs them into his pockets with a scowl. In the gloom, Huxley wonders why the news about Haley's fate seems to hold more weight than all of the rest. He wonders about their history.

"You and Haley..." he says.

"Haley?" For a second, Bracken's face pinches. "We had a thing."

"A thing?"

"Yeah, a thing."

He obviously doesn't want to talk about it, so the boy continues.

Huxley finishes his story at the moment when he opened the door and found Bracken chained to the wall. He looks up, trying to gauge Bracken's reaction in the night, searching for any expression, any hints or clues that might betray his thoughts, but all he finds is a blank, dour face. Maybe there a hint of sadness lingers, but he can't be certain in the dim light of the moon.

Bracken exhales and leans forward. He rubs his hands together and rests his elbows on his knees.

"You've been through a lot of in the last few days, huh?" he says. "Probably seen more ugliness than a kid your age should see. I'm sorry about that. I'd say none of this should happen, but that's spitting into the wind. We've all seen way more than anyone ever should. Doesn't make it right, but there's nothing we can do about that now, is there? We have to deal with what we have."

He looks at Huxley. In the darkness his black eyes gleam. "Some people will tell you that you need to push all of that aside, hide it, forget it, whatever." He shakes his head. "But you can't do that. Don't bury it. Don't forget it. Don't let it fade. Carry that stuff with you. You got to carry everything with you, the good and bad. If it's good, great, there's precious little of that going around in this world. You'll need that to get you through the long nights, through the quiet times when everything gets real heavy. Those are the moments you might get crushed when you think of the sheer overwhelming weight of how fucked we all are. That's when you need to think of whatever good times you have left, when you're on the verge of giving up on it all is when you'll need it the most.

"But be careful of that, you hear me? You have to be careful you don't get lost in them. I've seen it happen. The good times aren't what keeps you alive. They might keep you sane, but that's not going to keep you moving forward. Anger or revenge or hate or bad intentions, that keeps you moving, that'll keep you alive a lot longer. The way the world is, alive is all we can hope for. Alive is all we've got. Don't let go. Don't ever let go. Keep it close. Don't get distracted. It'll only get you killed. Use it. Use it for what you can. It won't be easy, but use it to keep breathing, keep moving, keep setting one next foot down in front of the last. A man has to have a reason. A man has to have a purpose, you hear me?"

The words come out like an argument and Huxley isn't sure who he wants to convince.

"You need to hold onto your memories. All of them. Aside from that, all we have is what's in front of us." He laughs and gestures with one sweeping arm. "And all that's in front of us is a goddamn shitstorm."

Silence descends over the top of them. Bracken shifts. "Now that I've thoroughly depressed you," he says. "Try to get some sleep."

Huxley knows its morning without opening his eyes. The sun seeps through his eyelids into the edges of sleep and the constant scream of the wind invades his ears like a swarm of insects. When he opens his eyes the only thing in his field of vision is the empty sky. He rolls onto his stomach. Bracken stands with his back to him.

"Time to get moving," he says without looking.

Much like the previous day, they trek across the barren waste at a steady pace. Bracken scans the distance, searching for any sign of life or threat, which, he explains with serious gravity, are most often and most likely the one and the same. They see nothing. Neither traveler speaks beyond a few words necessary to communicate their immediate needs to the other.

They stop only to eat and relieve themselves.

At night they make camp.

In the morning they wake and repeat the process.

The next day is the same. They barely speak. The constant shriek of the wind and their footsteps grinding into the dirt are the only sounds. Keeping covered despite the heat of the sun, and bundled up against the chill of night, they only pause to tear into their shrinking supply of canned food, sip tepid water, and try to sleep.

As becomes the regular pattern in their trek, Bracken takes the lead while Huxley trails a few steps behind. When they walk their footsteps sync up; their feet rise and fall in unison, creating a single sound. Grains of dust swirl in the wind around their boots. In this fashion, they slog forward across the dead, blanched land.

Unconsciously, Huxley imitates Bracken, adopting his mannerisms and characteristics. He carries his rifle at the ready, and he, too, searches their surroundings. Not entirely certain what to look for, he simply looks for any sign of anything at all. There's nothing to see, but that doesn't stop him. He volunteers to carry the pack and even when it gets so heavy, he feels crushed, the straps biting into his shoulders, his muscles and joints crying in pain, he never complains or gives up his burden easily. Huxley knows this makes Bracken smile as the man slings the bag over his own shoulders, even though the boy never sees it directly. But there's something different in the muscles of his jaw and the back of his neck and he knows when Bracken smiles.

Their path leads them to a small ravine carved out by a river. Any trace of water is a faded memory, but a deep groove remains in the earth. Huxley knows the supply of water in their jugs is steadily declining. He doesn't mention this fact, but knows that Bracken is well aware of the situation. They pause at the lip of the gully. Bracken squints his eyes against the sun, does a 360-degree scan of the distance, looks back to the furrow, and scans again.

With cautious steps, bracing himself, he descends into the ravine.

"I don't necessarily like this," he offers without turning around. "Things hide down here. But at least we can move without being spotted if there is someone out there watching for us."

"So we can hide, too," Huxley says.

"That's the general idea."

The gorge grows deeper as they move. The walls grow sharper and tighter, and the avenue bends and turns. Bracken grows ever more vigilant in these confines. Huxley, too, increases his guard. Their forward progression slows as they approach bends and corners. The wind cries and wails overhead and kicks a fine spray of dirt down on top of them like a light dusting of snow.

Bracken sweeps around a corner and stops, his body rigid. His eyes and the barrel of his gun focus on the same spot. He crouches down a few inches and takes two deliberate steps to the side. Huxley scoots up to the crook and peeks around. A few meters in front of them lies a body in a prone position. It used to be a man from the beard on its chin. Now it's mostly nude, but what used to be pants still cling to its waist, held in place by a weathered belt, though it's missing one leg. The deep blue skin is almost black. Wounds ranging from small slices to jagged chunks of absent flesh cover the emaciated back and rail thin arms.

Yet the body still moves.

What little muscle mass remains lifts the head back and works the jaw. A faint sound comes from the gaping, mostly toothless mouth, a sound somewhere between a hiss and a cry, which blends with the ambient sound of the wind. Hands full of broken fingers extend and reach out, trying to close the space to Bracken and Huxley. The boy watches, more curious than afraid. Different from the ones that attack him and his father, and the ones Bracken battled in the arena, nothing about this creature poses an immediate threat.

"It's starving," Huxley says not looking away from the decimated body.

"They're still like us," Bracken says. "At least in that one way. If they don't eat, they die. Simple as that, right?"

The two stand in place and contemplate the shriveled, writhing body lying prostrate in front of them.

"Are you going to shoot it?" Huxley asks.

Bracken shakes his head. "We don't have enough bullets to waste one when we don't need to. And we don't want to make any extra noise if we don't have to."

He takes a step forward, focusing on the weak infected. "You still have to be careful." He moves forward another step. "Even when they get like this, they're dangerous and can make you into one of them." He takes one more step and cocks his head, examining the decaying creature. A bony arm reaches for him. He pins it to the ground with one foot and in the same motion brings the butt of his gun down on the infected's skull. The sharp sound of the rifle stock on bone is hollow and parched. It only takes one blow and the body collapses face down into the dirt, motionless. The final remnants of life gone.

Bracken stands over the corpse, trains the barrel on its skull, and motions for Huxley to pass behind him. The sweet smell of decay clings to the body. He waits for the boy to completely clear the body before moving on.

"Does that mean there are more of them?" Huxley asks after a few minutes.

"They mostly hunt in groups, packs, three or four together. But the state of our friend back there might be a good sign. If there isn't enough food around to keep them all fed then hopefully any of them that were here have moved on to greener pastures, so to speak, and left him behind. Or if there are any more hanging around, they'll probably resemble that fellow and will be easy enough to deal with if we stay on our toes."

He sweeps around another corner, and Huxley barely hears him, says, "I hope."

They follow the ravine until it takes a sharp turn toward the south. Bracken scrambles up the steep wall and crouches, checking to see if anyone or anything lies in wait. Convinced the coast is clear, he leans over the lip and reaches one arm down. Huxley grabs his hand and Bracken hoists him easily out of the depression.

Ahead of them sun sinks again into the horizon, the sky grows dark, and the shadows lengthen at their feet. They walk until it's too dark to see any potential threats and stop for the night. The meager camp they set consists solely of removing the blankets from the pack, which then sits on the ground between them.

"You should eat something," Bracken says.

Huxley shakes his head. "I'm okay."

Bracken shrugs.

"You should eat something," Huxley says.

Bracken shakes his head. "I'm okay."

Huxley shrugs in imitation of his companion.

The two sit and listen to the howl of the wind; a sound so constant it disappears into the background leaving void that neither one tries to fill. Huxley doesn't try to sleep. He sits with one blanket over his head and wraps the rest around his body and shoulders. Despite the cover, his body still shivers in the cold. Bracken stands and walks over. He unfolds his blanket and flaps it out once. The corners snap with the movement. He drapes it over Huxley's shoulders and returns to his seat.

"Won't you be cold?" Huxley asks.

Bracken shakes his head. "I'll be fine."

"Thanks."

Bracken keeps the assault rifle at the ready in his hands, upright and rigid, even more alert than usual. His carriage betrays his concern; seeing that infected stirred up the same worries as in Huxley.

Huxley loses track of the time in the darkness. He tries to sleep but fails. Still, his attention drifts into a hazy, reflexive zone. His eyes lose focus and though they stare in Bracken's direction, they don't see anything specific.

Eventually, his thoughts wander where they always do: to his father and the monsters and what waits for them beyond the range of what he can see and what must be coming after them from Requiem. He thinks of his father pedaling his makeshift rickshaw from place to place along the hard, packed ground, sitting in the back watching the landscape slip by. He loses himself inside of his own skull.

"Do you still have that toothbrush I gave you?" Bracken asks. The sound of his voice snaps Huxley out of his trance. For a second, he thinks he has lost his mind and that the gloom is asking him a question.

Huxley nods. Unsure if Bracken can see him, he adds, "Yes."

"I haven't seen you use it this entire trip. You have to take care of your teeth. That's the only set you're going to get." He gestures to the hills around them. "I don't know about you, but I don't see any dentist's offices around here."

Huxley nods automatically then pauses. "What's a dentist's office?"

Bracken laughs and smiles so wide Huxley sees his white teeth gleam in the night. Huxley can't figure out what's so funny and feels like Bracken's laughter comes at his expense.

"Oh shit," he laughs again, but it subsides and he releases a heavy sigh and shakes his head. "It really is a different world, kid." A smile still on his lips, Bracken leans forward. He motions with one hand, "Okay, give it here. Time for oral hygiene 101."

Huxley shrugs, grabs his bag, and digs out the toothbrush and the tube. Squeezing the skin, it gives way under the pressure of his fingers, like it is full of some sort of thick goop. He makes a face and hands it to Bracken.

"And the brush," Bracken says.

When Huxley hands over the long, thin cardboard box, Bracken peels off a layer of clear plastic wrap and discards it on the ground. He looks up at Huxley. "What? There's nowhere to recycle."

Huxley starts to say that he has no idea what the hell recycling means, but decides he doesn't care and lets it go.

Bracken holds a skinny finger of blue plastic in one hand. White bristles protrude from one end. "This is a toothbrush," he says, flicking the handle once for emphasis. "You know what a brush is, and you use this to brush your teeth, obviously. You know why that is?"

Huxley shrugs. "I know what teeth are, and I know what a brush is. I can guess" He can't help but notice Bracken's enthusiasm about this topic.

"But do you know why?" Bracken laughs. "You brush your teeth to keep them clean and healthy, so they don't fall out of your damn head, because you need them to eat. And once they're gone, they're gone forever. I guess you could whittle some wooden teeth like George Washington, but other than that, no one's going to make you a set of dentures."

Huxley purses his lips and crosses his arms. "You enjoy talking about things I don't know about, don't you?"

"Well aren't you a sassy little bastard today," Bracken says. "Okay, here's the point of today's demonstration." He shows Huxley how open the tube of toothpaste, squeeze a dollop of bright green paste onto the bristles of the toothbrush, and wet the whole thing with a bit of water from one of their jugs.

"Isn't that a waste of water?" Huxley asks.

"No." Bracken shakes his head. "No, this is an important life lesson I'm teaching you. I can't believe your dad never showed you this stuff before." At the mention of Huxley's father, Bracken stiffens up but quickly moves on. Huxley notices the blip but focuses all of his attention on the toothbrush and Bracken's tutorial. The older man goes on to show Huxley how to hold the brush, position the head, and the proper angle to run the bristles along his teeth. It's difficult to see in the dark and Bracken has to repeat his instructions often.

Huxley holds the brush as he's been shown, giving Bracken one last, questioning glance, and for the first time in his life, starts brushing his teeth. The taste of the paste is hot and cool at the same time, and as he breathes the slight burning sensation travels into his lungs and up into his nostrils and sinuses. He frowns as the bristles, scratching back and forth against the smooth surface of his teeth, poke and prick his gums raw.

He stops and pulls the toothbrush out of his mouth. "I don't like this."

"You're not supposed to like it," Bracken says. "But it's good for you."

"Does it build character?"

Bracken laughs.

After a few more false starts, Huxley finishes brushing to Bracken's satisfaction.

"Now rinse and spit," Bracken says.

Huxley does as told.

"And there we go." Bracken claps his hands together once and arches his eyebrows at Huxley.

The boy examines the man in front of him, a man who has no qualms about killing a father in front of his son if it needs to be done, but who also just showed him how to clean his teeth with a giddiness that Huxley didn't believe existed anywhere inside of him.

After a time, Huxley asks, "Why are you so excited about this?"

Bracken stops and cocks his head to one side, considering the question. He shrugs and turns his hands up. "I don't know. I guess stuff like this makes me feel normal. Like it used to be. Showing kids how to take care of their teeth is something people used to do."

"Did you ever show your own kids?"

Bracken stops. He shakes his head. "Never had any. Never had the chance."

Neither Huxley nor Bracken sleeps during the night. Both remain wide awake until the sky slowly bleaches from darkness into daylight. Without a word they rise, fold up and repack the blankets, and break down their camp.

Bracken takes a jar out of the bag and hands it to Huxley.

"Breakfast," he says with a nod then turns to the bag and pretends to adjust one of the straps.

Huxley takes it. He knows they only have two left.

"Aren't you hungry?" Huxley asks.

Bracken shakes his head. "No, I'm good. I've never been a big breakfast guy. Now brunch." He smiles. "Brunch is a different story entirely. I used to fuck up some brunch."

Huxley devours what turns out to be a can of stewed tomatoes. Ravenous, the interior of his stomach attacks the food as soon as he swallows. Bracken hands him one of the water jugs. Dirt coats the exterior and only an inch or two of gritty water remains in the bottom of the plastic container. Huxley takes a large swig, swishes it around in his mouth, swallows, and hands the bottle back, noting Bracken puts it away without drinking.

They haven't seen anything, any leftovers from civilization, since leaving the car, not even an abandoned building or farmhouse. It's like people never existed here in this place and Huxley wonders if maybe they're the first people ever to walk where they've walked. Maybe their footprints are the first to ever break the surface of this earth.

Huxley scans the horizon, nothing moves. It looks a painting. The emptiness reassures him, the lack of flesh-starved creatures or cars driven by a madman bent on their destruction. He squints and asks, "Why did you work for him? For Elwood."

"I needed a job, he needed things done." Bracken pauses. "I didn't like myself very much, so I didn't mind putting myself in situations others wouldn't. Made it easier to do things that made me feel even worse. Until I got…" He shakes his head, looking for the word, "Numb."

Bracken finishes securing the pack, lifts it onto his shoulders, and tightens the straps. He looks at Huxley. "Ready to go?"

Huxley tosses the empty tomato container to one side and they walk without another word. They pause in the middle of the day, with the sun at its highest peak over their heads, and Bracken makes Huxley drink more water. This time he takes a small sip of his own. He swirls the scant contents before he puts it away and they continue.

When they crest a low-rise Bracken halts and indicates for Huxley to do the same. He lays down at the apex of the hill, his rifle against his shoulder, aiming in front of him. Huxley crouches into the grade of the hill and braces himself, the fingers of his hand sink into the loose dirt. He momentarily notes the soil, darker and lusher than most places, and slides up next to Bracken, flat on his belly. His heart speeds up and his muscles tense, ready to move.

Topping the hill, he sees what Bracken sees, though it takes a moment to register in his mind. A structure stands in the distance. His heart thunders in his ears and his palms sweat. It appears to be a house, a simple square with a flat roof, but definitely a building. Next to the house, at a distance, stands a skeletal windmill. The blades turn slowly but steadily in the wind. Huxley thinks he hears a low shriek of metal on metal as they cut through the air, but the sound could be his imagination. Something, now long dead, once grew out of this ground, and long, even rows of brown shoots stick out of the dirt.

"I didn't think anyone farmed out this far," Bracken says. "Most of the fertile land is farther north."

"They made something grow," Huxley says. The words evaporate into the wind.

They sit and watch for a long time. Nothing changes. No one arrives or departs. There's no more movement; there's nothing else to see. Nothing or no one enters or exits. The place is abandoned, dead. A shiver runs up the length of Huxley's spine.

Bracken purses his lips and exhales a stream of air. He rolls to face Huxley. "I'm going to go down there and check it out, okay?"

Huxley nods.

"Stay here. I'll signal you if everything is clear and if it's safe for you to come down, okay?"

Again, Huxley nods.

Bracken rises to a crouch, his gun at the ready, and slowly, painstakingly, descends toward the farm. Bracken shrinks with the distance and Huxley searches their surroundings for any signs of life. He makes himself take deep, measured breaths instead of the shallow, rapid ones his body wants. Blood courses through his veins, faster and faster as Bracken nears the building.

Once he arrives, Bracken circles the house. Huxley's hands tighten around his rifle for the short moment that he disappears behind the structure. His knuckles turn white with the pressure and he holds his breath. He licks his cracked lips and releases the air from his lungs as Bracken comes back into view.

Bracken's figure shuffles up to the door and presses his body against the wall. With one hand he pushes the door open and takes a quick step back, covering the opening with the barrel of his rifle. Sweeping as he goes, he creeps closer and closer until he finally takes a step inside.

Without realizing it at first, Huxley holds his breath again when Bracken vanishes into the interior of the house.

After an uncomfortable amount of time, Bracken emerges and shuts the door behind him. He scans the horizon and waves one hand, indicating for Huxley to come down. The boy stands, puts the pack on his shoulders, and, rifle at the ready, jogs down the hill.

The scene comes into clearer view as he approaches. Raw boards, whatever rough scraps the inhabitants could scrabble together form the main building. It has no windows and only the single door. It makes a certain amount of sense not to have windows in a land where the wind never stops. A crude storage shed juts from the backside of the structure. The windmill is similarly constructed, with a support structure of scrap lumber. A pipe runs down the middle into the ground, a spigot on the back. Mismatched pipes and hoses scroll out toward the skeleton fields.

The site was obviously once a farm. A field once grew, but now only the odd ends of some unidentifiable plant protrude out of the dirt. Brown and brittle tips ripple in the wind, dead and rigid like stubble. Nothing grows anymore and Huxley contemplates what it means that these people, whoever they are, managed to coax any living thing at all out of the cold, dead ground.

Bracken stands in front of the building with his back to the door, like he doesn't want to let Huxley see inside.

"Hey," he says when Huxley gets close enough to hear, something new and strange in his voice. "I'll scrounge what I can from inside, why don't you go see if that pump works and fill up all of our bottles."

Huxley nods and scampers over to the windmill.

"If you see anything," Bracken calls after him. "Anything at all, you yell. You got that?"

Already busy freeing anything that will hold water from the pack, Huxley nods without looking up.

Before he dumps the last bit of water out of their last jug he wants to make sure there's actually more. The spigot is shut tight and won't turn. He pulls and pulls, but nothing. He tries again. Nothing. Another attempt, and again, nothing. Overhead, the blades of the windmill churn steady in the wind.

Frustrated, he puts his hands on his hips and glares at the handle. He places a hand on each end of the handle, one pulling, one pushing, and braces one foot against the splintering wood of the windmill. With all of the strength he can summon he twists his entire body. Rust bites into his hands, and the muscles of his arms, legs, and back pull and strain.

With a groan, the handle gives way. Huxley falls backward to the ground as it rotates. He props himself up on his hands and looks into the black hole at the end of the spigot. A hollow gurgle sounds somewhere deep within the pipes then a spray of water erupts from the spout, hitting him full in the chest and splashing up onto his neck and face.

He lets out a shriek from the shock before he is able to roll to one side. On his knees, he watches the flood and breathes hard, wiping the water off of his face. He can't help but laugh as he stands up and goes about the business of rinsing and filling the containers. He looks over and sees that Bracken has rushed out of the house, ready for battle.

Huxley smiles and waves and indicates the steady flow of water, like anyone could have missed it. Bracken nods, a tight smile strains at his lips. He nods again and ducks back into the house.

When all four of their bottles are all full, Huxley raises one to his lips and tilts it back. The water is chill and gritty and sweet in his mouth. He swishes it around and spits it out, and then drains half of the contents. The coolness flows down his throat and spreads out inside, filling his belly. He feels the cold on the bottom of his lungs. When he lowers the bottle he takes deep, gasping breaths. His stomach bulges with the liquid. He smiles, pleased with himself, and refills the bottle.

Before he turns off the tap, Huxley sticks head underneath the flow. Water runs through his shaggy brown hair and down over his face. He works his fingers against his scalp until the accumulation of grit and dirt washes away. With his palms, he wipes and scrubs his cheeks and features until his hands come back clean. Rivulets run down into the collar of his shirt. The cold water feels crisp and clean on his salty skin.

He shuts off the spigot, careful not to turn it so tight he can't open it again, and shakes his head. Globs of water spray off of him and leave a wide circle of mud splotches in a circle pattern on the ground. He picks up a bottle to offer to Bracken and turns toward the house.

The door stands open, the interior dim and grey. Inside looks similar to the exterior, coarse and irregular, with a collection of rudimentary furniture made in a similar fashion as the house—a bed, a table and chairs, and a simple crib. Huxley stands in the doorway. In the middle of the floor, Bracken fills the backpack with cans and jars and supplies from cupboards that line one wall. Otherwise occupied, he doesn't notice Huxley standing there.

Feeling the presence, Bracken looks up from his pile of goods and freezes. Quickly, he stands and moves toward Huxley, placing himself between the boy and the inside of the house. Huxley steps back before the advancing man. Bracken steps out and pulls the door behind him, but not before Huxley sees the bodies.

Bracken looms over Huxley, looking down at the child, who gazes back up at him. Neither one speaks. Bracken breaks eye contact first. His eyes skip to one side and he exhales through his nostrils. He looks back at Huxley and cocks his head to the left. Huxley looks down at the ground and kicks at the loose dirt with the toe of his shoe.

"That for me?" Bracken says, indicating the water.

Huxley nods and raises the hand with the bottle. He struggles to lift the weight of the gallon jug with one arm.

Bracken takes it and drinks deeply. A stream runs down from one corner of his mouth and drips off of his chin. "That's good. Thank you." He sighs, reaches behind him, and opens the door.

Dust thickens the air inside; the room hasn't been opened in some time. Three bodies lay parallel to one another on the bed; a man, a woman, and a young boy, not much taller than Huxley. All three are long dead. The bodies have shrunk in death, their simple, functional clothes loose and too large. The skin of their faces and hands, all that Huxley can see, stretches taut and brown with age. They resemble leather or dried meat. Their lips pull back over their teeth, creating vicious smiles on all three faces.

The woman and the boy have puckered bullet holes in their foreheads. A ragged chunk of flesh is missing from the woman's neck, a bite. The boy's hands cross over his chest, a bite mark, a distinct half circle of tooth imprints, visible in the desiccated meat between the thumb and forefinger of his left hand. The man has one hand in his pocket. The other holds a dust-covered revolver beneath his chin. Behind his head, dried blood and brain stain the hand-sewn pillow.

Through the bars of the crib Huxley sees the still outline of a small body.

Dry and stale, the air doesn't smell like death. It doesn't smell like anything.

Huxley stands and stares. Bracken stands next to him. He puts his hand on the boy's shoulder and squeezes. Then he releases the pressure and returns to the task of loading up the bag.

He pauses and says, "Maybe you should wait outside. If you want to. I can handle this."

Huxley nods and backs out of the door.

Huxley sits in the dirt, his arms around his knees, and stares into the distance, not looking at anything. The sun creeps low and the day fades away. The top of his head gets cold as the wind dries his wet hair.

Bracken emerges from the house with the new bag slung over one shoulder. It bulges. He shuts the door gently and rests his forehead against the rough boards before walking over and setting down the bag. The contents clunk together and settle. He sits next to Huxley and rests his elbows on his knees, watching the same horizon. They sit in silence.

"Who were they?" Huxley finally asks.

"I don't know," Bracken says. He shakes his head and raises his eyebrows. "I do know one thing. Whoever they were, they just saved our lives."

Huxley nods. He knows this fact too well.

"Why did he do it?" he asks after another pause.

"Why? I'm sure it had to be done. I'm sure he didn't want to, but he didn't have a choice." Bracken trails off. "I'm sure it had to be done."

"Like you and my dad?"

Bracken's jaw tightens and he nods. "Just like that."

"Just like that." Huxley nods.

Behind them the house sits, still as ever; a tomb and a cradle, life and death within the same four walls.

CHAPTER 7

Huxley and Bracken sit next to each other, silent, facing away from the farmhouse mausoleum. Neither one pays any attention to the grains of sand the wind whips against their cheeks and eyes, blinking only on reflex. It sounds like a rain against their clothes. Without turning his head Bracken occasionally looks over to check on the boy. They remain at rest and watch the sky fade by degrees into dusk.

Despite the dwindling light, part of Huxley wants to load up, grab their bags, and get as far from here as they can. San Francisco waits for them, and even though it fills him with uncertainty and dread, and the nights are full of unseen horrors, he can't shake the air of death that surrounds this place. It reminds him of his father and he shivers in the wind. There are too many ways to die and he feels like he's just waiting for them; waiting for Elwood, for the infected, to starve, to die of thirst, to wander into a hole and never come out.

"We'll camp out here tonight," Bracken says, breaking the silence. He doesn't speak to Huxley so much as he talks to the wind. He puts his hands on his knees and stands. An audible crack sounds deep in the center of his joints as his legs straighten.

He looks at the house and says, "Wait here. There's something I need to do. Keep an eye on the stuff."

With his gun slung across his chest he walks over to the shed at the back of the house and disappears inside. When he emerges he holds a shovel in one hand. Even from the distance of his vantage point, Huxley sees the blade, brown with rust.

Bracken moves away from the house and begins to dig. Huxley listens to the grind of the shovel plunging into the earth. A brief silence follows, then a soft thud as Bracken dumps the scoop of dirt into a neat pile. The process repeats again and again in regular, measured strokes. Huxley falls into a lull under the spell of the hypnotic sound that draws him in until it occupies his entire mind. For once, he doesn't think about looming threats, mysterious cities, the nightmare list of possibilities, all of them bad. He just breathes and exists. His eyes lose focus and his head rocks imperceptibly with the rhythm of the work, forward with the initial penetrations, back with the silence, forward again with the dump, over and over.

When the digging stops, the jarring silence pulls Huxley from his reveries and back to reality.

By the time Bracken hoists himself out of the hole the night is almost entirely dark and the last of the light glows on the horizon behind. He's a black shadow outline, something other than a man, a shape, a thing. Huxley watches the silhouette move from the hole back into the house. When it reappears a moment later the form has grown and the shape has changed. It carries something long and indistinct, a body wrapped in a blanket. The shadow man places the body in the hole and climbs out again.

Huxley watches the process repeat a second then a third time. The third body is noticeably smaller than the first two, the corpse of the boy, similar in size to Huxley, similar in age, only he will remain frozen in time and never grow older. Huxley watches but has the feeling what he sees isn't real, that it can't be real. This is simply something vague in the distance that may or may not be happening, some loose dream or hallucination. The lines all blur and melt and when he thinks about it none of it seems real and for a moment it feels like he's the one being placed in the hole.

It becomes real again when Bracken exits the house for the final time. Bracken, that's who he is. Bracken, once again and not a blank shadow figure, a man and not a thing, shuts the door behind him. In his arms he carries the body from the crib, draped in a cloth.

Huxley turns away.

After a moment the sound of shoveling begins again in reverse. This time it provides no comfort, no distraction, no solace. He doesn't lose himself in the rhythm again. He can't let his mind wander off. He can only dwell.

When the hole is refilled, Bracken pats down the loose earth three times with the flat of the shovel blade. The metal rings three times like a bell. In the darkness, he stands next to the freshly turned earth and examines his handiwork.

Huxley rises and walks toward the grave. He stands next to Bracken and looks at the ground.

"Do you want to say anything?" Bracken asks.

Huxley shakes his head. "There isn't anything to say, is there?"

"No, no there isn't."

Huxley turns and walks back to their bags.

Bracken pushes the edge of the shovel into the dirt and leaves it standing there like a headstone as he walks away. Huxley thinks of the hasty shallow grave the man dug for his father.

In the morning, Huxley finds Bracken already awake and moving by the time he opens his eyes from a night of unpleasant dreams. No specific images stick in his mind. All that remains is a lingering sense of fear and loss and a vague terror that slowly dissipates in the morning sun. Instead of rising himself, he remains laying down, his head on his arm, and watches. Bracken has his back to the boy and bends over their bags. The contents of both lay on the ground in front of him and he moves items from one pack to the other, testing the weight. Finally, only one item remains, the small, wrapped parcel Huxley remembers seeing as he stuffed stolen food into his bag before escaping from the orphanage.

Quietly, Huxley stands and moves over toward Bracken. "What's that?"

Bracken straightens abruptly and turns, stuffing his hand and the package into the mouth of the boy's bag. When he sees Huxley, he puts on a wide, false smile.

"Jesus, kid. You're like a ninja." He closes the bag and sets it behind him.

Huxley looks as him and knits his brow, trying to get a look, but Bracken places his body between the boy and the bag.

"You probably don't know what a ninja is, do you?" He laughs to himself. "You hungry?"

Huxley shakes his head and looks through Bracken's legs at the worn bag. He turns away and folds up his blankets, making a conscious effort not to look at back at the empty house, or the shovel sticking out of the dirt, indicating the grave. Already the turned soil blends into the rest of the land and the lines between life and death begin to blur. He knows it's there and through deliberate effort he keeps the entire scene at his back.

"Here," Bracken says as he sets the new bag next to Huxley. Smaller than the original, made out of blue and black nylon, with a pocket at the top. "I split everything up. I'll take all the heavy stuff, but it'll be a huge help if you would lug this one around for me."

Huxley looks up, forces a smile, and nods. Bracken pats him on the shoulder.

"I put all of your stuff in there. I figured you'd want to keep it close." He pauses. "The gun, your father's gun, the revolver, and all of the bullets for it. All of that is in that top pocket there if you need it." He nods once and walks away.

The morning sun climbs higher into the sky as they walk away from the farm. Neither of them acknowledges the structure and it remains behind them, much as it was before they found it. They hunch forward underneath their burdens and trudge ahead into the waste, toward an uncertain goal, like a pair of bent pack animals. Huxley's arms ache from carrying their water bottles. The straps of his backpack bite into his shoulders. His back feels stretched out and tight, but he keeps pressing forward without complaint, adjusting his load as best he can.

CHAPTER 8

Two days pass in virtual silence. They walk and eat and camp with even fewer words than before. The wind and the steady churning of their footsteps in the dirt seem to converse with one another, saying things they can't possibly comprehend.

In the middle of the day they stop to eat. The farmhouse provided a bounty of canned food, things the occupants managed to grow themselves and preserve, and they sit in the middle of a wide-open valley, each gently chewing and swallowing the contents of their selected containers. Huxley shovels cold beans into his mouth, while Bracken consumes sliced pears.

When he finishes the fruit, Bracken holds the can out to Huxley. "Here," he says. "Drink this." Huxley is unsure. "Go ahead." He pushes the container forward. "It's sweet."

Huxley relents and accepts the offer. He lifts the rim to his lips and tilts it back. When the remaining syrup hits his tongue, he smiles despite himself. He takes another small sip, savoring the flavor.

"It's good," he says, still holding the can at his mouth. His words ring metallic and deep in the silver cylinder. "It's good," he says again, just to hear the distortion of his voice.

Bracken smiles and ruffles his hair and grins. He scans their surroundings and as quickly as the smile appears, it vanishes. His eyes widen and his entire face tightens. Looking at his expression, Huxley's own expression changes.

"Is it Elwood?"

Bracken shakes his head but doesn't say a word.

Huxley follows Bracken's eyes to see what he sees.

At the crest of the ridge in the distance behind he spies a black wall, a black wall moving toward them across the waste.

"Fuck," Bracken yells, standing and grabbing his bag and rifle. "Move."

Huxley follows Bracken's lead and grabs his own gear. They sprint into the heart of the valley, toward a collection of low structures surrounded by a fence. Huxley's bag bounces on his shoulders and his lungs suck deeply at the air, searching for every last molecule of oxygen they can find.

"What?" he stammers between breaths. "What is that?"

"Black blizzard," Bracken says. He turns his head, looking past the boy, over his head. "Sandstorm."

Huxley glances behind them. He's heard stories of black blizzards and even lived through a number of sandstorms that felt severe at the time. But what he sees now makes his mouth drop open. "Holy shit," he says.

A dark tidal wave of sand stretches upward. Black fingers reach up into the sky, much closer than he expected. It looks alive. The front edge boils and seethes, tearing up the surface of the earth trying to get to them. A static charge builds in the air around them and the hairs on Huxley's arms stand up. An angry, vengeful night shadows them across the floor of the valley, sweeping in on them from the periphery.

"We're not going to make it," Bracken says. "Over here." He steers Huxley toward a rock outcropping. Behind it they duck under an overhang. Bracken throws off his pack and pulls out their blankets.

"Goggles," he yells at Huxley. "Scarf. Now."

Huxley follows his orders and as soon as the rough fabric of his scarf touches the soft skin of his face the world explodes around him. In the space of less than a second the world goes from day to night, from silent calm to thunderous chaos. The wall breaks around their rock shelter. Sand collapses over top of them with a roar, like a crashing wave. It feels like someone dumped a bucket of earth over him. Even through his clothes it stings and dirt pours down the collar of his coat.

Bracken forces him against the wall of the rock, as far underneath the overhang as he can, placing himself between the boy and the storm. In the same motion he pulls the biggest blanket they have over the top of both of them, attempting to shield them from the fury.

Panic overtakes Huxley. He screams and struggles against Bracken's weight, tries to breath, but gets only a mouthful of sand. Coughing and convulsing he chokes. Tears stream from his eyes. He tries to push his goggles back to wipe his eyes, but gets a vicious blast of sand in the face and clamps his eyes shut with the pain.

Bracken holds the blanket tight around him. "It's okay. It's okay. It's okay," he yells over and over again, competing with the deafening howl of the wind.

Coughing, he holds Huxley's face to his chest, sheltering the boy as much as he can. "It's okay. It'll be okay. Just keep your eyes closed. Keep covered."

Eventually, the assurances do their job and Huxley stops hyperventilating and calms down as much as possible. Bracken does his best to keep the storm out, but he can only do so much against the onslaught as the wind tries to tear the blanket out of his fingers and expose them.

Huxley still can't get a real, true lungful of air, every breath shallow and halting. It feels like he's drowning and his panic rises again. The sand down the back of his neck feels like it is filling him. Grit forces into his mouth, grinding between his teeth and creeping down his throat. When he tries to spit it out more comes in, invading his nostrils, eyes, and ears.

Finally, he can't take it anymore. It's going to go on forever and never end. He writhes and kicks against Bracken again, who only presses him harder against the boulder.

"Hey. Hey. Hey," Bracken yells. "This isn't going to stop. We have to get out of here." He puts his forehead against Huxley's and grabs the boy by the sides of the face.

"Open your eyes," he yells. "Look at me."

Huxley cracks his eyes. Sand bites at them, even with his goggles, but he keeps them open, tears streaming.

"We have to move," Bracken says. He shakes the blanket. "I'm going to wrap you in this, and we're going to make for those buildings. Okay?"

Huxley nods.

"Smile, junior," Bracken says, a wry grin on his face like he is enjoying himself. "This going to be an awesome story to tell someday."

Huxley gives a cursory laugh, which results in another mouthful of grit, and another coughing jag.

"Stay covered. Keep your eyes closed. Cover your mouth." He looks the boy in the eyes. "I need you to be brave. Can you do that for me?"

Huxley clenches his jaw defiantly, and gives a curt nod. "I'm ready."

"I need you to trust me. Do you trust me?"

Another nod.

"Okay. We're going to be fine. Everything is going to be fine." He grabs Huxley by the hand. "I'm going to wrap you up. You don't need to see, I can see for both of us. Hold on to me and don't you even think of letting go. You hear me?"

Bracken tightens his scarf around his mouth and nose, tucking the ends into the neckline of his jacket, and grabs both of their packs and rifles, slinging everything across his shoulders. He winks at Huxley and wraps him in the blanket. Huxley feels tight, swaddled, and the fabric restricts his movement. One arm presses against his side, the other one protrudes and his hand clings to Bracken's as if his life depends on it. Which, it occurs to him in the moment, it does.

"Ready?" he hears Bracken yell.

"Just go already," Huxley yells over the noise of the storm.

"All right, tough guy, here we go."

Nothing in Huxley's short life, not even the seemingly dangerous storms he's experienced, has prepared him for the terrible squall they step into. In a trusting darkness, they move slowly away from the shelter of the rock. The middle of the storm is even louder; more than a shriek, more than a howl, more than a scream. It tears at the legs of his pants and the edges of the blanket and the wind almost shoves him over onto the ground. Despite the layers, sand still penetrates, piercing his body creating a rough film between his skin and his clothes, rubbing and tearing at his flesh and weighing him down. Raw blisters quickly form on his feet inside his shoes.

Blindly, he lets Bracken lead him through the blizzard of dirt. Every step a mystery, an exercise in trust. He trusts that Bracken leads them in the right direction. He trusts there's ground beneath him. He trusts, he has to.

He loses time in the storm. They may have taken ten steps, or they may have taken a thousand. A minute may have passed, or an hour, or five. He exists in a void with nothing around him to anchor him to reality except a single hand. It's like being back in the dark of the underground labyrinth. With nothing to orient him, he grows dizzy and stumbles. Bracken catches him.

"Hey there, buddy," he yells over the wind. "You're doing great. We're almost there." He coughs and pulls Huxley into his body. The feel of something solid, something concrete, reassures the boy, and he swallows his rising fear for the time being.

The blanket slips off of Huxley's head and he gets a brief glimpse into the storm. He has a firm grip on Bracken's hand, he can feel it, but he can't see it. The sand swirls so thick in front of his face that he can't see to the end of his own arm. The world closes him off, even from his own body. There's nothing but the storm, walking into oblivion, and he shrieks.

Bracken stops and pulls him closer.

"What? Are you okay?" Finally, no more than a few inches from the end of his nose, Huxley can make out the dark outline of Bracken in the storm. "We're almost there, promise." A pair of large, disembodied hands secures the blanket around him again. "Hold on."

Moving forward, Huxley's dizziness worsens. Every breath more sand than air, his head grows lighter as it slowly strangles him. With every step he almost topples over. Only Bracken's hand guides him in an unsteady line. When he can't take another step he hears the sound of metal rattling against metal. He must be imagining things, but then hears it again.

"Yes," Bracken yells. "We found the fence, kid. We just have to follow it and we can find our way to one of the buildings." A torrent of coughing follows his words.

Huxley extends his hand. The sand tears into the skin, but his fingers feel the cool, smooth surface of chain-link. He smiles underneath the blanket, still struggling for breath, and Bracken pulls him to his right. He trails his fingers along the fence.

"This is kind of fun," Huxley says, trying to sound tough and strong and make light of the situation like Bracken does.

He coughs and tries to breath.

That's the last thing he remembers.

Huxley's body convulses. His lungs burn and heave and struggle for breath. With every ragged cough, his entire frame bends forward and twists and folds over on top of itself. Sand coats his lips and mouth and throat. The bottom of his lungs feel heavy and no matter how much air he inhales, it's not enough, not anywhere near what his body screams for. Forehead against the floor, he jerks and hacks and coughs, his body expelling solid matter with each blow. Drowning on dry land, he breaks out in a panicked sweat.

A wide hand thumps him rhythmically on the back. It makes a solid echoing sound both inside his chest and around them. The sound bounces off of the walls, the walls of a room. They're inside.

When he tries to open his eyes and look around, he finds a thick crust fusing his eyelids shut, and he scratches madly at them until he pries the lids apart. He blinks the grit and dirt away as it flakes into his eyes, stinging. The room around him is dark. He can't tell if there are any windows, but the storm sounds quiet and far away.

"Where?" He pants and coughs, trying to catch a breath. "Where, where, where." This begins another prolonged coughing fit.

"You gave me quite a fright, kid," Bracken's voice comes out of the darkness. "You passed out back there and I had to carry you." He laughs. "At least you're not heavy. It was like carrying a sack of potatoes." He coughs and spits a mouthful of something to one side. In the darkness it hits something solid with a thick splat that sounds like more than just saliva or phlegm.

Huxley continues to cough and spit up.

"That's it," Bracken says. His voice stays rough, but even, as gentle as Huxley imagines it can be. "Get as much of that shit out of your body as you can."

The coughing continues, but between gasps and expulsions, Huxley manages a few words. "What is this place?" he asks.

"This?" Bracken says, his voice returns to its usual timbre. "This is prison."

"Prison?"

"Lovelock Correctional Center to be precise." Bracken chuckle. "I always thought 'Lovelock' was a funny name for a prison. I'm sure someone, someplace along the line referred to their marriage as a love lock and had a good laugh."

Huxley remains quiet in the darkness. He still can't breath and teeters on the verge of hyperventilating and falling into a full-blown distress.

"Don't worry if you don't get it, kid. Even if you did, it wasn't a very good joke. I've never been particularly funny."

Huxley starts to ask another question, but a new fit of uncontrollable coughing gets in the way. "Is it," he stammers, trying to catch his breath. "Is it safe?"

"I don't know." Huxley imagines Bracken shaking his head and staring at wherever the door is. "But we don't have much of a choice at the moment. I guess it's safer in here than out there right now."

Huxley pulls himself upright and pushes his head back against the wall. The concrete feels solid and cool through his hair. He turns his head and puts his cheek on the rough surface. Inch by inch he slides over until he feels Bracken's form against his shoulder and side. His presence provides comforting and for the first time since he woke up, he takes a real, true breath. The air rattles in his lungs, but it finds a home and helps him calm down and stem the tide of terror. He's happy to be alive and guilty as he thinks that his father is not.

"That wasn't pleasant, was it?" Bracken says.

Huxley shakes his head.

"You do realize I can't see you shake your head right now, don't you?"

"Oh, sorry," Huxley says. "Yeah, that was scary."

"Kind of an adventure though, huh?"

Huxley laughs, which only makes him cough more.

"What was it? I mean, why did it happen?"

"I'm sure there is some scientific reason for it, something about wind convergence vectors, or something like that, that I don't understand. But I'm no meteorologist, so I can't explain it. For whatever reason a bunch of wind picks up a bunch of dirt and it gets a little bit crazy somewhere along the line. And we had the misfortune to get caught in the middle of it."

"How long will it last?" Huxley asks.

"Don't know." Huxley hears noise from the collar of Bracken's coat and pictures him shaking his head. "I've seen storms that last a few minutes, and I've seen some that last a few hours. The longest I've personally experienced lasted almost an entire day. Before the infection, there were reports of storms that started in the Midwest and ran all the way out east, as far as DC." He pauses. "I guess that doesn't mean much to you. Basically they started in the middle of the continent and went east, all the way east, fast. Thousands of miles. Tearing up everything that got in the way.

"In the middle of the country," he continues. "This is every day. It's so flat and so dry in places that there's nothing to stop them, so the storms are almost constant. There used to be big cities in the middle, but most of them were abandoned, even before the plague hit. Chicago was pretty much a ghost town. And that, that is why I've always been a west coast kid. I like hills and mountains. Storms aren't usually this bad this far west."

"I've never seen one this bad before," Huxley says.

"They don't get a whole lot worse." Bracken sighs. "And now that you've survived that, you know you can survive whatever the world throws at you. Out here you find out what you're capable of, and from the look of it, you're capable of pretty much anything."

In the darkness, Huxley clings to Bracken's voice. The words provide comfort and he feels himself grow calm. Not even the words themselves, it's the sound that soothes, and he wants Bracken to keep talking.

"Once, I waited out a storm in a house," Bracken continues. "When it was over, we went out through the windows because there were giant drifts of sand blocking all of the doors. We had to climb out and shovel it open." Huxley imagines Bracken smiling to himself in his distant manner. He closes his eyes and finds that it is just as dark as when they are open.

Bracken coughs. "Like I said, the storms started even before the infections. All of the Midwest, that's the center of the continent for the most part, used to be farms. Just miles and miles and miles and miles of flat land that was fertile and would grow whatever you wanted. But then the climate changed. People called it different things. Water supplies started to dry up, and the rain stopped, and the winds picked up, and . . ." He trails off.

"When it changed, everyone left, headed to the cities on the coasts. It happened like that once before, in the 1930s, and the government put in a bunch of failsafe measures so it wouldn't happen again, but one by one they all failed." He chuckles once. "Failsafe. Nothing is really failsafe. Especially when greedy assholes purposefully take them away. And when everyone moved into the cities, they got crowded, and mean. Too many people in too small a space."

He stays silent for a moment. Huxley leans his head into Bracken.

"When the infections started." Bracken's voice is quiet when it starts up again. "When the infections started, there were so many people piled on top of each other that, well, you know what happened then. It just spread from one to the next to the next, like a forest fire. Before anyone even really knew what was going on, before it even had a proper name to be afraid of, everyone was infected and eating each other and the entire world ended.

"Some people called it 'Ivan' for a while. They were convinced it was the Russians. I'm sure there's some scientific classification of it in some abandoned lab somewhere, I just don't know what it is. And in the end it doesn't really matter what you call it."

Bracken continues to talk in the darkness, but Huxley fades under the vibrations of the speech, and sleep overtakes his exhausted body.

Huxley wakes up below one blanket, with another folded into a neat rectangle underneath his head. The room still dim, light trickles in through the open door. He looks up. All that remains of the furniture is a desk and office chair pushed against the wall and a black metal filing cabinet in one corner. The floor is linoleum, white, but covered in stains and dust. Some torn papers litter the ground and tacks hold a few yellowing pages to a corkboard.

Bracken sits with his back against the wall, one leg straight out, and on the other, on the raised knee, he props his rifle, the barrel pointing at the doorway. His eyes watch the opening.

"Morning," he says without turning to look at Huxley.

"Morning." Huxley sits up, yawns, and stretches his arms over his head. Sand falls from him with every movement. He looks over at where he spit and coughed, and moist piles of dirt, black and much larger than seems possible, cover the floor. The scene looks like someone knocked over a bucket of potting soil. Looking at it makes him cough again, but it's lighter in nature. He points at the piles with one hand and covers his mouth with the other, and says, "All of that?"

"Yup. It all came out of you," Bracken says, completing the thought.

"Wow," is all Huxley can think to say.

"Indeed."

Huxley notices the sound, or rather the absence of sound. The constant screams of the wind have fallen silent. The quiet is shocking, and somehow deafening. He stares out the door, as if an answer will present itself to him and make sense out of everything. His shoulders begin to bounce slightly and he feels the coughs build deep in his chest.

"The storm?" he asks before giving into the coughs.

"As far as I can tell, it's over," Bracken says.

Bracken instructs Huxley to take off his clothes and they shake the sand out of every last item. The process takes much longer than he imagines. With the amount of sand that pours out of his boots, he's not sure how there was room for his feet. When all of their clothes are as clean as practicality allows, piles of sand litter the floor. They both laugh at the sight, but the laughter makes both of them cough again. Huxley rinses his mouth, but even afterwards, grit covers his teeth.

Before they gear up to move on, Bracken takes both of the rifles and cleans them as best he can.

"Nothing more worthless than a gun that won't kill anything," he says as he hands the bolt-action rifle back to Huxley.

When they leave, Bracken checks the hallway outside of the room. They walk down a short corridor toward the source of the light, and round a corner. In front of them, at the end of another corridor, two sets of double doors lead outside. Each door has two panes of glass, one above and one below. Beyond them, Huxley sees high chain-link fences topped with razor wire, and a knocked-over flagpole that's almost completely buried.

The bottom pane of the left door is broken out and sand creeps in and covers much of the floor. Outside it piles up against the door and walls.

"Had to let myself in," Bracken says. "They forgot to leave a key under the mat for visitors. They're going to get a bad Yelp review for this."

Huxley looks up at him.

"Remember when I said I wasn't funny?" Bracken smiles. "Come on."

"We can't stay here for a while?" Huxley asks.

Bracken shakes his head. "This place is too well known. People tried to hold up here for a minute, figured a prison designed to keep people in might keep monsters out. It didn't. If Elwood hasn't checked for us here yet, he probably will before long."

With his back he presses into the door, which only swings open an inch before the sand stops the momentum. He pumps his legs and the door grinds slowly through the sand leaving a foot of open space.

"Good enough," he says, sucks in an exaggerated breath, and slips out.

"Are you sure the storm is over?" Huxley asks. His pulse quickens, too vivid images of the storm in his mind. Bracken doesn't respond.

Huxley follows him through, though, and emerges into the world. The wind is strangely still. Around them a layer of dirt and sand covers everything. The squall tore up the surrounding land and spread it over everything. Scanning the surroundings, it looks as if the world rearranged itself.

Bracken begins to walk west, searching the horizon as he goes. Huxley falls in step behind him, nervously scanning on his own.

They come across a round post mostly hidden by sand. A sign, most of the paint worn off by the weather, advises against picking up hitchhikers.

"What's a hitchhiker?" Huxley asks.

Bracken thinks about the question for a moment. "Well, they were travelers. They would wait by the side of the road and try to get rides from strangers." He stretched out his arm and put his thumb up in the air. "They'd hang out until someone passing by picked them up in their car."

"What happened if no one wanted to give them a ride?"

"Well, then I guess they had to walk."

"So they were kind of like us."

"They weren't usually being chased." Bracken smiles. "But yeah, I guess they were kind of like us."

CHAPTER 9

Throughout the entire day that follows the black blizzard, Huxley lives in continual fear of another. He constantly scouring their surroundings as they trudge westward, looking for any sign of an approaching storm. For the moment anyway, this new worry replaces the any concern over roaming infected, Elwood and company pursuing them, mummified bodies in a cabin, or anything else, in the forefront of his mind.

At the crest of a far-off ridge he sees a shaft of sand caught in an updraft, spinning and rising into the afternoon sky. He stops dead in his tracks. His eyes grow wide and his body breaks out into an immediate sweat. Panic settles in his stomach like liquid metal.

He stares without blinking, until his eyes quickly dry out. The discomfort shakes him back to his senses and he bounds over the sand after Bracken. He tries to raise an alarm, but he stammers syllables instead of forming actual words or sentences. When he's close enough, he reaches out, grabs Bracken's coattails, and tugs.

Bracken whirls around, rifle up and ready to fire, instantly prepared for trouble. But seeing no immediate threat, he looks down at Huxley with a question written across his face. Panting, Huxley points toward what he's sure is certain death chasing them down from behind.

Bracken follows the boy's finger, unsure of what he should be seeing. "What is it? I don't see anything."

Huxley breathes in deep, collects himself, and says, "There, a storm. Another black blizzard. It's coming for us. It's going to get us, we have to hide." His frantic voice cracks, and he's on the verge of tears.

The concern on Bracken's face evaporates as Huxley's words sink in. His shoulders relax and he smiles.

"That?" he shakes his head and points in the direction of the ridge. "That's not a storm. It's just another little dust devil."

"No, it is, we have to hide." Huxley's voice breaks, his body shakes, and tears form in the corner of his eyes. "We're going to die."

Bracken crouches down until his eyes are even with Huxley's. He puts a heavy hand on the boy's shoulder and squeezes. Despite his overwhelming panic, Huxley finds this gesture reassuring, even though Bracken looks annoyed.

"I promise that's not a storm. That's just some dust in the wind, dude." He chuckles to himself. "It'll be okay."

"Are you sure?"

"A hundred percent. Take a look at it." He pulls the boy closer and nods toward the ridge. "See, that's the wind coming over the point of that hill. It just picks up some sand and dirt and junk and blows it around for a little bit.

We live in a windy, windy time, it happens."

Huxley watches for a moment. Nothing more happens. The small-scale tornado dances and twists, but it stays in the distance and remains small until he watches it weaken and break apart. Gradually his fear subsides and his heart rate returns to normal.

"If that was a storm," Bracken continues. "You'd know it. There wouldn't be any doubt." His voice is calm and even.

"How will I know?"

Bracken smiles. "Because I'll be running and hiding and shitting myself."

Huxley grins.

"Besides, a little fear can be a healthy thing. It can keep you alert and alive."

A trail of similar exchanges occur over the next few hours. Huxley thinks he sees death lurking over every hill and on every ridge, until, finally, Bracken's reassurances sink in and he gradually sheds his worry. Walking along behind Bracken, he feels lighter, less weighed down with his concerns. Deep, cool breaths sooth his raw throat and lungs, and Huxley feels good. He still scans their surroundings, but with a sense of exploration as opposed to one of impending doom and destruction.

Looking to the north, Huxley sees something, unsure exactly what, but it makes him reach out for Bracken.

Bracken stops, tilts his head skyward, and inhales deeply. "Seriously?" he shouts as he spins around. "Remember when I said a little fear can be a healthy thing? This is not healthy. This will not keep you alive. Keep this up and I may kill you my damn self."

Huxley stares to their right, and raises his hand, pointing into the distance.

Bracken exhales, and when he speaks, his voice is a low growl. "What. The. Fuck? What is it this time? I guarantee you it's not a fucking storm."

Huxley swallows and continues to point. He's seen this side of Bracken directed at other people, but never at himself. He nods, trying to make Bracken look in the appropriate direction. "Over there." He gestures with more urgency. "Someone's there."

Bracken, newly alert, turns to see what Huxley points at. In the distance, barely visible, a human form walks out of the emptiness, directly toward them. The small silhouette hovers just above the horizon line. It shakes and blurs in the dying rays of the sun, but it's unmistakably a human form, or at least something that used to be human.

"Fuck," Bracken says, sighting the shape with his rifle and stepping in front of Huxley.

"Told you," Huxley says.

Without taking his eyes away from his target, Bracken points back and to his left, toward a small mound of earth topped with a boulder big enough to hide behind. "Move. That way."

They creep backward and keep low. Huxley peers around Bracken. He can't tell if it's a man or a monster that approaches them. He's also unsure which scares him more, which option is more dangerous, or if there's even a difference between the two out here.

"Is it Elwood?" he whispers. "It's Elwood, isn't it? He found us. Is he going to kill us? He's going to kill us." Horrific images fill his mind. Imprisonment and torture, pain and agony. He imagines being chained to a high table by his throat, Elwood looming over him, a monstrous smile on his face as he burns him, pulls out his teeth, and slowly saws off his fingers, knuckle by knuckle. The joints in each digit ache with the phantom pain and he flexes his hands to chase it away. In his head, he's buried alive, confined in a tight, airless box deep in the ground. His eyes are cut out, but not before the tip of the rusty knife, coated with dried blood, hovers over the sockets, taunting his twitching eyeballs. His tongue is sliced off so he can't scream.

"I don't know who that is. Or what," Bracken says. His eyes dart over the landscape. "I don't see signs of anyone else, and I doubt Elwood is out here alone. And it's coming from the wrong direction." He leaves the thought to dangle in the wind. "I really hope it's an infected," he says quietly as they duck behind the boulder, taking solace in the minimal amount of cover it provides. Against his every instinct in his body, Huxley agrees with the sentiment, though he asks himself how do you pick between two nightmares?

Time slows down to a crawl as the figure approaches. The wind is the only sound. Huxley crouches behind Bracken, clutching the bolt-action rifle in his hands, and watches the outline grow. It still heads directly for them.

The profile raises one arm into the air.

Bracken glances back at Huxley. "Did he just wave at us?"

"I think so."

As the form approaches, it comes into sharp focus, and it is indeed a man. A human man. He wears clothes similar to their own, only more faded, dustier, and somehow more beaten and broken down even than their rags. A small bag sits high up on his back, a double-barreled shotgun strapped across his shoulders, and a machete dangles from his side, bouncing with each step, slapping against his thigh. Tall and gaunt and exhausted looking, his clothes hang off of his body. Creases run across his face, deep lines worried into his skin by time and exposure; he looks carved out of a block of wood. A wide smile on his lips exposes brown, broken teeth.

Bracken stands and steps into the open, his rifle trained on the man.

The stranger stops, raises both hands above his head, and shrugs. "Hey there."

Bracken nods. "Nice gun."

"My personal preference in firearms," the man says. "Fewer parts means less to break down."

"Simple. I like simple." Bracken lowers his gun to his hip, still pointing the barrel at the man. "That's about close enough, I think."

The stranger nods and stops, slowly lowering his hands to his sides. "That your boy?" He tips his head at Huxley, who, even though he stands behind Bracken, aims his own gun at the intruder.

"What are you doing out here?" Bracken asks, ignoring the question.

"Just wandering," he says, still smiling.

Behind Bracken, Huxley whispers, "He smiles too much."

"What do you want?" Bracken asks. His voice is flat. There's no anger in his tone, but the words carry a definite force.

The man shakes his head. "I just saw you folks, thought I might pop over and say hello. Don't get much opportunity to practice my conversation skills. Fact is, sometimes I go so long without uttering a word that I start to wonder if I even remember how to talk." He laughs to himself, but his smile dims a shade. "But, if you aren't in the mood for company I understand." He looks them over then nods to himself. Neither Bracken nor Huxley makes a move. His eyebrows arch. "I guess I'll be on my way then. Always nice to know that there's more of us alive out here in the world. Getting to be a rare thing."

Huxley pulls on the back of Bracken's jacket. He looks down at the boy then up at the man's retreating shape.

"Really?"

Huxley nods.

"Okay." Bracken nods. He yells after the man, "It's late."

The man pauses and turns, looking at the fading sky. "It's not so bad."

"Maybe you should camp with us tonight."

He turns and strolls back, pausing in front of them. "Much obliged."

Bracken nods. "I won't hesitate to kill you."

The stranger laughs. "Never doubted that for a second. You look like hard man."

"Just so we're clear."

"Crystal."

They scrape together what fuel they can and light a fire. Bracken and Huxley sit across the small gulf of flame from the man. In the firelight, the folds in his face cut even deeper, a relief map of canyons and riverbeds. They stay quiet, watching each other. Bracken never takes his finger off the trigger. No introductions are made; there are to be no attempts at connection.

Huxley digs into his bag and comes out with a silver can. He stands and walks over to the stranger and extends his hand. Bracken's eyes track the movement, like he doesn't approve, but Huxley does it anyway. The man looks up and smiles, an easy, natural smile, not the broad, forced grin he wore when they first encountered him.

"Well that's very generous of you, young man," he says.

"You looked hungry," Huxley says.

"That I am." He nods. "That I am." He pulls a can opener and a worn looking spoon from his pack. "Rations have, admittedly, been pretty slim as of late."

Sitting down, Huxley retrieves a can for himself. Digging through his bag, he notices the package among his things. He offers one to Bracken who shakes his head at the gesture, and he puts the food back in the bag.

"What are you doing out here?" Huxley asks through the crackling flames.

"Just traveling," the man answers between bites. He eats like he hasn't eaten in weeks.

"Why do you travel?"

"Just what I do. To tell the truth, I was always a bit of a wanderer even back in the before times. Never stuck around in one place very long. Used to hop trains, hitchhike, dumpster dive, shoplift, live by my wits, and all that noise." He chuckles. "When I think about it, my life hasn't really changed all that much. More walking, I guess. Same destination."

"Where are you going?" Huxley leans forward, his elbows on his knees, listening to the traveler, trying to understand the aimless wandering.

"Nowhere," he shakes his head. "Found out long ago that no matter what my destination was, regardless of my what my goals were at the beginning, it always changed before I got there anyway."

"If there's no end, how do you know when you're done?"

"Every journey has an end. Just like every journey has a beginning. It isn't always as cut and dried as folks make it out to be. You can start a journey and another journey and another and so on before you ever finish a single one. And you can end in the middle of another, and take all manner of left turns and right turns and backs and forths. Hell, you might finish something you didn't even know you started in the first place."

"Will you ever be done?" Huxley asks, wondering if this makes sense or if it's madness.

"I suppose I'll be good and done when I'm dead. That's a pretty good indication that you're finished," the traveler says with a grin. "But listen to me go on. You must think I'm a damn fool. I apologize. Like I said, haven't spoken much of late." He smiles to himself and settles back.

The fire cracks and spits and burns down to ash and ember. Huxley wraps himself in blankets and lies down in the sand with his eyes closed.

"He asleep?" the traveler asks in a quiet voice after a few minutes of silence.

Huxley keeps his eyes closed. Bracken must nod, because the man continues.

"I'm not going to ask you where you're headed."

"I wouldn't tell you if you did," Bracken says.

"And I didn't want to say it in front of the boy, but I heard of some people looking for, well I assume looking they were looking for you all. A small crew of bad, bad boys, with one woman in tow, and a couple of particularly nasty gentlemen leading the pack."

"I figured they were out here someplace. Let me guess, a guy with black and gray hair who insists on wearing white, despite the fact that he's in a constant windstorm of dirt."

The stranger chuckles. "That is the one." Huxley imagines him nodding.

"Then there will be the guy that wears all black with the tattoos along his jaw and a burned-up arm."

"Among others. Whatever you did, you managed to piss them off something fierce. They're scouring the desert looking for you, in cars, too. Using up more gasoline than I thought there was left in the world. They are plenty mad at you, young fella."

"I have a tendency to rub people the wrong way." He laughs. Huxley imagines that Bracken's face pinched tight, his expression clashing with his laugh.

"Why did you come down here?" Bracken says. "There are more people farther north."

"I don't much care for most of the people I meet out there on the road." Huxley hears both men stand and move a short distance away from the fire. He cracks his eyes and watches them. They stand with their backs to him, too far away for him to eavesdrop on their conversation. He watches their posture and gestures until his eyes grow heavy and he falls asleep.

Bracken and the traveler are up and moving when Huxley wakes up.

When Bracken sees him stir, he says, "Hey, get packed up, we're heading out."

Huxley nods and scurries to the task.

Bracken and the traveler stand next to each other and talk.

"There's a farmhouse a few days hike that way," Bracken says, pointing in the direction they came from. "Nothing left alive. We took what we could carry, but there are still some supplies you could use. Food. Water. A few blankets we didn't need. Shelter for a night or two."

The traveler nods. "Thank you."

Huxley runs up and hands him another can of food then returns to folding up his blankets.

"You got a good boy there," the traveler says.

Bracken nods.

"He's kind, despite everything that surrounds him. I've been a lot of places and that's a rare commodity in this day and age. You got to protect that. You raised him right."

Bracken chuckles. "I guess someone did."

The stranger eyes him, a question on his lips, but one he thinks better of asking.

Huxley, pack on his shoulders and, ready to move, slides up next to Bracken. The three stand in a rough circle in silence.

The traveler nods at them and walks away without another word.

"You stay alive," Bracken yells after him.

"That's the goal," the traveler replies without turning. "That's always the goal."

They stand with their packs on their shoulders, guns in their hands, and watch the stranger shrink into the distance and disappear over the hill.

CHAPTER 10

After the encounter with the traveler, Bracken stays more alert and on edge than ever. He never stops searching, he never lowers his gun, he sleeps even less, and never lights a fire. As much as they can, they proceed under cover, even at night, by the blue light of the moon and the stars. They wake up early, before the sun, and make camp later and later. They spend entire days hiding in washes and caves, like insects under rocks, or in whatever out of the way shadows the arid, parched landscape provides.

Huxley stares out at the landscape from the mouth of the cave they slept in. He has to crouch to get in or out, but once inside the space opens up and he can stand at his full height. Bracken has to hunch so he won't hit his head on the ceiling. The cave isn't deep, but the air is cool and musty in Huxley's nostrils.

Huxley finds it comforting to be in an enclosed space, to have walls surround him on every side. He feels held and protected, cradled. The rock walls create a welcome shelter from the constant torrent of whipping sand and the burn and sting of the sun and wind. He rubs his cheeks and feels the skin, raw and red and chafed and scurfy, under his fingers. If he closes his eyes and pretends, the cave almost feels like a house and part of him grows sad because he knows they have to leave soon. Is this what it will feel like in San Francisco, like home? He's come to think of home as wherever Bracken is, not necessarily a specific place. Maybe that's what it means.

"Anything out there?" Bracken asks, sidling up behind him.

Huxley shakes his head. "Nothing I can see."

"Well that's a start. Go ahead and pack up, and we'll get a move on."

The moment Huxley steps outside, sand assaults his eyes. He squints and leans his face forward until his chin touches his chest. With one hand, the other holds his rifle, he pulls his scarf up and over his mouth and nose then pulls his goggles down over his eyes. Shallow scratches crisscross the lens, which tints the entire landscape a light orange. Grains of sand make an audible sound as they collide with the window. The plastic clip that adjusts the elastic strap is set as tight as it can go and bites into the side of his head right above his left ear. He fidgets with it while the wind howls in his ears, trying to make it comfortable.

Bracken crawls out of the cave and stands next to him. Motionless, they explore their surroundings with their eyes. With sharp breaths, Bracken tries to blow grit and sand out of his nostrils before pulling his dirty bandana over his face.

Everything around them stays still, except the wind tearing across the dead land. Always still. Sometimes it feels like they're walking through a picture, where nothing ever has or ever will move.

They approach the outskirts of what was once a large town. For the first time in their journey they come close to a city this size. Large collections of trailers give way to tracts of similarly constructed suburban homes, land parceled out and separated by boundary markers. On the outskirts the houses are in full decay. The paint has long since peeled off under the constant barrage of sand and wind. Wood siding rots and wears away. Fences lean at odd angles and earmark where a yard once stood. Here and there backyard playground equipment sticks up. Rusty swing sets jut from the earth.

The high mountain desert is well into the process of reclaiming the valley, and has already taken back much of the metropolis. Sand piles up and covers everything, blocking doors and hiding driveways and streets. Almost every window has been broken.

Bracken stands on high alert, moving forward deliberately, all of his senses searching for threats.

"This is a bad idea," Bracken says. "I don't like going into cities, but we need food, and this is quicker than walking around."

Huxley hears the words, but stays silent.

"Welcome to the biggest little city in the world," Bracken says.

"I have no idea what that means," Huxley says, shaking his head.

"Well, this town's called Reno, and that was their motto, or catchphrase."

"They didn't have anything else to worry about than coming up with a slogan?" Huxley asks. The idea seems strange to him, that people, more people than he has ever seen by the look of the place, would waste time and energy on something so silly and pointless.

"It was a different time, kid," Bracken says. "You could relax. The entire world wasn't out to kill you every minute of every day. When I think of all the things I took for granted." He shakes his head. "You could go into a store and pick anything, literally anything, you wanted to eat off of a shelf. We all lived in nice, safe houses where you could turn a knob and fresh water just came out of a faucet. In your house. Flip a switch and everything lit up. Flip another one and your house would get warm. It all seems so insane now." Bracken grows silent, and continues forward. "But, man, it was awesome."

At a few of the houses that haven't been obviously looted, the ones without kicked in doors, they enter and forage for food or anything useful. Here and there they find a few leftover cans and replenish their dwindling stores. They never stay inside for longer than it takes to search the kitchen and pantry, and Bracken always makes sure to clear before they exit.

They stop when their packs are replenished, full to bursting, almost too heavy to carry.

As they near downtown, the buildings grow taller. Bracken steers them down the center of the street, putting as much space between them and any structure as possible so they have the most warning for any potential attacks. The ever-present wind whips over them like they're walking through a canyon.

The walls are all dull colors, weather beaten grays and tans that blend in with the muted hues of the desert around them, as the old and new worlds unite and become one. Again, most of the windows are broken out. Doors are kicked in. Multicolored shards of glass lurk beneath the surface.

"Did people live in all of these?" Huxley asks.

"Some of them." Bracken nods. "Most of these were businesses, casinos and hotels mostly. A hotel's a place where you could pay for a room for a couple of nights and then move on. A kind of momentary house. A casino's . . ."

Huxley interrupts. "I know what a casino is."

After so much time in the wastes, their footsteps on the firmness of the concrete sounds and feels strange to Huxley. Every time they pass the dead hulk of a car, he expects something or someone to dart out after them. He tries not to notice the body in the cab of a pickup truck, but through the dust-coated window he sees the shape hunched over the steering wheel as if in prayer. He swallows hard and continues to follow Bracken deeper into Reno.

They cross a bridge over the empty bed of a river that once flowed through the heart of downtown, and the buildings become even taller and bunch closer together. These structures are also the most ravaged. More cars line the streets here, and more dead bodies. All of them protrude from the sand to various degrees, an arm or a leg or just the shape hidden beneath a layer of dirt. None of the corpses are fresh, a huge relief to Huxley.

"Back in the day," Bracken says. He does not turn all the way around and his voice is loud enough to be heard, but nothing above that. "At night, all of this was lit up. This was all bright, flashing lights. They blinked in patterns that looked like movement, all competing, all trying to get you to go into their place. Everything, and I mean everything, had lights stuck to it.

"I can't even explain it to you in any way that will make sense. You don't have anything to compare it to. There was every color imaginable, every shade of pink and green and red and blue and orange. Shit." He shakes his head. "Colors I haven't seen since. Hell, I probably forgot about most of them. I used to think it was so ugly, so gaudy, but now, what I wouldn't give to see this street lit up just one more time, teaming with people having fun."

A sound from the left snaps him around and he aims the barrel of his rifle in the direction of the disturbance. Huxley goes through the same motion only in miniature, though it's more difficult for him to keep his gun level, and the muzzle sways in his small hands.

The noise comes from a man. At first Huxley thinks it's one of the infected and almost pulls the trigger. The creature that emerges from the gaping mouth of one of the tallest buildings is a mess, ragged and worn down, uncomfortably thin, and looks like something wholly unnatural, but it is still a human man. Barely.

His head sticks through a hole cut in a brown blanket that sits on his shoulders like an improvised poncho. Huxley can see through the threadbare garment in places. The top of his head is bare with the exception of a wisp of grey hair like a puff of smoke sticking up from the middle of his scalp. Along the rim of his skull and down over his chin and face, hair grows in long mats. The strands have grown together into large chunks. The dirty skin of his face stretches tight across his skull.

He approaches with his arms thrust out to the sides; his grubby hands turn skyward and his skeletal fingers wriggle. His eyes are wide and bloodshot, and he makes Huxley's skin crawl. A cackle escapes his mouth, trying and failing to form words. His lips suck in and puff out over his gums, and it's clear that he doesn't have a single tooth left in his head.

"Stop," Bracken says. His voice sounds deep and hard, and the single word contains all the necessary menace. He doesn't need to finish his sentence with, "Or I will kill you where you stand." Huxley shivers.

The apparition freezes in his tracks. A wide, manic grin spreads across his face like it will continue until the two ends meet at the back of his head. Huxley sees his tongue flick back and forth like a worm in the black chasm of his mouth. The man tries to talk, but what comes out is a series of clicks and groans that sound vaguely mechanical.

"What the fuck do you want?" Bracken says each syllable words slow and even. He does not shout, but force lies behind his words.

"Just saw you passing through," the old man says. His voice, high-pitched, creaks like old wood. "Don't get many visitors. Thought I might just pop out and say hello. Hello." He waves his fingers and laughs a rickety laugh to himself, and takes a step forward.

"Don't do that," Bracken says.

"Heh, heh." The man chuckles, and grins. "I can see you're not a man to be trifled with."

"I most certainly am not." Bracken eyes the man. "What's your name?"

The man shrugs, his hands still skyward. "The last guy stopped through here called me 'Coot.' Guess that's my name as much as any." He raises his eyebrows and slowly lowers his arms to his side. They disappear beneath the poncho. "Coot."

Huxley flips his eyes back and forth between the man and Bracken. Bracken keeps his aim steady. "I'd prefer it if I could see your hands." He gestures with the gun. "You understand, I'm sure."

The Coot chuckles again and takes his hands out. He tosses the front of the poncho over his shoulder. Beneath it he wears a sweater with green and red stripes so dingy and caked with filth it's difficult to tell where one color ends and the other begins. The garment dangles off of him like a hanger. Huxley notices the man's wrists are as thin as his own.

"Much obliged." Bracken nods.

"Much obliged to oblige." He seems incapable of speaking without laughing. "Why don't you and your young fella come with me to my house?" He turns and shuffles forward, barely picking up his feet out of the dirt he kicks up a small cloud with each step. Huxley notices he doesn't wear shoes, but flaps of leather wrapped around his feet and tied with frayed lengths of rope.

His house sits in the middle of the street, a collection of boxes, bins, and scruffy furniture arranged around a fire-pit in an intersection, beneath the arch that boasts, "Reno: the Biggest Little City in the World." Behind them, in the middle of the block set off to one side, is a high, uneven mound of earth. Huxley makes out a long bone in the sand next to the base.

"Make yourself comfortable," the Coot says, busying himself rummaging through a blue plastic bin.

Huxley sits on a torn couch that reeks like fresh urine and stale armpit, and he has to swallow the bile that creeps up his throat when the smell of the couch hits his nostrils.

The Coot flails his arms and cackles in frustration. He makes a final noise of aggravation, picks up a cardboard box half full of papers, and sets in the middle of the ashes and coals. Embers still glow in the middle and it only takes a moment before the box begins to smoke and flame.

"Ha ha. There we go." The Coot claps and rubs his hands together. The chapped skin grates like sandpaper.

"Aren't you worried about attracting attention?" Bracken asks.

The Coot bends over, groping through a bin, tossing things left and right onto the street. "Attention? There isn't any attention to attract."

"You don't worry about the infected in these parts?"

"Infected?" He looks over his shoulder at Bracken, shakes his head, and returns to his task. "No no no no no. They don't bother much with me. No no, don't bother me much."

"Really," Bracken says. "I've never come across any that didn't want to tear out my throat. Are there many around?"

"No, no, haven't seen any in . . ." The Coot trails off and shrugs. He mutters again, but his words grind together in an incomprehensible mass. Huxley wants to ask what he said, but the coot stands bolt upright, holding three tin cans.

"Dinner," he says, crowing triumphantly. He turns and smiles at Huxley.

Huxley looks away from the mad eyes. Everything about their situation makes him uncomfortable. Why do they linger here instead of moving on?

The old man cuts the tops off of the cans and sets them in the fire with his bare hands. After a few minutes the contents start bubble. He picks them up, again with his bare hands. The metal sizzles against his skin and the smell of burning hair offends Huxley's nostrils. He hands a can of beans to the boy. Huxley looks at Bracken, who nods, then the boy covers his hand with the end of his sleeve and takes the food, feeling the heat of the cylinder through the fabric.

The Coot hands one to Bracken, takes a one for himself, and sits down in a chair on the opposite side of the flames.

"Have many people been through lately?" Bracken asks.

"Here and there."

"Anyone recently? Maybe a group of them? In cars? Probably have face tattoos, dress in black?"

"Can't rightly say," the Coot says. He slurps and swallows his beans. Juice runs down his chin, seeping into his beard.

Bracken leans over to Huxley. "Watch him gum his food," he whispers. "You want to wind up like him?"

Huxley shakes his head.

"Toothbrush," Bracken says then sits upright. "We're not going to get anything out of him. Finish your food and we're out of here."

Relief settles over Huxley and he nods and speeds up his eating.

"So, old timer," Bracken says, leaning back. There is less business in his voice. "What's a guy like you do around here for fun."

"Fun? What's fun? Hasn't been fun in this world since a long long time ago. Not that there was even much fun then. Fun wasn't never as fun as the fun as everyone always claimed it to be." The old man mutters and stands and shuffles from container to container, pawing through piles of what looks like garbage. "I forage, I rummage, I scavenge, I search, I scream heresies at the sky."

"You scream heresies at the sky for fun?"

"Heresies at the sky." He pauses and looks at Bracken then turns to the sky and shakes his fist. "Someone has to hold God accountable for what he done. He can sit up there and watch and laugh and judge, but never can he help, no, never. He can cause all of this, send his creations sinking head first into the shitbox that he made for us, but he will do nothing to pull us out, wipe us off, clean the stench from his world, no, no, that's too much to ask."

"Isn't it a bit redundant to be a heretic in a godless land?" Bracken leans back, a wicked smile on his face, prodding at the old man.

The Coot stops and looks at Bracken. "Oh, a nonbeliever"

Bracken nods.

"Well tell me then, son, what was it made a man such as yourself come to deny the existence of God, our Lord and Savior."

"The moment I put a bullet through my wife's brain. That was when I knew there was no God." He pauses, his face changed from a light expression to a tight, grim look, and then he lets out a loud, forced laugh.

This information stuns Huxley and sucks the air out of his lungs. Watching Bracken in disbelief, he examines his companion for any hint or sign of emotion. In the flickering light, his face looks darker, the creases deeper, but he can't tell if it's his mind and the flames playing tricks.

Is he even telling the truth? Did he only say that to throw the old man off balance? It's a deep personal detail to share with a stranger. But maybe that's why, maybe a stranger makes it easier to say. Something about the words, the gravity with which he says them, makes them ring of fact.

Silence hangs in the air after the echo of Bracken's laugh fades. The only sounds the crackling of the fire and the mournful howl of the wind.

The old man nods. "Could see how that might do it," he says and turns back to digging in his boxes. "Could see that indeed."

Darkness settles around them. Maybe it's a trick of the fire, the flames and shadows dancing across his features, but Bracken's expression hangs more severe than usual, heavy and sorrowful. Huxley wonders if he really killed his wife.

Bracken sits and stares into the fire. He glances at Huxley, catches him watching, and says, "You done?"

Huxley nods. Bracken stands up and brushes off his pants.

The Coot notices the movement and turns. "What? Where?" he stammers. Bits of spittle fly out of his mouth. "You can't, you can't go." He rushes to them, his arms outstretched. "No no no, you need to stay here for the night. Here." Desperation sounds in his cracked voice. "I need, I need, I need you to stay. Haven't had company in so long, yes, so lonely, yes, lonely." He smiles a toothless smile. "The boy, the boy needs to rest, the boy is tired, see."

"No, I'm not," Huxley says.

"You heard the kid," Bracken says. He turns to Huxley, "Let's get the fuck out of here, I don't want to wake up in Reno."

"No no no no," the old man pleads, moving to block their path with his hands raised above his head. "Hey, friends, we're friends, right?"

"No," Huxley says. "We're not."

Bracken looks at the boy and laughs. "You heard the kid. Thanks for dinner."

Something catches his eye. In the same motion the smile drops from his face and he brings his rifle to his shoulder. "Motherfucker."

Huxley spins around and raises his own weapon, seeing movement at the periphery of the firelight. At first he only sees one, a shadow lurking at the edge of darkness, the shape of a man, but crouching, stalking like an animal. Then he sees the second, third, fourth, and fifth outlines creeping in a semicircle. He jumps as Bracken's gun erupts. One of the shadows falls to the ground, but it gets up and continues to move, limping and hissing. The others take up the cry, spreading out to the sides, trying to completely encircle them before they attack.

"You fucking shit," Bracken says.

The old man giggles wildly behind them. "I brought them for you," he yells over their heads, at the shadows. He cackles until his entire body quivers and bounces uncontrollably. The laughter and the hissing combine.

"Look, I brought you a child." He grabs Huxley. "Fresh and soft and juicy." He lets go and clasps his hands. "So tender."

Huxley swings the barrel of his rifle wildly. It connects with the old man's jaw with an audible crack. The Coot stumbles backward a few steps and laughs, clutching the side of his face.

"Fuck fuck fuck fuck fuck," Bracken mutters under his breath. His eyes bounce from one target to the next.

The infected creep forward and Huxley makes out the details of their appearance in the firelight. Three of them used to be men, two were women. Two of them, a man and a woman, are completely naked, while the others wear varying degrees of rags. The naked woman only has one arm. In the night, their blue skin looks like charcoal. All of them miss large chunks of flesh. Wounds and filth and carnage cover their bodies.

Bracken's gun roars again and the clothed woman's head explodes. Her body goes limp and falls to the ground. The others barely notice.

"Get ready to run," Bracken shouts to Huxley.

Bracken rotates to take a shot at another infected, but as he does another comes at his blindside. Huxley, reacting without thinking, raises his rifle and pulls the trigger. The creature's head whips backward, the outstretched limbs go limp, and it crumples to the ground in a wilted pile. He hadn't planned anything, it just happened, and he stares at the corpse, surprise swelling over him even as he expels the spent shell from his rifle and racks a new bullet.

Bracken takes care of his target, turns and winks at Huxley, before he raises the butt of his own rifle to beat back an oncoming infected. Huxley sees the Coot pull a long knife from below his poncho, and with a manic, almost joyful sound, he rushes Bracken from behind.

Again, with an automatic reaction, Huxley swings his rifle and catches the Coot in the stomach. The ghost of a man bends in the middle and crumples to the ground. He struggles to get back to his feet, cackling, but by now Bracken has turned and shoots the Coot in the knee. The laughter turns to cries of pain, though the transition from one to the other isn't so great. The withered body crumples to the ground, flopping around in the dirt.

Huxley's arms go limp and fall to his side. Shock is all he feels as he looks at the man writhe on the ground. A hand on his shoulder snaps him out of the momentary reverie.

"Move," Bracken yells, and Huxley turns and runs in the opposite direction of the creatures.

Bracken fires his gun one more time then catches up with Huxley.

Behind them the old man yells, "No, no no no no no, you're my friends, I brought you presents, no no no, no you can't." Screams and snarls and cries follow. "I feed you, care for you." His words change to choking cries.

Running as fast as his legs will move, Huxley glances over his shoulder. In front of the fire the silhouettes of three creatures converge over the body of the fallen Coot, ripping and tearing and biting. Bracken must have killed one more. Their hissing sounds like jeers, mocking the old man's death screams.

They don't slow down until Huxley thinks he's about to collapse. Still they do not stop, walking forward in a near jog.

"You," Huxley says, panting. "You shot him and left him there."

"Yes I did."

Huxley continues forward.

"Good."

Huxley can't help but glance over his shoulder every few steps and look into the darkness at their backs. Exhausted, but fueled by adrenaline, there's no chance of sleep and they do not stop.

"He really thought that they would leave him alone," Huxley says. "Didn't he?"

Bracken nods. "He certainly did."

"Why?"

"That I don't know. Maybe he'd been out here long enough, survived long enough, he started to think he was invincible, or protected, or different and special somehow. Maybe he was always a little bit off his rocker and the strain finally got to him and he went full blown bat-shit crazy. Hell, maybe he was just so far gone even those fucking monsters didn't bother with him. Didn't look like he would have been much of a meal anyway."

He continues. "I've seen a lot of madness. None of it makes sense. I've seen people want to be bitten, want to turn into one of those things. Saw a guy get bitten and fall to ground, screaming in ecstasy, like it was the best thing that had ever happened in the history of the world. He just kept screaming, 'thank you, thank you, thank you,' over and over again, and laughing."

He shakes his head and falls silent. "Sometimes I feel like I don't know a god damned thing."

They stop briefly to rest and Bracken makes Huxley drink and eat. He sits and stretches his legs as the boy slurps down a can of salty green beans.

"I didn't know you were married," Huxley says.

Bracken looks at him.

"Was that in San Francisco?"

Bracken looks away, scanning the perimeter.

"I'm sorry about your wife."

Bracken stands up. "We should keep moving."

The sun rises behind them. In front of them mountains loom, taking up the entire horizon, blocking their path like a massive stone wall.

Bracken pauses. His breaths aren't heavy, but they are deep and purposeful. Exertion and the thin air of elevation combine to make his lungs crave oxygen. He looks at Huxley then up at the mountains.

Huxley asks, "We have to go in there, don't we?"

Bracken nods, turns, and trudges forward, into the mouth of the mountains.

CHAPTER II

After leaving Reno they don't slow down. Bracken sets and keeps the fastest pace of their journey so far. Huxley breathes hard and his lungs burn in the mountain air, more and more as they climb. His heart pounds inside of his ribs. The straps of his pack bite into his shoulders and he leans forward against the weight of his load. He struggles to keep his legs moving, to maintain the velocity, even to continue setting the next foot in front of the last.

More than before they remain on the remnants of the interstate that winds up and into the Sierras as he learns to call them. Torn up concrete rubble remains in places where the earth gave way beneath the road, and support columns have collapsed in places, leaving large gaps in the thoroughfare. Bracken explains that the terrain is much too rough to proceed any other way for any length of time. Huxley feels exposed walking in the middle of the road, out in the open for anyone or anything to see. The wind whips through the pass, the walls focus the natural power. At times it seems as if he would lift off if not weighted down by his bag.

They stand in open, unsheltered space. Still, the landscape feels close and presses on them. Mountains loom on either side, pinning them in. Huxley examines the walls. There are far too many places to hide and precious few directions to run. Even though they don't encounter anyone, he feels like someone's out there, watching. He feels eyes on him. He can't know, maybe there is someone lurking behind every rock, or prowling in the shadow of every dried out, wasted tree. The possibilities start to overwhelm him and he jumps at every sound that carries on the wind.

Beneath his clothes his body sweats, creating a layer of moist warmth. With one hand he loosens the collar of his jacket and feels the cool air flow down and in, spreading across his neck and chest.

At a bend in the road they pause. The level area drops off steeply to one side. In the barrier there's a gap where something tore through the guardrail, something big travelling fast. Below them sits the corroded remains of a station wagon. Golden paint peels off of the metal and most of the side windows are broken. The front rests against the trunk of a large tree, folded back on the body. A mess of spider-webbing cracks crawls across the front window, except on the passenger side, where an oblong hole punches through the safety glass. In front of the car, a surprising distance from the wreckage, and beneath a thick layer of silt and ash and detritus, lies a broken human body with its head bent backward at a horrific angle. Huxley's body squeezes in on itself once with visceral revulsion and his knees get weak. What remains of the flesh has dried and browned, and remnants of clothing cling to the corpse. There's no sign of the driver.

Bracken stops and looks down on the wreck. He checks the surroundings, examines the hills, then looks up at the sky and furrows his brow. The sky grows dark overhead and the encircling crags accentuate and exaggerate the shadows and the fall of night.

"Let's stop here for the night," he says.

Huxley looks around for himself and nods.

Carefully, they sidestep down the embankment, away from the road. Bracken peers into the car as they approach. It's empty. He grips one of the handles on the back door and pulls. It sticks. On the third try it opens with a dry tearing sounds and the metal on metal shriek of the corroded hinges.

When the time to sleep comes, Bracken pats the long back seat. "This yours for tonight. Almost like a real bed."

Huxley gladly sprawls across the stale padding of the bench seat. His body and his mind are spent, and almost before he has a chance to think about it, he falls into a deep sleep, full of dark dreams and images of the Coot flailing on the ground, being torn apart.

Huxley wakes up shivering beneath his blankets. When he tries to sit up, he finds his own blankets, as well as Bracken's, wrapped tightly around him. An instant of panic shoots through his constricted body. He squirms and wriggles to free himself. The blankets fall away as he sits up. In the air his breath forms clouds that billow and dissipate.

As always, Bracken is up and packed and ready to go. He notices Huxley's awake. "Finally awake? I let you sleep for a while longer, you looked like you could use a little extra rest."

Huxley stretches his arms and yawns, the taste of morning clings to his teeth and tongue. He climbs out of the car, blinking the sleep out of his eyes, and the images around him clear and take shape.

"Do you ever sleep?" he asks.

Bracken laughs.

"Seriously, do you actually sleep?"

Bracken laughs again. "Buddy, there'll be plenty of time for me to sleep when I'm dead."

Huxley chuckles, too, but it's forced.

To make up for time spent sleeping, they continue on well into the night. The blue light of the moon and stars casts enough illumination on the surface of the road they easily spot obstructions and maneuver around sporadic abandoned cars that litter the roadway. They stick to the periphery as much as is possible, conscious of the visible shadows they cast even in the dead of night.

"Fuck," Bracken whispers.

He comes to a complete stop, crouches down, and slowly side steps to his right, toward the edge of the road. When he reaches the end of the concrete, he slides his legs and body down the gravel shoulder, into the ditch at the side of the road. He lays flat on his belly, trains his rifle on a spot in the distance, and swears to himself again.

Huxley shadows Bracken, echoing his motions, coming to rest beside the older man. He looks in the direction Bracken points his weapon and examines the hillside, finally seeing what he sees, what gave him such a start.

In the distance, up one side of the hill, burns a small fire.

"Fuck," Huxley whispers.

"Told you so."

An orange circle glows in the black and blue hillside. Huxley imagines he hears the crackle of the flames and the smell smoke on the wind. They stay still and watch. Aside from the fire they are no other signs of life. They don't see any other movement and are too far away to notice anyone around the fire.

"What do we do?" Huxley asks.

"For now, we wait."

"Should we go over there?"

"No. I don't like this. It's too obvious, like they lit the fire in the spot where it would be most visible from the road."

"You don't think it might be someone else travelling?"

"No."

"Do you think it's a trap?"

"Yes."

"Who do you think it is?"

"Cannibals."

"Oh."

"Now the real question is," Bracken whispers. "Which way to we go. Did they light the fire to draw us in, to bring us over toward them and spring the trap on us there? Or, did they light it assuming we'd stay as far away from it as we can and try to sneak through the woods on the opposite wall, and that's where they're waiting for us?"

"How did they know we were coming?"

"Either someone we didn't see saw us in Reno, or this is just something then do when they're hungry and out of food. It's pretty risky. We're not the only ones attracted to fire."

Huxley nods in the darkness. "Which way do we go?"

Bracken shakes his head. "If I had a coin, I'd flip it."

After a few more moments of consideration, Bracken rises to a crouch. He looks at Huxley and asks, "Do you still have your father's revolver?"

Huxley looks up and nods. "It's in my bag."

"Get it out. Keep it in your belt." He looks away, at the fire in the distance. "If they catch us, you'll want to shoot yourself in the head."

He stands. His knees crack. "Come on. Quietly."

Huxley digs the weapon out of his backpack and stuffs it in the front pocket of his coat. The gun feels heavy and tugs the fabric toward the ground, but the solid weight provides comfort.

Bracken leads them back, away from the road. They sidestep down from the asphalt surface until they reach the forest floor below. Slowly, deliberately, they move forward through the trees. He keeps low, sweeping the path in front of them with his eyes and the barrel of his gun moving as one. Huxley keeps his own rifle up, despite the weight and the protest of his muscles.

In the dead of night, their breathing and footsteps, no matter how hard they try to mask them, are the only sounds he hears. He keeps his ears open, searching for any indication of danger. The muscles in his arms are tight and he tries not to imagine what's waiting for them in the darkness. Every painstaking inch that passes weighs heavy on his small shoulders and he wants to run, to sprint for as long and far as his body will let him, but he knows he can't. A tremor runs through his body with the effort of maintaining their gradual pace.

On their left, they draw even with the orange glow of the fire. When it slips past, when they start to leave it in their wake, Huxley breathes easier. He thinks Bracken is being paranoid, overly cautious. A nervous smile breaks across his lips and he almost laughs to himself in the gloom.

The sound of a shotgun racking chases all joy from Huxley. A single whimper escapes his lips.

Bracken freezes and sighs. He sounds more impatient and annoyed than afraid or anxious.

Ahead of them a lantern flares up. In the jarring burst of light, Huxley turns his head away while his eyes adjust to the invasion. When he looks up, Bracken has his hands above his head, holding his rifle by the barrel. Huxley looks at him and thinks he looks bored more than anything else.

A hand rips the rifle out of Huxley's hands and he returns to the moment. He twists around, taking in their situation. Four people surround them, three men and a woman, all heavily armed. Soot covers them from head to toe and he can't tell what color their clothes used to be. Under the weak flicker of lamplight, their faces are all maps of thin lines and it's impossible to tell how old any of them are. Like everyone else, probably even himself, they look weathered.

One of the men takes Bracken's weapon and slings it over his shoulder. He has one milky, dead eye, and a tangle of beard on his face. "Hands on your head, cowboy."

Bracken shrugs and does as ordered.

The woman stands directly in front of Huxley. Most of her hair is up inside of a black wool cap, but a single strand hangs down, bisecting one eye. The end touches her chin. Around her neck she wears a necklace. Huxley's blood runs cold when he realizes it's the bones of a human hand, stripped of flesh, drilled, and laced together. She holds a shotgun and stares the boy directly in the eyes, ignoring the activity of the men around her. He can't take his eyes off of her, starts to shake, and wants her to move or say something or do anything.

"Is that a fucking kid?" the man with the dead eye says.

Finally, not taking her gaze off Huxley, the woman smiles. Beneath the cracks on her lips her teeth are brown and broken, pointed like fangs. Her smile terrifies him even more than her stare and Huxley almost falls down in his fright.

"Yes," she says, a crack of glee in her voice. "Yes it is."

"Well fuck yeah, we got us some veal."

Huxley takes a step back but a hand shoves him forward.

Bracken looks over Huxley's shoulder, his hands on the top of his head. He shakes his head. "Don't do that," he says. His voice, flat and calm, sends a shiver up Huxley's spine.

"Fuck you, tough guy." The man behind Huxley steps forward.

"Cody, stop it," the woman says. She doesn't yell but there's an inherent force in her voice. The man stops. She has a quality similar to Bracken, an air of authority and power that others know on some gut level is not to be challenged.

"Sorry, Apple," he says. He slinks back.

"This your boy?" Apple asks Bracken.

Bracken shrugs. "He's as much mine as anyone else's."

She nods then turns to Dead Eye and says, "I imagine you should probably search this one."

He nods and pats Bracken down, finding a pistol and two knives. He tucks the gun into his belt. They don't bother to search Huxley.

"See?" Apple gestures to the weapons.

"Are you going to eat us?" Huxley asks. He keeps his voice as steady as he can, but the words still tremble when they leave his mouth. He swallows hard.

"Of course we are, dear," Apple says. Her voice takes on a false matronly air.

"How did you know they were going to eat us?" he whispers to Bracken.

"Lucky guess."

Panic takes hold of Huxley. His muscles tense for flight, but he knows he can't run. They have all the guns and longer legs and there's nothing he can do. Helpless, he keels over and throws up into the dirt at his feet. The men laugh.

"Oh, don't worry, sweetie," Apple says. Her lips twist into a smirk. "Winston over there used to be an army medic. Seen some shit, even before the world went to hell."

"Not to be rude," Braken interrupts. "But I don't give a shit about your life story." For which he receives another whack on the shoulder.

Apple smiles and continues. "He knows all sorts of other shit, and he's real good about taking a piece off here, a piece off there, and keeping the blood loss to a minimum. We're going to take our time with you, so you'll still be around for a while. Well, some of you will be around for a while." This time she joins the men in their laughter.

She turns and walks forward. "Come on."

They push Huxley up next to Bracken and they all follow Apple. "You okay?" he asks.

Huxley stares up at him, his mouth open, vomit still wet on his lips.

"Ask a stupid question."

Alarm subsides and all Huxley feels is dumb shock and terror, knowing he's about to be tortured, killed, and eaten, and not in that exact order. He thinks he should feel something more, but all that remains is a dead emptiness and a lingering sense of nausea. He's dizzy and sweating, about to hyperventilate.

"Just breath, kid," Bracken says. "It'll be okay."

Behind them, Cody laughs.

"Cody, is it?" Bracken looks over his shoulder. "I'm going to kill you last."

Cody cracks Bracken in the back with the butt of a rifle. Bracken's body jerks, but he doesn't make a sound and continues walking. He glares at the other man, who glances away, a scowl on his face, and a look in his eyes that frightens Huxley.

"Play nice back there," Apple tosses back at them.

Cody mutters curses under his breath.

Bracken takes a deep breath and looks forward, smiling. Huxley notices and stares, wondering what possible reason there is to smile.

Bracken notices Huxley watch him. Without looking down he whispers, "Remember when I said we might not be the only ones who noticed the fire?" He glances at the boy and winks. It's a sinister gesture that makes Huxley's blood run cold for a split-second.

Then Huxley hears it, a low hiss in the darkness, barely audible. He straightens up and clenches his jaw by reflex. His eyes widen with fear but his carriage doesn't betray what he knows.

Dead Eye stops and looks around. "What was . . ." Before he gets out the rest of the phrase, an infected tackles him to the ground and latches on to his throat. A cry cuts short and dies in a gurgle. His legs kick and twitch as the infected rips out his esophagus. It used to be a woman. Naked and missing one arm, in the dim light, her skin looks almost black. These are the infected from Reno.

In a single motion, Bracken grabs Huxley, pulls the boy behind him, punches Cody, who stares dumbly at his fallen comrade, in the throat, and grabs the bolt-action hunting rifle out of his hands. The cannibal drops the lantern and falls to his knees, grasping at his neck, gasping for air. The lamp bounces and rolls, throwing out a haphazard spray of light across the ground, trees, and human forms.

Another infected attacks the other guard, Winston, and sinks its teeth into his arm. He screams and wrestles the monster to the ground. It struggles beneath him and chomps on his forearm. He tries to raise his gun, but the creature clings to him, pinning his arms to

his body. Out of other offensive options, he head butts the monster in the mouth. Bracken raises the rifle and shoots the infected. It goes limp.

"Look out," Huxley yells too late. A third infected wraps its arms around Bracken from behind. It bites down but only gets a mouthful of his hearty jacket. He spins instinctively and catches his attacker in the temple with an elbow. It's just enough that it releases its grasp and Bracken sends the unbalanced creature toppling head over heels onto Cody and Winston.

Apple turns and unleashes an angry scream. She kicks the one-armed infected off of Dead Eye. It hisses, gore clinging to its chin, and lunges. She knocks it back with a boot to the chest, raises her shotgun, and pulls the trigger. The walking corpse collapses into a headless pile with heavy thud.

In a quick, practiced motion, Bracken shoots his infected in the head, ejects the spent shell and reseats the next, and fires into the back of Winston's head. The two bodies crumple on top of one another as Bracken racks another round. Cody, still choking for air, reaches into his belt and pulls out a pistol and raises his arm. Bracken pulls the trigger first, before Cody can aim and fire. Red bursts from his chest and his pistol shoots harmlessly into the forest. His body slumps backward, a look of mild surprise on his face. He blinks once then his dead eyes stare into the night sky.

Bracken freezes as Apple racks her shotgun behind him. He grimaces and swears silently to himself. Easing his finger off the trigger he raises his hands and slowly turns around.

Apple pants, a splash of blood on her cheek, aiming her shotgun at Bracken. "Motherfucker. You just killed two of my friends."

Bracken shrugs but doesn't say anything. What is there to say in a moment like this?

"On your knees," Apple says. Her voice is flat and even, but her body quivers with rage and adrenaline.

Bracken doesn't move.

"On. Your. Fucking Knees." she screams, a tremble beneath the words. She's breaking. Her eyes are red and it takes everything she has to not cry. The barrel of the shotgun quakes in her hands as the tremor inside of her worsens. She's about to pull the trigger.

Huxley reaches down and pulls the revolver out of his pocket. Her focus solely on Bracken, she doesn't notice. Huxley stares down at it, cold and heavy. It's comically large in his small hand.

Bracken told him to shoot himself if cannibals captured them. This might be his last chance. He looks up at the rugged woman with the shotgun, over to Bracken, then back at his own gun. He blinks back tears and raises the barrel of the gun.

"Say good-bye . . ." Apple starts. Her words cut off short as Huxley fires a round into her torso. The report echoes in the darkness.

She turns her head slowly and looks at the boy, her mouth open. A thin line of blood rises over her lip and runs down her chin.

"Guess I forgot about you," she says, air in her voice. Her arms go limp. The gun falls to the ground. She slumps, bracing her body with one arm, then lowers herself to her knees. She coughs a mouthful of blood into the dirt and lies down on her stomach.

Huxley's hands shake. He drops the gun. Silent tears well up in his eyes and run down his face.

Bracken steps between the boy and the litter of corpses. He looks around quickly then crouches down in front of Huxley. The boy doesn't look up. He stares at the dead body face down on the ground.

"Don't look," Bracken says. He pulls Huxley to him and presses his face into his shoulder. "Don't look." He grips Huxley and holds him back at arm's length. "I know this is hard, but I need you to grab our stuff. We have to go. We don't know how many more of them there are. We don't know what the hell else is waiting out there."

"Which ones?" Huxley asks, his voice scarcely a whisper. He doesn't look at Bracken. He still stares past his shoulder at Apple's corpse.

"Does it matter? Do you want to run into more of either?" Bracken stands. "Get our stuff. We have to move."

Like an automaton, Huxley retrieves their belongings. Bracken retrieves their weapons and frisks the dead bodies for anything useful. He gets a couple of bottles of water, knives, bullets, and he takes Apple's shotgun and shells, slinging it over his back. You can never be too well armed.

They move, as fast as possible, paying only minimal attention to being quiet. The key now is to put space behind them.

Huxley follows Bracken. He doesn't look up or around, he simply trails behind. Though he keeps his eyes on Bracken's feet, he doesn't notice anything. Terror and dread and fear have all been taken over, supplanted by deadness, by numbness, by cold.

CHAPTER 12

When they can, Bracken takes them off the road, and their path leads them through a stretch where fire ravaged the remnants of the forest. The dried and desiccated corpses of trees provided the perfect food for the flames that tore through the long dead woods. All that remains is an expanse of blackened trunks sticking out of the ground.

Huxley thinks the burned-out husks look like the exposed bones of animals that couldn't escape the fire, like giant creatures born of the inferno, clawing out from the belly of the earth. He tries to imagine what the fire looked like. Giant flames leaping across the space between trees, from one crackling dry branch to the next and so on until the entire dead forest was vibrant with yellow and orange fingers reaching up into the night sky. The forest must have looked more alive than it had in years.

Ash stains the ground a rainbow of grays, all across the spectrum from light hints of cinders to deep charcoal black. Behind them, they leave a trail of white footprints in the dark soot as they make their way between the trees.

Without branches or needles, Huxley can see almost to the horizon through the trees. His view feels like layers upon layers moving independently from one another as he moves; continually startled by the illusion of movement in the distance as the black stalks cross and dance through his eyes, claustrophobic and disorienting. His heart beats faster, his breathing rushes, and his body leaks sweat. He makes a conscious effort to suppress the panic that forms deep in the pit of his stomach and the back of his head. Only the lack of other footprints in the scorched earth helps quiet his fear. It would be easy to see if there is anything alive or moving in the vicinity. He stares down at the ground in front of him to lessen his disorientation.

He passes near a trunk, reaches out his left hand, and drags the tips of his fingers along the charred bark. Soot, so black it glistens, sticks to the ridges of his fingerprints. He rubs his thumb and middle finger together and stares at the smear. When he wipes his hand on his pants, he leaves five smudges, five fingerprint streaks across his thigh.

That night the sky darkens early. Black clouds storm in and choke out the sun. Huxley and Bracken take refuge in the mouth of a shallow cave. Around them an angry tempest stirs to life. Huxley scarcely notices, stuck in his own head until the rising ruckus drags him out.

It's a dry storm. Bracken sits with his back against the wall, his elbows on his knees, cradling his rifle. White light falls across his face every time lightning streaks across the sky, leaving deep, jagged shadows. Instead of his normal face in these quick instants, it looks like he only has a grinning skull. Huxley sits next to his travel companion and watches until the sinister illusion becomes too much and he has to look away.

Thunder crashes over them, so loud Huxley fears the cave will collapse or that an unseen avalanche is about to spill down and trap them underground. He feels the rumble deep inside of himself, in his stomach and organs and bones, and he pushes himself against the rock at his back. The sound claws to live in the distance then crawls closer, growing louder and louder until the roar hurts his ears and rattles his teeth. He attempts to stand up and flee in a panic.

Bracken reaches out, grabs a fistful of the back of his jacket, and pulls the boy back to the ground. "It's just a storm. You're fine. There's nothing it can do to us. It will pass." He sounds tired and unconvinced, and every time he blinks his eyes close a second longer than before.

A canvas of stark contrasts waits beyond the lip of the cave. Moments of absolute blackness follow brilliant spurts of white, blinding light. Huxley sees everything or nothing in split-second bursts as his pupils struggle to adjust to the constant barrage. Within the eruptions of light, the shadows dance back and forth, shifting with each new explosion.

Huxley's senses swim and leave him, the storm hypnotic and terrifying. Between the flashes in front of him, the constant rumble originates in the air and the ground at the same time, from nearby and far away, from everywhere at once. He feels unstuck in the world, floating, rolling over and again in the force of the storm. He squeezes his eyes shut but the lightning pierces through the thin lids. He presses his hands over his ears to block out the thunder, but instead of penetrating his eardrums it invades the rest of his body instead. He shakes and quivers with each blast.

He opens his eyes and sees movement, not just the illusion, but a definite human shape moving between the charred skeleton trees. The shadow jumps from tree to tree with each flash, and the collection of still images betrays motions. He watches.

Then, through the constant thunderclaps, he hears it. He hears a voice. At first, it's nothing more than another tone underneath the sound of pandemonium outside, but it grows louder and more distinct.

He sits forward and strains to hear. The thunder is painful, but in the down moments between eruptions of sound, he can almost make it out. When he finally deciphers a word, distinguishes one sound from another, he falls back against the wall, his jaw slack and open, unable to believe his own ears. It has to be a hallucination. It can't be real. It must be a dream. He slaps himself across the face. He's awake. But then he hears it again, clearer and closer this time.

"Huxley," yells the voice of his father from the middle of the storm.

Huxley looks over at Bracken, but his head leans to one side, asleep.

Huxley twists around again and searches the storm. The shadow man has gone, but he can still hear the voice, growing quieter with every yell, interrupted by thunder and trailing off. The voice moves on, moves away, misses them. It is going to miss them. He spins around and looks again at Bracken, still asleep. He can't let his father wander off. He may never find them again.

Huxley scrambles to his feet, slipping once and landing hard on his knees and hands, and bolts out of the cave, into the heart of the storm.

Tumult engulfs him from all sides and falls over the top of him. He runs in the direction he thinks the voice originates. "Dad," he screams. The competing wind and thunder swallow up his cries. "Dad." In the flashes and darkness he stumbles on, bouncing off of the charcoal trees, stumbling in the loose soil, falling and picking himself up. "Dad." He twists from side to side, frantic. He has no idea what's more than a few feet in front of his face, but he thinks he hears the voice again behind him, spins, and heads in a new direction.

Is that movement to his right or just a trick of shadow and light? Did the voice come from in front of him or from the left? He turns into a tree, bounces off the trunk, and falls, sprawling to the ground. "Dad." He stands and moves forward. He thinks he sees his father's shape and reaches out his arms, only to hug a tree. Tears stream down his cheeks as he turns away. "Dad."

He's lost. He can't see anything. He can't hear anything. All he can do is run and scream. His voice tears at his throat, fighting against the din of the storm. The flashes of lightning blind him. He spins and shrieks and cries, dizzy and disoriented. In the end he can't even form words. All he can muster are formless grunts and yelps.

From behind an arm grabs him around the waist and lifts him off the ground. Bracken tosses him easily over his shoulder. The boy kicks and screams and flails his arms.

"It's okay," Bracken says. "It's okay."

The more Huxley thrashes and struggles, the tighter Bracken holds him. By the time they reach the cave, his body and arms fall limp, and his head bounces against Bracken's back.

Bracken sets him down and looks into him. "Are you okay?"

"He's out there," Huxley says, spittle flying out of his mouth. He tries to stand, to push Bracken back and continue his search. "He's out there. He's out there and he's looking for me."

Bracken's face tightens and he grabs Huxley by the shoulder, holding him in place. "Who's out there?"

"He's out there and he's looking for me and he's not going to be able to find me if I don't find him." Again he tries to stand. Tears stream down his face, leaving trails in his dirt and soot stained cheeks.

"Listen to me," Bracken says. He squeezes. "Who is out there?"

Huxley goes limp and slumps against the wall. Snot bubbles out of his nose. Saliva clings to his lips. "My father." He sniffs. "My father is out there."

Bracken softens in an instant. He still has a hold on Huxley, but his grip and his expression ease. He looks at the boy.

"I'm sorry, kid," he says, his voice gentle. "But your dad isn't out there."

"No, he is, I heard him. I saw him."

"I'm sorry, but your dad's dead."

Huxley stops wriggling. He looks into Bracken's eyes. For the first time they're full of sympathy and sorrow. He looks into those eyes, bursts into a new fit of tears, throws himself forward, wraps his arms around Bracken's neck, and buries his face in his jacket. Bracken freezes, unsure of how to respond, but ultimately returns the embrace. They remain like that all night, hidden from the storm that rages on around them, indifferent to their existence.

By morning the storm has gone. Huxley and Bracken emerge from their shelter, into the wind and sun.

Huxley is numb. He feels nothing, and has nothing left inside of him, like he cried everything out in the night, like everything left him and he's nothing more than an empty shell wandering randomly in a haphazard, empty wasteland.

They walk through the day in silence. Huxley follows Bracken like a dull echo as they move beyond the reach of the burned forest and continue their winding way through the mountains.

CHAPTER 13

They don't stop. They can't stop. The ruggedness of the terrain forces them back onto the asphalt of the freeway and they walk on through the night and the next day. All they can do is push forward, push onward. If they don't continue to move forward, death will catch up with them. In the quiet moments, Huxley dwells and turns inwards on himself.

"Are we the good guys?" Huxley asks.

"What?" Bracken says, without slowing his pace or turning around.

"Are we the good guys?" Huxley looks up.

Bracken takes his time answering. "I don't know." He pauses, breathing heavily. "I don't know if we're the good guys." He shakes his head and his words hang. "But we might be as good as it gets."

The wind fills the silence around them. Huxley bends his head forward, tucking his face into the rough fabric of his scarf. The fibers scratch at his lips and the chapped skin of his cheeks. He pushes his goggles down over his eyes. He won't let Bracken see him cry.

He tries to blink as little as possible, every time his eyes close, he sees images of Apple, face down in the dirt, blood seeping out of the wound in her chest, her last breath escaping her lungs, and her body going limp one final time. The image remains etched into the back of his eyelids, waiting for them when he blinks, when he most needs rest, reminding him of what he did, that he shot another human being, that he killed someone, not even an infected, but real living person. An actual person died by his hand. His actions took a life. *He* took a life.

Bracken stops walking and turns around. He squints in the sun and looks at Huxley. "Are you hungry?"

Huxley shakes his head without looking up.

Bracken nods and rotates back. He takes a deep breath, and says, "I didn't think you would be."

Huxley struggles to keep up the pace. His short legs churn underneath him, his muscles scream and throb, and his arms hang limp at his sides. The steps come automatic, unconscious, and he remains unaware of anything around him. Within his clothes sweat pours from his skin and soaks through layer after layer. For a moment he feels like he's cooking, boiling inside of his own skin.

At least the physical discomfort distracts him. The visceral irritation, the bodily distress, and the screaming in his limbs take up space in his mind and he diverts other thoughts to the darkest recesses of remembrance, pushing them until the demons are vague ghosts in the corners. It focuses him. When his mind wanders away from the pain all he sees is death; bodies on the ground, corpses leaning against walls, storms screaming overhead, faceless killers pursuing him, decaying blue monsters reaching out with bloody hands, mouths full of broken teeth trying to tear his flesh. Elwood and his henchmen tracking them with bad intentions in mind. His father. Dead on the ground.

He shudders at such thoughts. Thrusting them back and away, he concentrates again on the pain of his blister covered feet, hunches forward into the strain on his small shoulders, and keeps walking. His body is heavy and he stumbles and catches himself.

Bracken stops and looks at the sweaty, pale child, and says, "Okay, it's time to take a break."

Huxley protests, he doesn't want to stop, but he breathes heavily and rocks on his feet. Bracken pats him on the back and slips the straps of the backpack off of the boy's shoulders. He motions toward the edge of the road and Huxley shuffles over and lowers himself to the asphalt, leaning against the concrete barrier with his head in his hands, trying to keep his eyes open.

They sit in the middle of a curve of the road, the level space cut out of the side of a mountain. The perch hovers over a steep drop to the valley floor below them and they stand on a platform high in the air, exposed. No shelter protects them from the wind and the air whips over them, tearing and clawing at the loose ends of their clothes like it's trying to drag them away.

Still, the sensation of air moving over his sweat covered body feels good. Huxley closes his eyes, loosens his scarf, and lets the furious wind cool his skin. For a moment he floats far above the world, far away from everything, so high nothing bad can ever touch him. When he opens his eyes his entire field of vision is the gray of concrete between his legs.

Bracken touches his shoulder and hands him a water bottle. "Drink."

Huxley takes the bottle and drinks. Tepid and gritty, the water tastes like dirt, but it's wet and soothes his cracked lips and raw throat and a cool feeling blooms and spreads inside of his chest.

A gust of wind tears over him and his body gives an involuntary shiver.

With a cracking of joints, Bracken sits next to him, and they stare out into empty space above the mountains.

"You had to," Bracken says. He continues to stare into the void. "You know that, right? You had to do it. You didn't have a choice."

"I know," Huxley whispers.

"You say that, and on that surface level, that removed, rational, logical level, I know you know."

"I know."

"But you need to know it deeper, down in that gut layer, that visceral layer, where you know it wasn't even a choice to be made, that it was a matter of your survival, pure and simple."

"I know." His voice is louder. He shakes.

"They were going to eat you. They were going to tear you into jagged little pieces and swallow you without even stopping to chew."

"I know." The words come through gritted teeth. He balls his hands up into fists.

Bracken turns his head and looks at Huxley. His voice is calm and even. "You had to."

"I know."

"You had to."

"I know."

"You had to."

Huxley looks up at him, tears flowing from his eyes, and screams, "I know. I know. I know." He buries face in Bracken's chest, grabbing fistfuls of his coat with his hands, sobbing into the coarse, dusty fabric, and punches weakly at his torso. His small body heaves with sobs, and everything pours out. He did what he had to do, what Bracken would have done, and Huxley can't be sure if he's upset because he killed someone, or because, after all this time of wanting to be like Bracken, he's finally on his way, and that scares him.

Bracken puts his arm around the child and holds him close.

Huxley cries himself out, and sits back. His eyes burn red and his nostrils are raw. He wipes his nose on his sleeve and hiccups. Looking up at Bracken, he asks, "Does it get easier?"

Bracken blinks and stares out at the mountain wall in the distance. He breathes deep. "I hope you never get to know how easy it can be. You're too good for that." He coughs into one hand and spits a glob of phlegm to his left.

"I've done horrible things," he continues. "A lot of horrible things. Things that should keep me up at night. But they don't. And I didn't think twice about them. Any of them. They used to bother me, but that was a long time ago. More times than I can count I've done things that you can't even imagine. Things I hope you never have the imagination for. Every single time it was them or me." He nods. "Them or me. At least I told myself that, tell myself that. I rationalized every life I've taken that way.

"I tell myself that I'm the good guy, but I know I'm not. I'm not a good guy. I'm just the hero of my own story. We're all the hero of our own story, and maybe that's the best anyone can hope for, and maybe we do what we have to keep our own story going long enough to hope it means something."

He laughs and lets his head sag. "It's all going to catch up with me at some point. Eventually." He looks at Huxley and smiles. "At least now I have the chance to maybe do something good for this world one last time before I die."

CHAPTER 14

Bracken continues to drive them forward, but now they proceed at a more manageable pace, and Huxley no longer struggles to keep up. He stays closer to the boy now, watching over him, a look of concern on his face, the wrinkles and creases deeper and more severe. His beard has grown thick and wiry, sitting along his jaw and throat in a dark tangle. This comforts Huxley, the closeness, the proximity, and he feels a new security wrap around him.

He walks in Bracken's shadow and follows him along the highway, twisting and rising and falling through the mountain pass, bouncing along behind. The wind and sun burn their skin. The high mountain cold sets in around them and each breath creates a cloud in front of their faces, even when the sun sits at its zenith in the sky above. Huxley enjoys the bursts of vapor and tries to make them last as long as possible, wishing that they could stay.

At night they don't light fires, but Huxley huddles near Bracken for warmth, often falling asleep leaning on the man's shoulder or leg.

Huxley has no idea how long they've been on the road; he stopped counting after two weeks, which feels like years ago. Each day becomes its own. He doesn't know how much farther it is to San Francisco. It dawns on him they could be walking aimlessly or in circles and he wouldn't know. They might wander forever and if Bracken remains, the boy's not sure he minds.

The idea of the city frightens him, thinking about it upsets his stomach. As positive as his father was, he instilled in him a sense of wariness of people. Not intentional, but after an entire life of avoiding them most of the time, giving towns and settlements a wide berth, the habit formed.

Beneath their feet the concrete of the freeway cracks and crumbles. Without human hands for maintenance it succumbs to the forces of nature and the elements. On an elevated stretch of road Huxley picks up a boot-sized chunk of asphalt and hurls it over the edge. There's a long silence then the sound of far impact below. The crack of a solid hitting another solid bounces off of the mountain walls. He nods to himself and walks on.

They round a curve and Bracken stops.

Huxley stops behind him, looking up. "What's wrong?"

Bracken looks over his shoulder at the boy and gestures in front of them. His hand sweeps in a wide arc.

"Oh," Huxley says. The road ends. A collection of key supports have given way and a portion of the bridge has collapsed, leaving a wide gap in their path. Rebar juts out from the jagged end, reaching out into space. A section of road lays bent and broken on the ground below them. It looks as if a giant hand reached down and tore a chunk out of the road.

They stand on the edge of the precipice in silence. The wind grabs at their clothes as they look out over the valley. Bracken laughs. It begins quietly, deep inside, but quickly bubbles out until his laughter rings off of the mountain walls. His laughter infects Huxley, and soon the boy laughs along.

"Of course," Bracken says. He wipes a tear from his eye. "Of course the road is gone. Why wouldn't it be gone?" He shakes his head. "It's all so fucking absurd."

Huxley stops laughing, but still smiles. "What do we do now?"

"Go back a little ways, drop down, climb up the other side, keep moving." He laughs once more. "Of course. It's laugh or cry at this point, huh?"

Bracken's expression changes when they slip over the edge of the road and his mirth subsides. The gravel grinds beneath his boots. He examines the crumbled remnants of the support beams, and Huxley notices his posture change and he becomes more alert.

Bracken leans close to Huxley and whispers, "These columns didn't fall on their own. They had help." He indicates the rubble. "Those black marks are from something explosive."

"Why would someone blow up the road?"

"It's a trap. You have to get off of the road and they wait for you down here."

"Fuck," Huxley says under his breath. His stomach sinks and he immediately starts to sweat. "Was it . . .?"

"I don't know." Bracken shakes his head. He searches the rocks and scrub and hidden corners. "I haven't been this way in a while, so I don't know how recent it is. Just be careful, watch where you step."

Huxley nods and they creep forward, toward the other side. Bracken sweeps with his rifle. Huxley's heart pounds in his throat. He swallows and swears it reverberates off of the underside of the bridge. Every step, every pebble that comes loose and rolls down the hill, betrays their presence and position.

Bracken peeks around the edge of a boulder and stops. He looks quickly at Huxley and back in front of him. Huxley tenses and readies his own rifle.

Bracken raises a hand behind him. "It's okay. But you may want to stay there."

Huxley ignores the warning and sidles up next to Bracken. On the other side of the giant rock he sees the charred remains of a campfire. Pressed against the wall of the boulder are the leftover pieces of three bodies, two men and a woman. Maybe. They've been eviscerated and eaten. One of the men is short an arm. But the corpses aren't fresh, the flesh crusty and dried out and brown, torn away in large lumps. Teeth marks ring the wound where the woman's throat was ripped away from the rest of her neck. Ribs and fingers and other bones stand out stark white. The bodies have been completely decimated, little flesh remains on the skeletons.

Huxley's stomach lurches, but he catches it and forces it back down. He checks behind them, nervous. Bracken looks back at him. Huxley looks up and nods, steeling himself.

"Who did this?" Huxley says.

"It was infected."

"How do you know?"

"Cannibals would have taken some along with them for the road." With the barrel of his rifle he indicates a collection of bags and equipment. "And it doesn't look like anything was taken. Infected don't need supplies, but humans do. Even those people-eating fuckers."

Huxley nods. "Are they still here?"

Bracken looks up, searching their surroundings again. "I don't think so. This has been here a while."

"Did the infected set the trap?"

Bracken shakes his head. "No. They're not that organized. Someone else probably did it, and these poor bastards had the misfortune to stumble into a trap that just keeps setting itself." He shrugs. "Or maybe these are the ones who did it and their plan came back to bite them in the ass. And everywhere else."

"Cover me," Bracken says.

Huxley stands guard while Bracken quickly rifles through the bags and pockets of the cadavers. When he finishes searching, taking what's useful, they continue on to the other side of the gap in the road, and climb back onto the asphalt surface.

"I know it gets cold," Bracken says. "But now you see why we don't light fires. They tend to attract a lot of unwanted attention."

When they can, they climb back onto the surface of the road and continue to follow the pavement, winding down through the mountains. Eventually they pass through the foothills and spill out into a wide, open valley at the base of the mountain range.

Free from the confinement of the stone walls of the mountains, Huxley feels light, like he can breathe again. The wind across the flat of the basin lacks the vindictive focus is has when it flows through the peaks. Instead of tearing at him, the moving air caresses his head through his shaggy, dusty hair.

Sand covers most of the road, and now that the mountain corridor no longer restricts their movement, Bracken leads them off of the concrete path, along a less obvious trajectory. A wave of relief settles over Huxley as they have more freedom to roam and stray. He feels like they can avoid trouble now, go around it instead of following the force of necessity, directly into danger.

When they pass a derelict gas station Bracken and Huxley duck inside and do a quick search for supplies. The shelves have been toppled and garbage and debris are strewn across the tile floor. Huxley opens a cooler but finds nothing there but a long empty beer can. There's nothing to unearth or discover in the store, the contents long since plundered by some survivor or group of survivors. Bracken scans the horizon as they exit the Plexiglas-paned doors. He squints in the sunlight.

Passing houses that sit alone or in clusters, they perform similar actions, scouring empty rooms for every last scrap of food or for anything that might prove useful on their journey. They are gradually able to restock their supplies, disregarding obviously corrupt and punctured tins of food.

They stop and sit on top of a gentle knoll, resting their weary joints and limbs. Huxley takes off his boots, peels off the multiple pairs of socks he wears, and lets his feet breathe. He wiggles his toes in the cool air, closing his eyes and leaning his head back. For once he actually enjoys the warm feel of the sunlight on his face and skin.

"What do we do when we get there?" he asks, basking in the sun, his eyes lightly shut.

"When we get where?" Bracken says.

"San Francisco."

"Oh yeah. I guess we'll find your people." After a pause he mutters something that sounds like, "If they're still alive."

"But what do we do then?" Huxley lifts his head and opens his eyes.

"Get back to my life, I suppose." Bracken laughs. "I'm in a whole mess of trouble that should probably try and find a way out of. I made some people you don't want mad at you very very mad at me. But you probably noticed that."

Huxley sits up. "You're not going to stay?"

"Of course not." Bracken shakes his head.

"You mean you're just going to leave me?" Desperation and anger seep into Huxley's words.

"It's not like I'm just going to abandon you on the side of the road," Bracken says. "We're going to find your family, your people, and you'll be safe with them. I'll stick around long enough to make sure you're all settled in. Everything will be fine, I promise."

"Everything will not be fine." Tears of frustration well up in the boy's eyes. "You're bringing me all this way just to drop me off and leave? What the hell?"

"Hey, hey, hey." Bracken puts his hand on Huxley's shoulder. "Don't worry, don't worry. You'll be surrounded by people who care about you, people who will look after you and who will want to take care of you."

"I want to stay with you."

"No you don't. It'll be great, kid, everything will be how it should be. No more running and hiding and fighting. You won't have to worry about any of the shit you have to worry about out here. You'll know where your next meal is coming from, there's nothing hunting you, nothing trying to eat you. Maybe you'll have a house, maybe your own room. Won't that be great?"

Huxley stares at him.

"You don't need me. Hell, I'm might be the worst thing that will ever happen to you. The places I go, the people I know." He shakes his head. "They aren't for you. You're better than that, you're better than this, better than this life."

"You're better than this," Huxley replies.

Bracken shakes his head. "Listen, you'll have a family, a real family. You don't need me hanging around. Give it time and you'll forget all about me. After a week of sleeping in a real bed you probably won't even remember what I look like, you'll just be glad you're not still out here."

Bracken shakes his head and continues, "That's not for me, not anymore. I need to keep moving."

"You're just too fucking selfish to stay."

Bracken laughs and sighs. "Maybe, kid, maybe."

Huxley pulls his knees to his chest, wraps his arms around his legs, and glares at Bracken.

Bracken sighs. "You didn't really think I was going to stay, did you?"

Until this moment Huxley never even contemplated the possibility that Bracken wasn't going to stay, that he wasn't always going to be around. He assumed that the man was a permanent part of his life, an enduring fixture of the landscape.

"I'm sorry, Huxley," Bracken says. "But that was never part of the plan. I have to get back to my life. And you, you have to get started on yours, and I shouldn't be a part of that. I just shouldn't. You're a good kid, and I'm sorry if this hurts you, but that's the way it has to be."

He stands and leaves Huxley to himself for a while. Huxley stares up at him. First, his father left him, now Bracken is, too. He has no one; he's alone, truly, inescapably alone.

A wave of dejection, gloom, and anger crashes over Huxley, and he sits up, puts his shoes on, and stumbles to his feet. He stands for a moment and stares at Bracken. Eventually he shoulders his pack and walks past the man.

"Fuck you," Huxley says as he walks past. "I don't need you. I can get to San Francisco by myself."

With his head down, he walks. He walks because there's nothing else that he can do, and he's done trailing along behind a man who is only going ultimately abandon him. He walks because it's what he's been doing for so long it feels like all he's ever known.

He keeps his head down. An angry army might surround them on all sides and he wouldn't notice. Right now, he wouldn't even care. He only wants to lie down on the ground and go to sleep for a year and forget that his entire life ever happened. He's vaguely aware that Bracken follows him at a distance, giving him space.

Images of Apple, dead on the ground, mix with imagined images of Huxley standing on the top of a hill, looking down at an empty valley, the wind crying in his ears, talking to him. He is alone. He will always be alone. Apple and the Coot and Reno and the prison and the lightning and the family at the farm and Elwood and Haley and Lexi and his father wander through his mind. His head gets heavier and heavier. It feels thick and numb and it floats away from his body. Images of everything he's seen drift in and around and mingle together in a blur.

He pants and gets dizzy, sweating and shaking and so completely, completely alone. He stops, bends at the waist, and throws up on the ground between his feet. Sucking in deep breaths and trying to spit the foul bile taste out of his mouth, Huxley stands with his hands on his knees. After a few minutes, Bracken's boots step into his field of vision. Huxley looks up. Bracken holds his rifle and looks at the boy. His expression betrays nothing. When he turns and walks away, Huxley straightens up, wipes his mouth on his sleeve, and follows in silence.

They walk past the ruins of a large city, skirting the main body, sticking to more open areas on the outskirts. Huxley barely sees the rubble. He looks up long enough to acknowledge the skyscrapers rising into the sky from out of the earth like the thick fingers of some long dead and buried giant that died trying to dig out of its own grave. From even the most cursory glance he can tell that nothing still lives in the city, nothing good at any rate.

"This used to be the capital of the state," Bracken says. He looks back at Huxley over his shoulder.

The boy stays silent, he doesn't know what a state is, or was, nor does he care.

Bracken nods to himself and looks forward. "Sacramento," he says to the wind.

They walk in silence for days, passing through a collection of low foothills. Huxley says nothing, eats little, and scarcely notices the passing of time and distance. Momentarily immune to the surrounding world, he's separate from everything. It flows around him without touching him. He's not hungry or tired or happy or sad, he's come loose and drifts away from the concrete reality around him. He's an empty space. In his enclosed state, the smell of the air changes around him.

Bracken stops. Huxley steps up next to him.

Bracken nods, indicating something in front of them. Huxley looks up.

They stand at the apex of a hill. The remains of a massive city scroll out in front of them. Then there's water. More water than Huxley has ever seen. More water than he imagined ever existed in all of the world. Across the water sits more land, an arm of soil jutting out into the bay, another city. Bridges, long skeletal conduits, reach back and forth across the bay. A thin veil of haze hovers over the buildings, reducing them to outlines. It looks more like a shadow, more like a dream than anything concrete or real. Beyond the peninsula there seems to be nothing but water stretching on into forever.

He stares at it, eyes wide, nothing like it in his store of memories. He has nothing to compare the sight to. Behind the city the sun sets over the water, the light catching in the fog, and everything is so bright he has to squint his eyes.

In this moment nothing else matters. Nothing else even comes close in his mind. There's only room for this new, exciting sight.

"San Francisco?" he asks.

"San Francisco," Bracken says.

CHAPTER 15

Huxley stands with his mouth open, staring down at the bay and the cities below. It isn't real. It can't be real. The whole scene looks like someone created an elaborate illusion just to fool one small child. He rubs his eyes with one hand to make sure that they aren't playing tricks on him, that what he thinks he sees is really real. Wide roads run in every direction, looping back and forth over one another like ribbons of concrete, running toward unseen destinations.

"Never seen anything like this before, huh?" Bracken says. He smiles down at the boy.

"I didn't know there was so much water." Huxley shakes his head. "Can you drink it?"

"No." Bracken shakes his head. "Unfortunately not. Almost all of the water we can drink is long gone. Or in Canada."

They wait and watch, Huxley staring in awe taking it all in.

"Close your mouth," Bracken says. He laughs. "You look like a hayseed."

Huxley closes his mouth and swallows. He breathes deeply through his nose. The air is different, thicker, wetter; he can't place his finger on the disparity, but it fills his lungs and throat and nostrils like nothing else ever has. Closing his eyes, he loses himself in the cool sensation.

"Do you really think they're down there?" he asks, without opening his eyes. "Do you think anyone is down there?"

"I guess we're about to find out."

Huxley opens his eyes and peers up at Bracken. The older man looks tired and worn down. For the first time Huxley sees the toll their journey has taken on Bracken. And something else waits there, something Huxley has never seen in him before—nervousness. He tries to control it, to keep it in check, but the boy can tell that it's there, that it's bubbling inside of him. Bracken tries to hide it, but it is written across his face and in the way he holds himself.

"If there are still people down there," Bracken says. "Then they aren't the only things down there. You understand me?"

Huxley nods.

"Good. I need you to be quiet, quieter than you've ever been, and I need you to be alert. Can you do that?"

Huxley nods.

Bracken breathes in deep and exhales. "Smells good, doesn't it?"

"Yeah," Huxley says, quietly. "It does."

"All right then. Onward, little soldier."

They move forward, down the hill, through sparser landscapes, into residential neighborhoods, full of decaying buildings and houses. Bracken keeps a swift pace and they proceed as quickly as they can while maintaining a safe level of silence.

Huxley spies a body against a fence. Face down in the dirt, one arm reaches up, the dead fingers clutch the chain-link. He keeps his eyes on it as they pass. Most of the flesh is gone, but he can tell it was once a man. Blood coagulates on the bones and around the pulpy remains of muscle and tissue. This body isn't dry and leathery like all of the others they've encountered.

"That looks fresh," Huxley says in a low voice.

Without looking, Bracken says, "Yeah, I noticed that, too."

And they push forward through the streets, always forward.

Sprawling neighborhoods full of family homes and apartments give way to the core of the city. The buildings become taller and concrete, skyscrapers bunching together on each block. Many of the windows are broken out and the buildings have been looted. Rusting hulks of cars line the streets. Some are parked orderly against the curbs, while others were left askew in the middle of the avenues, doors left open, a layer of dirt and grit over all of them.

Huxley tries not to notice other sets of footprints on the ground. They run back and forth across the streets and intersections. Some of them are recent and hurried. He knows that Bracken sees them, too, so there's no need to mention them. The overall effect of being downtown is like walking along the bottom of a deep, lonely canyon. The screaming wind their constant companion.

"Are we going to go over one of those giant bridges?" Huxley says, almost hopeful about the possibility.

Bracken shakes his head. "No. They couldn't fortify them securely enough. They couldn't guarantee that they could keep the infected out, so they blew big chunks out of the middle of all of them."

"How are we going to get across the water?"

"We're going to head to the waterfront and hope we find something that resembles a boat."

Huxley nods. Then he stops and asks, "What's a boat?"

Moving beyond the downtown core, they come to the edge of the bay. Huxley can't help but stop and stare out across the water, he knows he should be looking behind them for threats, but the view draws all of his attention. Waves rise and fall, and the wind rips at the crests, creating white caps and spraying foam into the air. The deep blue water fades into black as the daylight fades into the western horizon.

The back and forth dance of the current hypnotizes him and Bracken has to drag the boy out of his momentary trance.

"This way," he says and leads them north to a thin finger of land that curls out into the bay, creating an area of calm and shelter in the water. Docks line the spit and reach out into the water. Most of the slips stand empty.

"When everything went to shit," Bracken explains. "A lot of people took to the water. Figured at least that way there was no way the infected were going to get to them on a boat."

Many of the remaining crafts are submerged, their shapes and shadows visible under the water, nothing sticking out besides a few stray masts, antennas, and an occasional bow, still tied to the dock.

"We've got to move," Bracken says. "I don't want to be fucking around here when it gets dark."

He leads them down a thin dock. Huxley peers over the edge at the water and sees a face staring back at him. It takes a moment to realize it's his reflection, broken and rippling in the choppy surface. They go down a ramp and onto a palate that floats on the surface of the water. It bobs gently. Huxley plants his feet and steadies himself, rocking with the movement beneath him. A small queasy feeling forms the center of his stomach and he takes short, unsure steps as he follows Bracken away from shore.

Bracken pulls himself onto one of the few remaining boats. "I'll be right back," he says. "Wait right there." He disappears then pops his head out. "And be careful you don't fall in."

Huxley nods and waits. Bracken emerges a moment later, hops down to the dock, and climbs aboard another boat.

The boy stares into the dark surface of the water. Carefully, he inches toward the edge of the dock, pausing to reset and steady himself with each move. He glances over the edge and pulls back, repeating the motion again, and then again. He crouches down, with his knees on the rough surface and his hands curling over the edge.

Hesitating, he reaches down toward the surface of the water. The tips of his fingers brush the top of a ripple. He pulls his hand back.

"Cold," he says to himself. He smiles and rubs his middle finger against his thumb. He wipes his hand on his sleeve and reaches out again. This time he pushes his entire hand into the water and holds it there. The cool water prickles his skin and makes him smile. Beneath the surface his hand looks pale and waxy, thick and clumsy. He wiggles his fingers.

Cupping his hand, he raises a palm full of water to his lips.

With a jolt, Huxley's fingers spread and the water runs out of his hand.

"Don't drink that," Bracken says from behind him. He stands on the back end of a large luxury yacht, the cabin of which has been burned. A covered rowboat sits on the deck. He knocks the hull with his knuckles and nods, "Fiberglass."

Bracken shakes his head. "You can't drink this water," he says. "It'll make you sick." He nods. "Take a little taste of the water on your finger."

Huxley touches his tongue to the tip of his finger. The water tastes salty and briny, and he recoils, making a face.

"Told you so," Bracken says. He pushes the dingy toward the edge of the yacht, a foot at a time. "We're going to have to row, but it looks like we have a worthy sea craft. Yargh." He winks at Huxley, who looks back at him with a confused expression on his face.

Bracken ties a coil of rope to the front of the rowboat, checks that it's long enough, and gives the small vessel one last heave. With a heavy splash, the white fiberglass craft slaps against the water, throwing foam and spray in every direction. It bucks but settles quickly.

Bracken grins. "Hold this," he says, and tosses the coil of rope to Huxley. He jumps down to the dock and stands next to the boy, patting him on the shoulder and nodding as the boat bounces gently in water.

"Looks like we got ourselves a boat." He grins and takes the rope from the boy. Crouching down, he removes a synthetic cover from the boat and tosses it into the bow. Inside wait three slat seats and a pair of oars that stretch along most of the length of the small vessel.

"You want to row?" Bracken asks.

Huxley looks up at him. "I don't know what that means." He looks back at the boat, rocking on the surface of the water. "How does that thing float?"

"Magic." Bracken grins and twinkles his fingers. The expression is too wide to be real and his enthusiasm rings false by a note. Something bothers him. He shakes his head, nervous, but trying to overcompensate for it. "Just kidding. I'm sure there's a scientific reason for it, but I'd be lying if I said I knew the physics behind it." His jaw continues to work as if he's chewing a small mouthful of food, and his fingers fidget with the rope in his hands.

"Take off your pack," Bracken says. While Huxley removes his, Bracken slips off his own pack and drops it into the front of the boat. The bag thuds against the artificial skin with a dull clunk and a wet echo. Huxley follows suit.

Bracken pulls the boat over until it bobs parallel to the dock. Taking great pains to remain steady, he lowers himself into the craft. Beneath his feet the boat gives way, rocking back and forth, and his legs rise and fall in an attempt to remain stable. When he finally has a purchase, he squats down and sits on the slat in the middle of the boat.

"I guess I don't have my sea legs anymore," he says. He grips the edge of the dock, holding the boat in place.

Huxley considers the craft for a moment, unsure about the whole situation.

"It's perfectly safe," Bracken says. "Cross my heart."

Huxley nods and inches toward the edge of the dock. He puts one foot over the precipice and bends down. His supporting leg quivers and he stands back up. Once more he tries the same approach, with the same results. Rotating a quarter of a turn, he attacks the problem sideways, crouching down, reaching for the bottom of the boat with the sole of his boot. Again, his stability wavers and he returns to a standing position.

"Need a hand?" Bracken says, reaching up for Huxley.

The boy shakes his head, he wants to do this on his own. He turns his back to the edge and stoops down onto his knees with his feet hanging over the side. Supporting himself on the palms of his hands, he scoots his legs back, until he's on his belly with his legs dangling loose below him.

When he feels the bottom of the boat under his feet he pushes back with his arms and stands straight up. The boat lurches to one side beneath his weight. Huxley tries to correct his stance, but only makes the boat pitch back the other way. He stumbles backward, balancing on one leg, arms flailing wildly, about to topple overboard, into the water.

Bracken grabs a fistful of the front of Huxley's jacket. The boy feels the fingers dig in and clench and the arm pull him upright, holding him straight up in the middle of the boat until the rocking subsides. His heart rate spikes, both of his little hands clamp over the large one sticking out of the middle of his chest, and he holds on for dear life.

"Why don't you sit down," Bracken says. "Gently."

Huxley swallows and nods and lowers himself onto the plank seat at the back of the boat. Bracken holds on until Huxley sits firmly on his perch.

"Thanks," Huxley says.

"Think nothing of it." Bracken has a smile on his face, an authentic smile this time. He looks over Huxley's shoulder, at the city across the bay, and the smile retreats. The shadows of night fall across his face.

With Huxley secure, he lets go of the dock and allows the boat drift away with the current. He takes up the oars and slips the collars into the oarlocks. Holding a beveled end in each hand, he looks at his companion and uses a single oar to turn the boat until his back faces San Francisco. He inhales a single deep breath, blows it out, and begins rowing across the bay.

At first, his motion is awkward, an uneven jerking movement. The blades twist and slap against the surface of the water, and the forward momentum of their small craft falters and lurches. Over time Bracken falls into a rhythm. The strokes become smooth, measured and even, and they cut through the darkening water toward their ultimate goal.

Night falls down over the top of them.

Huxley's body jostles and rolls with motion of the boat and the waves beneath them. Nausea grows in his stomach and spreads through the rest of his body. A light sweat breaks through his skin, and he takes deep breaths, holding them in for a moment before releasing them. Over and over again, it helps him maintain and finally, his stomach settles. He closes his eyes and lolls with the movement, his body loose, maybe falling asleep, verging on unconsciousness.

He opens his eyes when he feels they're no longer moving forward. It's completely dark, they've stopped, and the bobbing of the boat in the blackness is surreal and disorienting. He puts his hand on the edge of his seat to anchor himself.

"Are we there?" he asks.

"No," Bracken says. "We're going to stay here tonight."

As his eyes adjust, the black outline of the city emerges out of the darkness, looming close over them. Skyscrapers cut swaths into the night sky. Next to them bobs a skeletal shadow sticking up out of the water.

"We're going to tie up to this buoy," Bracken says. He pounds the flat of his hand and it rings with a hollow metal thunk. "I want to check things out. I want to know what's out there before we dive in head first."

Huxley rocks back and forth, watching the city. In the darkness it appears completely blank. There's nothing to see, no lights, no signs of life. Looking at the city, the goal, their destination, he isn't sure what he feels. This is what they've been looking for, where they've been going, and there it is, hovering right in front of his face. What waits for him he can't imagine. More than anything, the city of San Francisco has come to mean one thing to him, abandonment. This is where Bracken leaves him.

Huxley doesn't sleep. He sways with the tide all night, fighting sporadic waves of nausea, staring into the city. Behind him the sun rises. In the light he can see the buoy. The base is round and flat, with a metal frame rising into the air. At one point it was red, but the majority of the paint is gone, stripped away by the elements, leaving only rust and stray flecks of color. Crusts of salt coat the surface and eat away at the metal.

Bracken stays awake, too.

In the boat, they bob up and down with the waves, sleep deprived, rocking in unison with the buoy. They sit in the bay, surveying the city in front of them. They wait and watch for hours, rising and sinking, rolling and pitching with the smallest movements of the water. Neither one in any rush to proceed.

Huxley puts his hand against the skin of the boat. The cold of the water radiates through the fiberglass. It feels good. He puts his cool fingertips against his cheek. He moves his hand and presses the palm against his forehead and closes his eyes. He sways and breathes in the sea air, steadying himself for whatever waits for them.

"I don't see anything," Bracken says. The sun sits high above them. "Anything." He furrows his brow. "You?"

Huxley shakes his head. "No."

"Do you want to go check it out?"

"We should."

"We didn't come all this way just to turn around and go back."

"No, we didn't."

"If there really isn't anyone left, looks like you might be stuck with me for a little while longer, kid."

Huxley tries to suppress his smile.

All he knows about Bracken are pieces and shards, but the more he collects, the clearer a picture they give him. Huxley knows Bracken's old life was here. It isn't much, but from that, he infers this is also where he killed his wife. Huxley wouldn't want to go back there either and imagines what it takes out of him to be here again. For a moment he allows himself to hope Bracken will turn the boat around.

Bracken stares at the city and swallows as the boat bobs and pulls against the rope like it wants to free itself. "I wonder if everyone really is gone." He scratches his face. Huxley's sure that he wipes away a tear.

CHAPTER 16

They see no signs of life as Bracken rows toward the docks that reach out into the bay like grasping fingers. After each stroke he pauses and turns to examine the approaching cityscape. Huxley isn't sure if he's being cautious or looking for a reason not to proceed. He glances back at Huxley, who shakes his head, confirming the absence of any movement or indications of life. The closer they get, the more he clenches his jaw.

Bracken pulls the oars one last time and the boat slides up to the float. He holds onto the edge and ties off to a heavy metal cleat. Bobbing in the water, the boat scrapes against the black rubber bumpers, creating a light shriek with each rise and fall. Bracken tosses their packs onto the dock and sits there without moving. Eventually he motions for Huxley to climb out of the boat.

Standing on solid enough ground, Huxley stretches, twisting from side to side. He's stiff from the night in the boat, and his spine pops inside of his body. A few other boats, larger crafts, bounce with the water. All of them look corroded, rife with damage, and he can tell why these particular vessels were left behind.

Something about the scene, the sun, the wind, the boats, the piers, creates a feeling of normalcy, like any moment someone might pop into view carrying a rope or other nautical supplies, tip his cap toward them, and go on about his business as if nothing is wrong. But there's nothing besides the cry of the wind, the lap of the water, and what appears to be an empty city looming over them.

"You see that?" Bracken says. He stands beside the boy and stares across the water at a small island. "That used to be a famous prison."

Huxley nods as if any of that means anything to him.

"You ready to go exploring?" Weapons at the ready, they start forward, into the concrete canyons of San Francisco.

Like the other times they entered cities, they stick to the center of the streets and give wide berths to the shells of cars that litter the boulevards and rust in the salty sea air. Both Bracken and Huxley keep their guns up, at the ready, and scan the windows, doorways, alleys, and anywhere else someone or something could possibly hide and lie in wait.

Bodies, and the remains of bodies, populate the city like refuse. A thin layer of silt covers most of them, but many others are more recently dead. They pass a delivery van. Inside the cab a body slumps over the steering wheel, and a thick, blackening coagulation covers window where the driver shot himself in the head. Huxley swallows hard, his mouth dry, and he pushes the image from his head before he continues on. His back draws tight and the muscles of his limbs poise for immediate action. Fight or flight, his body is ready to react in an instant.

"If there is anyone," Bracken says. "They'll see us coming a mile away. We're not exactly concealed. I don't like that. But I also don't like things jumping at me out of doorways."

Huxley nods his silent assent, even though Bracken can't see it.

"This used to be one of the main streets," he continues.

Huxley ignores Bracken's words. They seem to be for his own comfort, not for Huxley's, and he pushes the sound into the background.

The wind carries a smell to them, sweet and sour and overwhelming all at the same time. It intensifies as they turn off of the main street and head to their right, closing in on the origin of the stench.

In a few blocks, the smell overpowers them and Huxley pulls his scarf up over his mouth and nose. This does little and he hunches forward a few degrees, hoping the added pressure will keep his stomach from spewing its contents all over the street. They pass a corner and in the midst of the towers and giant buildings stands an open square. In the middle of the free space is the source of the stink. A massive mound of bodies, dozens, maybe hundreds, piled up on top of one another, rotting together in the sun.

These are fresh bodies. This is recent.

The scene looks false, surreal. The limbs don't seem to be limbs, but pieces of some bizarre meat sculpture. Corpses fit together like a macabre puzzle, as if each one was placed there intentionally and with great thought. Faces with dead eyes stare out from the stack, looking at nothing. Huxley's stomach convulses and heaves, but he steels himself and forces the bile back down to where it belongs. He can't be weak right now. He can't let anything get to him. He has to be cold and hard and prepared.

He forces himself to look at the mountain of flesh until his entire body shakes, until the rattle of his teeth threatens to deafen him, but he does not look away until Bracken touches him on the shoulder. This is the signal that they are going to continue on, leaving the smell and the mass open-air grave behind them.

"I used to love that place," Bracken says. "I'd sit there for hours and just drink a cup of coffee and watch the entire city pass by." His eyes are red and blink rapidly as he remembers things long past. Huxley watches him and wishes he would stay focused.

They continue to wind their way through the city, weaving left and right at random, without heading toward an obvious end goal. In their travels they see more and more corpses, more than Huxley has ever seen in one area. He tries to imagine this place when all of the bodies were alive, people roaming back and forth between the buildings, going in and out. He wonders what it's like to peer down from the top of one of the skyscrapers, how small everything must look and feel. Could you see to the end of the earth if the sky was clear?

The bodies produce a strange feeling in Huxley. Despite the fact that they haven't seen any signs of current life, the presence of the bodies makes him feel like they're not alone, and he keeps thinking the bodies are about to stand up and either say hello, or try to kill them. Even though nothing looks to be alive, he feels like something follows them, tracking them as they shuffle forward through the endless maze of city streets, and he knows he should fear it. A couple of times Huxley thinks he sees something move, behind a window, in a building, darting around a corner, but nothing ever holds up upon closer examination, and he passes it off as paranoia. Still, the rifle in his hands and the weight of his father's revolver tucked into his belt reassure him.

Bracken's body coils tightly as they proceed, always at attention, always watching and alert for danger. Huxley worries he might snap.

They come to a point where Bracken stops in the middle of an intersection. He turns and looks up and down each avenue, examining and assessing each possible route. Anxious. He exhales and looks down at Huxley, pinching his forehead, and drawing his brow together over his eyes. He looks away, breathes out again, and looks back at the boy.

"There's nothing here." He shakes his head and looks away. "Nothing alive anyway. Fuck this. Fuck this place. I left for a reason. Why the fuck did I think it was a good idea to come back?" He sweats and his breathing is rapid and shallow, on the verge hyperventilation. He swallows hard and clenches his hands around the stock and barrel of his gun, but Huxley still sees them shake. The panic, the stress, the anxiety is something he's never seen in Bracken, something that never seemed to exist in him before. He's usually so stolid, and Huxley has to quell a wave of his own apprehension that threatens to overtake him.

Huxley watches Bracken spin and turn, staring down one avenue then the next, and begins to worry. Bracken may sprint away in some random direction. Reaching out, he takes a step forward, raising one hand until it touches Bracken's hand on his rifle barrel. Gently he pushes the gun down and looks up. Bracken blinks and looks down at him, confusion and distress on his face.

"It's okay," Huxley says. "It'll be okay."

Bracken looks at him with a blank expression. His face is flush and his eyes are wet and bloodshot. He cocks his head to one side.

"Breathe," Huxley says.

Not taking his eyes away from Huxley's, he inhales, holds the air in his lungs, and releases it, one breath after another.

After a moment, after he's calm, he smiles and looks away with a laugh. Again he looks down every street, but not in a panic like before.

"I hate to tell you this, kid," he says. He looks back to Huxley. "But I think your people are dead."

The boy nods. That's more like it. "I think they're dead, too."

"What do you say we get the fuck out of this death trap hell hole?"

"I'd like that."

Bracken nods and goes to take a step. He pauses and looks over his shoulder at Huxley.

"Thanks."

Huxley smiles and doesn't say a word.

They make their way back to the boat as quickly as possible, racing the setting sun to the west. Their pace isn't quite a jog, but they move as fast as Huxley can without having to run, and they take a direct route instead of exploring.

"What are we going to do now?" Huxley says.

Bracken shakes his head. "I have no idea. You have any thoughts on the matter?"

Huxley considers the question for a moment. "No. Right now I just want to get out of here. I don't like this place." A feeling akin to relief creeps over him. He will not be left here.

"I couldn't agree more."

They round a corner and see the dock a few blocks ahead of them, and the water of the bay and the hills in the distance beyond that. When Huxley sees this, he breathes out a long stream of air, realizing that he has been holding his breath for much of their exploration of the city.

Passing a block, they freeze as a shotgun racks behind them.

"I thought I might find you here," a man's voice says.

Bracken squeezes his eyes shut and he swears quietly. His fingers tense around the pistol grip of his rifle and his index finger touches the trigger. Huxley knows he's considering his next move, thinking about spinning and spraying bullets everywhere.

He releases his grip and holds his finger away from the trigger.

"Motherfucker."

"That certainly is one name I've been called."

CHAPTER 17

"Huxley, meet Elwood," Bracken says. His head slumps forward and he curses to himself. "He's a dick."

"Always with the name calling," Elwood says. "I know you're not stupid, but just in case you're thinking about some end-of-the-movie, hero, hail of gunfire kind of shit, it's probably not the best idea for your immediate health."

Bracken rotates to face the voice and in the same motion he reaches out and pulls Huxley behind him. The boy peeks around his leg.

"Well isn't that fucking noble?" Elwood says with a laugh. "What the fuck happened to you, son?" He leans against a wall with his arms crossed, the ends of his salt and pepper hair flapping in the breeze, clad head to toe in spotless white, unconcerned with the filth and dirt of the world around him. He shakes his head. "You used to be such a fucking badass."

"Come a little closer and I'll show you what I can still do."

Elwood chuckles and gives Bracken an incredulous look. The sound sends a cold shiver up the length of Huxley's spine. "Oh, please."

On either side of Elwood stand six men with guns, all aiming at Huxley and Bracken, mostly at Bracken. All of them wear the similar black outfits of Elwood's personal guard. A few have shaved heads, while the rest have a tangle of matted hair and dreadlocks, and they have a various number of black dots tattooed along their jaw lines. The older, more grizzled and rough around the edges members of the group have more tattoos, and Huxley cringes at the thought of what they had to do to earn each of these grimy badges of honor.

Elwood wears a pistol slung across his chest. He uncrosses his arms, clasps his hands behind his back, and pushes away from the wall. His authority is so absolute and inclusive that he doesn't need a weapon in his hand to command the complete attention of his soldiers.

"How about you give me what I want?" Elwood says.

"How about you go right on and fuck yourself?" Bracken says.

Elwood laughs. "I didn't think it would be that easy." He shrugs. "But it never hurts to try."

"I can make it hurt plenty if that's what you're going for."

"You can hand it over and, well, I won't exactly let you go, it's far too late for that. Things have progressed far beyond the letting you go stage. But I might be so kind as to make your death relatively quick. Not entirely painless, mind you, that metaphorical ship has also sailed, and I hate to deprive myself of that one small joy. But nonetheless, quicker than it is otherwise going to be."

"Thanks for the offer," Bracken says. "And I'd like to consider it, but I keep going back to that whole you fucking yourself idea."

Elwood sighs and turns back to face his forces. "A tough guy until the very end. I guess I *would* be disappointed by anything less." He actually seems legitimately tired of playing along with the back and forth.

He continues, "Normally I could stand here and banter with you all day long. Nothing would give me more pleasure. The art of witty repartee is truly lost these new-jacks." He waves at his soldiers. "The problem is, I've been looking for you for a long time. I'm tired, I'm far from the comforts of home, and frankly I'm a little bored by it all. I just don't have the energy. So, here's what we're going to do."

Elwood waves his hand and the most grizzled, tattooed, rough looking soldier steps out from a doorway. He holds a woman in front of him, and a pistol against her temple.

"Haley?" Bracken says. "I thought you were dead?" He looks down at Huxley, "I thought you said she was dead?"

Huxley stares, open-mouthed, at her. "I saw you die," he says.

"Yeah," Haley says as the guard pushes her forward. "Well, right now I kind of wish."

"The kid said he saw you die," Bracken says.

"The kid saw me get shot. A bunch." Haley grimaces as the soldier pulls her head backward by her hair.

"Hey, Cyrus," Bracken says to the guard, who now has a fistful of Haley's hair. "Do that again and I'll fucking kill you."

Cyrus smiles. "That went so well that went for you last time?"

One of Haley's eyes is swollen almost completely shut, her lips split, and a serious looking gash runs along her hairline, dry blood caked in her hair. She looks awful, but despite what reason tells Huxley, she is obviously alive.

Elwood spins on his heels and smiles. "So, I believe you were about to hand your weapons over to my boys here," he interrupts.

Bracken closes his eyes in a long blink and grinds his teeth together. He pops the clip out of his rifle, ejects the cartridge from the chamber, and tosses the weapon on the ground at Elwood's feet.

"Search him," Cyrus says to the phalanx. "And be thorough."

Bracken laughs and puts his hands on his head. One of the guards comes forward. The youngest of the group, probably still only in his teens, he has the fewest markings on his face. He wears a scared, wary expression, and his body tenses as he pats Bracken down. He pulls a pistol from inside his jacket, one knife from his waistband, and another from one boot.

"Unless you want to get shanked," Cyrus says. "I suggest you check his check his forearms as well."

The soldier pulls another knife from inside Bracken's sleeve.

Bracken shrugs, a wry smile on his lips.

Huxley hides behind Bracken, clutching the tails of his jacket, clinging to the vague hope that no one notices him.

The young guard looks at him. "Yours too, kid."

Huxley only clutches his rifle tighter. The guard reaches for the barrel. In a sharp motion that's more instinct than plan, Huxley twists his hips and whips the stock around, catching the guard square on the knee. The wood makes a dense crack as it collides with bone.

"Aww, fuck," the guard yells, collapsing to the ground, grabbing his leg. "You little shit."

In the same motion, Huxley takes a step back and raises his rifle, aiming at Elwood's chest. Bracken looks impressed, he chuckles once and gives a little tip of the head.

Elwood laughs. "I like this kid," he says to Bracken. "I can see why you keep him around. Some of your feistiness rubbed off on him. That may or may not serve him well." He crosses his arms. "Do you mind?"

Bracken nods and turns to face Huxley. "Kid, you should probably give them the rifle." His voice is gentle. "Nice try, though."

Huxley looks up at him with only his eyes. His features stretch tight, and the rifle trembles visibly in his hands. He shakes his head. The bad guys watch him with tense expressions, the bad guys that is, besides Elwood and Cyrus. Their faces remain untouched by worry. Elwood looks amused more than concerned.

"You did a good thing." Bracken nods at the guard, limping back to the wall. "And that prick isn't going to forget you any time soon." He laughs again.

"I can kill him right now," Huxley says. "I've done it before."

"Ooh, tough guy," Elwood says. "I'm shaking, I'm sure."

"You have no idea," Bracken replies. He turns his gaze back to Huxley, his voice soft and soothing. "I know you have, but this isn't the right time. Right now, this will just get us all killed. I promise, we'll get to kill every single one of these pieces of shit soon, real soon, and when the time comes, I won't leave you out of that. You can kill as many of them as you want." He points to the biggest guard, a hulking brute at the end of the line. "How about that big fucker right there? Want to kill him? He's yours, cross my heart."

"Promises, promises," Elwood says. He taps his wrist.

"Give me the rifle," Bracken says. His tone warm and even. "*Just* give me the rifle." He winks.

Huxley inhales. As his torso expands with the breath, the metal of the revolver tucked into his belt bites into his skin, reminding him it's still there.

"Give me the rifle." He reaches out and wraps his fingers around the barrel. "All I want is the rifle."

Huxley loosens his grasp and releases the weapon to Bracken. He flashes a quick smile then looks to the ground, stuffing his hands into his pocket, trying to fashion an expression of defeat on his face. Bracken pats him on the shoulder, ejects the cartridge, and tosses the hunting rifle on the ground.

He puts his hands on his head again, laces the fingers together, and turns to face Elwood. Huxley slides up next to him and puts his hands on his head, mimicking Bracken.

"Now aren't you a pair," Elwood says.

Bracken spits to one side.

"Come on," Elwood says and turns to walk.

The guards herd Huxley and Bracken along in front of them. Cyrus releases Haley and shoves her ahead, next to them.

Bracken looks over at her with a smile. "Hey."

She looks at him. Huxley can't tell if it's disgust, pity, anger, or simple exhaustion written on her face. "Hey." She smiles and looks away, almost as if she's mad at herself for the expression. Her gait is awkward and she moves with pain radiating from multiple places. "You had to involve me, didn't you?"

"Who else do I know that would take care of a kid? I did shoot his father after all, I felt a little responsible for him."

"That has to be a first. You picked a hell of a time to grow a conscience."

"I know, right?"

"Shut the fuck up," Cyrus says from behind them, more annoyed than angry.

"Oh now, Cyrus," Elwood says. "I can't believe you, of all people, doesn't appreciate this rekindling of a long-lost love. And here I always thought you were a hopeless romantic at heart." He laughs. "But seriously, feel free to shut the fuck up any time."

"You do have a plan," Haley whispers. "Don't you?"

"Of course I have a plan," Bracken says. "Who do you think you're talking to?"

Haley shakes her head and keeps walking. As they continue to move forward Bracken kicks an empty five-gallon bucket. It rattles across the concrete and bounces off the fender of a wide, green Buick, with a loud clang. When their captors steer them near an abandoned sedan, he kicks off the side view mirror, again creating a burst of noise. He looks back and glares at Elwood.

Huxley glances over his shoulder. The gang walks along behind them. Most of the guards hold their weapons loosely, and the one Huxley clubbed limps along at the rear, which makes him feel warm inside. Only Cyrus remains fully alert. His eyes bore holes into Bracken's back, and he holds Bracken's rifle, pointing it at the prisoners. Elwood's eyes burn with a malicious, bemused fire beneath his bushy eyebrows. With a wicked smile across his lips, he looks sinister, evil, yet entirely pleased about something.

"I can tell you where it is," Bracken says over his shoulder.

"You'll tell me, all right," Elwood returns. "But it isn't going to be that easy. The time for easy has come and gone. Did you forget who you're talking to?"

"It was worth a shot, wasn't it?"

"You do have to try. I'll give you that."

Haley squeezes her eyes shut and shakes her head. "I really hope that wasn't your entire plan."

"Oh ye of little faith," Bracken says. He looks over at Huxley. "At least you still trust me, don't you?"

Huxley looks up at him, his face weather-worn, covered by a wiry beard twisting into knots. He looks broken down and beaten and led them into a trap, but Huxley still has faith in him. Just looking into his eyes offers reassurance. "I guess."

Haley laughs. "Jesus, even your minion doesn't believe."

"Damn, kid," Bracken says in mock indignation. "You really know how to hurt a guy. I thought I raised you better than that."

"No," Huxley protests. "I do, I do."

"Oh, shut the fuck up," Cyrus yells. He jabs Bracken in the ribs with barrel of his gun.

Huxley isn't sure what's going on, he can't begin to divine Bracken's plan, but he wishes whatever it is, that it will just happen already. He tries to be brave, to be hard, to not cry and tremble and wail uncontrollably, but it's more difficult with every step they take toward what looks like their inevitable doom.

Haley smiles and laughs quietly to herself. "At least you're not going to die in that raggedy fucking poncho."

Huxley chuckles without thinking.

"Hey," Bracken says, his voice a low hiss. "I pull that off."

Haley and Huxley laugh and look at each other.

"No," Haley says. "No you don't.

Bracken looks legitimately hurt at the derision of his wardrobe. They march on in silence along the waterfront, past an endless line up of piers. Long neglected boats bob in the deep blue water that turns black as the sun sets and the night encroaches upon them from the edges.

"Here we are," Elwood says. They stop in front of an expansive dock. To one side sits a long, low structure that once sold nautical supplies. Inside the broken windows are rows of shelves, some looted and wiped bare, others still stocked like the store is merely closed for the evening and will open again in the morning. The shop connects to a warehouse in the back. A metal gate bars their access to the pier, and at the end a large white yacht bounces in the water.

"Not bad," Bracken says. "Your boat is way nicer than ours."

"I do like to travel in style."

"Speaking of style, you remember you beloved SS? She's rotting away in the middle of the desert somewhere. We did quite a number on her before we left. Remember, kid? That was fun, huh? What was her name? Margaret? Martha? Madonna?"

"Maggie," Elwood says through clenched teeth. "And I certainly didn't forget about her. I'm going to kill you a little extra, just for that." He takes a long, deliberate breath and closes his eyes. When he speaks again it is barely a whisper. "I loved that car."

"Can I please just shoot him now?" Cyrus asks. "This is getting old. I'm sick of listening to you two jerk each other off."

Huxley freezes for a second at the insult, expecting some swift outburst of violence from Elwood. He watches in anticipation, but nothing comes.

Elwood barely registers the slight. Cyrus must be the only one who can get away with talking like that to him, and Huxley wonders why.

"Relax, my good man," Elwood says, and pats him twice on the shoulder. "Don't you worry your pretty little head about it. You'll have plenty of time to work out your frustrations on your dear old friend."

In the midst of the back and forth banter Huxley hears it. A sound that makes the flesh along his spine crawl and the muscles in his arms and legs tense up into ropes. A low hiss, a rasp, so quiet it might otherwise blend in with the background white noise of the wind and the water at the docks. He scans the faces of the others to see if anyone else notices, but they all focus on the back and forth, waiting to see what happens next. He hears it again, but again he appears to be the only one.

Bracken, his hands still on top of his head, casts a quick sidelong glance, and Huxley knows he hears it too, and he knows that this is all part of his plan. That explains the bucket and the mirror, all of the intentional noise. Bracken was trying to attract them. Huxley inches closer to him.

Bracken talks louder and louder, speaking faster and becomes more and more insulting. As Bracken questions the sexual practices of Elwood's mother, something shifts in the shadows behind Elwood's crew, a ghost of movement. Huxley's heart jumps, his instinctive reactions kick in, and his body quivers with a surge of adrenalin. Poised to flee, he tries not to respond, tries not to betray the threat, and prepares to react to whatever happens.

The guard Huxley clubbed hangs back behind the rest of the gang. Leaning against the concrete wall of a low building, next to the entrance of an alley. He watches what happens in front of him, entertained by the whole situation, holding his held rifle low and easy. A hand and arm reach out from the confines of the alley, grab his throat, and jerk him off his feet and into the passage. His rifle flies out of his hands, clattering to the concrete, and he screams. The initial sound gurgles in his mouth and chokes off. More shrieks of pain and terror, guttural and visceral, follow from around the corner, and Huxley imagines the teeth of the infected digging into his flesh.

With the cry, Elwood and his team of goons spin automatically to see the threat. The soldiers all swing their weapons toward the mouth of the alley and the screams of their comrade. Infected pour out of the lane and the soldiers begin to fire and fall back.

Without hesitation, Bracken springs into action. He grabs Huxley, pulls him over, and in the same motion reaches inside his coat and pulls out the boy's revolver. Pushing Huxley and Haley toward the entrance to the store, Bracken raises the gun and fires. The bullet hits the guard closest to them in the back of the skull and his face explodes forward over the man in front of him, who turns just in time for Bracken to fire a second round into his eye.

Even as the two bodies fall to the ground, Bracken, Huxley, and Haley sprint toward the shelter of the store.

"Move," Bracken yells.

Huxley and Haley duck through the door and keep low, moving toward the rear of the store. Before he follows, Bracken pauses and fires one more shot. Elwood draws and fires as Bracken dives through the door. The bullet ricochets off of the wall and necessity compels Elwood to turn his attention back to the swarm of infected coming at him from the alley.

Yells and gunshots follow Bracken into the building. Huxley and Haley crouch behind an empty shelf in the back of the store. Bracken stays low and joins them. Garbage and boxes knocked off of the shelves in haste and panic litter the tiles of the floor.

"See," he says. "I told you I had a plan."

"Great plan," Haley says, rolling her eyes.

"Like clockwork." Bracken looks at Haley and smiles. He looks like he enjoys this. "As much fun as this is, we should probably get the hell out of here." Pointing, he says, "Back there, through those doors."

With the sound of the melee boiling outside, the trio scoots toward the back of the store. Haley pauses and picks up a long wooden pole with a metal hook and spike on the end. Bracken grabs a small, galvanized anchor with sharp triangles at the ends off of a low shelf. He swings it back and forth once and nods to himself. Huxley searches through the piles of items as they move. His foot kicks an orange plastic case and it clatters across the floor.

"Hey," he yells after Bracken and Haley. They keep moving. Quickly, he looks behind him, pauses, and opens the pops open the box. Inside sits what looks like an orange plastic gun, and four shotgun-size shells. "Hey, I found . . ." He trails off, curses under his breath, and follows them, stuffing the shells into his pocket, loading the gun and trying to watch where he is going.

Bracken pulls the door shut behind Huxley. They stand in a long, dark warehouse fabricated out of sheet metal. The noise from outside, the cries and yells of men and the hideous undead noises of the infected and the sound of gunshots, echo off of the walls inside the tinny space. Huxley snaps the gun shut and listens to the sounds rattle around, muted like they're far away.

Quickly, Haley leads them down the length of the warehouse. In the darkness, Huxley trips on something. Falling to the ground he hits his knee with a deep thud. Pain shoots up and down his leg. Bracken helps him up and he limps along with him as fast as he can, a grimace on his face.

Haley reaches the end of the warehouse first and throws her shoulder against the heavy door. It gives but doesn't break. She growls, steps back, and kicks the door with a heavy boot. Still it holds strong, and she kicks it again.

"She's kind of badass, huh?" Bracken says to Huxley, watching the display with a grin. The older man is actually having fun.

With a final guttural noise, Haley throws one last kick, the frame splinters, and the door slams open. She takes a deep breath, looks at Bracken and Huxley, and shrugs. "Door's open." She gestures with one hand. "Women and children first."

Bracken pokes his head through the door, pistol in one hand, anchor in the other, then steps out. He motions for the others to follow him. They move away from the sound of fighting and screams. They stick close to the walls of buildings while they jog in the direction of the dock where they left their boat.

"Where are we going?" Haley asks.

"We have a boat," Bracken says. "Well, we have a dingy."

"A dingy?"

"Luxury watercrafts are hard to come by these days. Let's go."

They round a corner and a find a pair of stray infected. Without pausing, Bracken swings his arm and the anchor in a wide, overhand arc. It connects with the monster's head and imbeds in the skull. He yanks it free with a moist ripping and cracking sound. Haley swings her pole. The butt slaps against the neck of the other infected and it topples to the ground with a roar. She stands over the creature as it snarls and reaches for her. With both hands she drives the metal spike through the face and into its brain. For good measure she twists the pole before pulling it out.

The whole encounter is over so quickly they barely have to slow down.

Ducking behind a tall green dumpster for shelter, they find one of Elwood's guards already there, cowering, a dark, wet stain down the front of his pants.

"Freeze, freeze," he says. He shakes, an obvious bite mark on his arm, and he points his pistol at Bracken. His hand shakes so bad Huxley expects him to drop the gun. "Don't fucking move."

Bracken holds his hands up and slowly approaches the young man. "It's okay. I don't give two fucks about you. We just want to get the fuck out of here, same as you. If you don't mind, we'll be on our way."

Huxley looks away from the standoff. Over his shoulder he sees a collection of infected heading in their direction.

Bracken's eyes flip away from the soldier to the encroaching mass. "Sorry, pal, don't have time for this. If you don't mind, I'm going to go fight with these undead fuckers for a bit." He nods and turns away. "But I'll be back."

The guard looks past Bracken and mutters something to himself that might be a prayer, closes his eyes, and shoots himself in the head. His brains paint the wall behind him. Meaty chunks cling to brick and gravity pulls them slowly toward the ground, leaving streaks behind. Huxley cocks his head and looks at the scene. His only thought is that this makes him feel nothing and that makes him feel strange, like he should have some emotion at seeing a man blow off his own head, but he can't conjure anything more than a slight twinge of envy.

Without missing a beat, Bracken grabs the dead man's pistol, and tosses it to Haley, who catches it. In the same motion, shoots the infected closest to her in the head. It topples over into a limp pile and the others continue to advance over the corpse of their companion.

The trio falls back and Haley continues to shoot until the clip is empty. She tucks it into her belt at the base of her spine and steps forward, swinging her pole. Bracken buries his anchor in an infected skull and knocks another one back with a straight kick to the midsection. It stumbles back into another creature. They snarl at each other and reach forward.

Huxley hangs back as Bracken and Haley fight. He wants to help, but isn't sure what to do. Something grabs him from behind. He spins just in time to put his hands up and block the jaws of the infected that has a hold of him. He lets out a scream as he presses against the decaying face. The skin is blue and torn and softer than he thought, and his fingers press into the spongy flesh. His face lurches so close he can smell the rancid stench of its breath, hot like rotten meat. The creature bends Huxley backward, forcing him to the ground, clawing and snapping at his face.

Bracken tussles with an infected when he hears the boy's cry. "Huxley," he shouts, and kicks the fetid creature away from him. He takes one long stride and dives over the top of Huxley, knocking the creature back, off of the child. The anchor falls to the ground with a clatter.

Huxley rolls out of the way and regains himself enough to look over and see Bracken grab the infected beneath the chin and force its head back. With a visceral cry, a brutal, feral sound, Bracken wrenches the head backward with a grotesque crunch. The jaw still works, but the body goes limp. Bracken grabs a fistful of stringy hair and beats the loose head against the concrete until it dies completely.

Huxley starts to breath, but another creature grabs Bracken from behind.

Spinning onto his back, he kicks at the knee of the creature. The joint folds back the wrong way and it collapses on top of Bracken. They struggle and it forces its mouth toward Bracken's neck. He grabs the creature by the throat, throws his weight to one side, and rolls over on top with a mangled yell.

Huxley rushes forward, picks up the discarded anchor, and swings it with every bit of strength he can muster. One metal triangle crashes through the forehead and the monster wilts to the ground. He looks up to see another infected, the last one in this group, heading toward them, reaching for them with a hand without a thumb.

Haley's rod bursts through its chest. She pulls back, the hook latches on to the clavicle, and it can't continue forwards. It claws madly at them, but she keeps it at a safe distance. Bracken stands, jerks the anchor out of dead skull, swats away the infected's hand, swings his weapon, and one more body falls.

Haley stands over the corpse, puts her foot in the middle of its back, and yanks the boat hook out of the body with the sound of breaking bones. They stand there, a pile of corpses at their feet, breathing heavy.

"Are you okay?" Huxley asks.

"Let's go," Bracken says.

Haley looks at him. "Are you . . ."

"Let's go," he says again and starts toward the boat, not waiting for them, and not giving an answer.

Bracken leads the way, moving at a trot. Haley runs next to Huxley, looking back and forth between her two companions. They pause at the end of the appropriate dock.

"And here we are," Bracken says.

"Here we are, indeed," Elwood says, stepping out from a shadow. Somehow his clothes remain meticulously clean and free from stains. His pistol is gone, but he doesn't have a mark on him. Standing at his shoulder, Cyrus isn't nearly so tidy. Viscera covers him from head to toe, gleaming in the final strands of light. His eyes burn with a fury and a wide smile cuts across his face, like he lives for moments like this. He aims a shotgun at Bracken.

"Are you fucking serious?" Bracken says, a look of disbelief on his face. "All I want is one little fucking break. Jesus." He seems frustrated with their predicament, more so than frightened or concerned.

"Can't thank you enough for killing all of those undead fucks," Elwood says. "I appreciate it. Now, if you don't mind dropping . . ." he motions with his hand and Bracken lets the pistol and anchor clatter to the ground. The chrome weapon rattles against the concrete and Huxley stares at it longingly, but it's too close to Elwood to grab.

Elwood sneers. "Cyrus, would you do the honors?"

"Gladly." Cyrus steadies himself and pulls the trigger.

Huxley flinches, but the only sound is a hollow click as the hammer falls on an empty chamber.

"Oops," Cyrus says. He shrugs with mischief in his eyes. "Had you going there for a second, didn't I?" He tosses the empty shotgun to the side.

Before the weapon hits the ground, Bracken charges forward, howling like a wild beast. He buries his shoulder in Cyrus's midsection and tackles him to the ground with an audible groan. He rears back and rains downs punches and elbows. Cyrus's head snaps back and thuds against the concrete; his nose breaks, flattening across his face. Blood pours out and coats Bracken's fists.

Elwood stands to the side, arms crossed. He watches the two men grapple on the ground, almost amused, an expression of curiosity on his face. With a wry grin, he looks at the gun on the ground in front of him and up at Huxley, taunting him, daring him to try.

Cyrus slips his head to the side as Bracken throws another punch that connects with the pavement. He traps Bracken's arm, rotates his body, and throws his legs over Bracken's head. He arches his back and tries to break his arm. Bracken twists, trying to roll out and free his arm. As his arm flexes in an unnatural direction, he bites Cyrus's leg. Cyrus winces but keeps his hold on the arm.

Haley makes a move towards Elwood and the gun on the ground, but stops and turns back to the flailing pile when she notices Bracken in trouble. She cocks her arm and throws her rod like a spear. It hits Cyrus in the neck and his grip slackens enough for Bracken to free his arm. In a flash he is back on top of Cyrus, traps one arm beneath him and grips his throat in his hand. Cyrus gurgles and slaps weakly at Bracken and pries at the fingers locked around his esophagus.

With an animal yell, Bracken sinks his fingers in and pulls out, tearing out a chunk of Cyrus's windpipe. Cyrus sputters and burbles, pawing at where his throat used to be, trying to keep a hold on his breath and blood. Desperate for air, his eyes go wide and his body heaves and writhes.

"You just got Daltoned, motherfucker," Bracken yells and punches Cyrus in the face one final time.

Elwood steps quickly over to Bracken's discarded revolver and bends to pick it up. When he stands, Huxley points the bright orange gun at him.

"A flare gun? Really?" Elwood says. He laughs. "You're a resourceful little guy, I'll give you that."

Bracken rolls off of Cyrus's body as it flops, dying on the concrete. He doesn't stand up, watching from the ground. Elwood smirks and points the revolver at Bracken. He opens his mouth to speak, for one final bit of mocking banter before he puts a bullet through his enemy.

Before he can utter a syllable, Huxley fires a flare directly into Elwood's chest. The burst of light from the end of the orange gun surprises the boy almost as much as it surprises Elwood. In an instant, flames engulf his spotless robes. He cries out in pain and terror. Flailing his arms, batting at the fire, he drops the revolver. It skitters across the concrete and comes to a stop next to Bracken.

He picks up the gun and aims it at Elwood. The burning man drops to his knees, tearing at his face. His screams echo in the increasing dusk. Bracken watches him writhe and suffer for a moment longer, a curious expression on his face, then fires a round into Elwood's skull. The cries cease and to body slumps to the ground, silent and still.

"That's for putting me in that damn arena," Bracken growls.

Bracken rises and walks over to the body and stares down at it. The flames dance and cast shadows across his face. Creases and lines crisscross Bracken's face like someone drew a spider web on him. He inhales, holds it, exhales, and puts another bullet into Elwood. He looks up at Huxley and Haley. They stare back at him. No one says anything.

Finally, Bracken speaks. "Let's go. Boat. Now."

CHAPTER 18

Bracken rows them out into the bay. Huxley and Haley sit side by side in the back of the boat. The boy leans his head against Haley's shoulder. She wraps her arm around his shoulders and both of them watch Bracken.

Bracken stares past them, at the ghost of a city receding into the darkness. Huxley tries to read his expression, but he can't find anything solid or specific to grab hold of. Whatever language is written across the older man's face, it's one Huxley still can't read.

They don't talk. The oarlocks creak with each stroke and the sound fills the air. Water slaps at the bow of the boat as they cut through. Over the top of them the wind howls and they hunker down low, letting it pass high above their bowed heads.

Once they're a safe distance from shore, Bracken slows his pace. His movements are smooth and even, but any ferocity or urgency evaporates when it becomes apparent nothing follows them. There's no one left. He rows and rows, bending forward, pulling back, slicing the blades through the water. The rhythm soothes Huxley. Between that and the gentle rocking, he drifts off to sleep.

Somewhere in the middle of the bay, it's impossible to tell where in the night, Bracken stops rowing and pulls the oars into the boat. The small craft bounces and rolls with the waves and wind. Huxley wakes and sits up. For a moment Bracken watches his companions and they watch him. No one speaks.

Bracken leans forward with his elbows on his knees and rubs his hands together. He picks up Huxley's pack from the floor of the boat. It takes a moment of rummaging around inside, but he eventually finds what he's after and removes a small, tightly wrapped package, the parcel he picked up from Lexi. He spins it over in his hands a couple of times as if trying to make sense of something, trying to wrap his mind around what this one specific thing means. Failing to find any reason, his head slumps down and hang limp between his shoulders.

Finally, he raises his head and tosses the package to his left, into the water. It lands with a splash and a bit of foam that gleams in the moonlight and quickly sinks below the surface and fades from view.

"What was that?" Huxley asks. "What was this all about?"

Bracken looks at him but doesn't respond. He turns, grabs the oars, and starts rowing again.

"What was that?" Huxley asks, looking up at Haley.

She smiles down at him and pulls him tightly to her.

Huxley opens his mouth, about to ask again. He looks at Haley, looks at her watching Bracken, and then he too looks at his guardian. He closes his mouth and nods to himself, so slight a nod that he's not sure if it's a conscious act or simply his rocking with the motion of the boat. Some things, he decides, are better left unknown.

At dawn Bracken heaves the oars one final time and they glide up alongside a floating dock. It may be the same dock they set sail from, but Huxley isn't sure, they all look the same to him. Bracken ties the boat off to a cleat as if they're coming back and helps Huxley and Haley out of the boat. Huxley wonders if the action of securing the boat is necessary, if there will ever be cause for anyone to use it again, and he briefly wants to unfasten the line and set the small craft free. It served their purpose well and freedom feels like a just reward.

In the growing light Huxley sees blood on Bracken's arm, soaking through the sleeve of his coat. He stares at it as Bracken climbs out of the boat after them, and a shiver creeps up and over his entire body. Bracken notices the gaze and turns his body, placing the injured arm on the opposite side from the boy.

"Time to move," he says, slinging the pack onto his shoulders and nudging Huxley down the length of the dock toward land.

Huxley looks over his shoulder. Despite the chill of the morning, a layer of sweat coats Bracken's face. He takes rapid, shallow breaths. Maybe it's only the result of a long night of rowing without sleep, the exertion of the journey, and his body is simply trying to recover. He hopes, but fear and reason overtake any optimism. Hope didn't help his father.

Haley touches his shoulder. She places herself between the two and he turns his eyes forward again.

After a few hours of walking north, they stop. Bracken's condition has visibly worsened. His skin hangs pale and pallid and his face looks molded out of sweaty wax.

"Here," he says, handing a can to Huxley. He takes great pains to hide the wounded arm. "You need to eat something." He tousles the boy's hair and looks at Haley. The two of them walk away from Huxley as he tears into a can of salty green beans.

Bracken and Haley stand in the distance and talk. They glance quickly over at Huxley and look away. Momentarily the meet each other's gazes and fall silent, but again they look quickly in the other direction. Huxley tries to watch without making it obvious what he's doing, trying to figure out what they are saying by the way they stand, by how they move their hands, by the expression on their faces. He has ideas about their conversation.

When they come back, the look on Bracken's face confirms his fears.

"Hey, kid," Bracken says. He crouches down and looks Huxley in the eyes. For a moment he remains quiet, searching for the words. "I don't know what else to say, so I'll just say it. I have to go now."

Huxley swallows hard. His jaw quivers, but he clamps it down and wills his eyes to hold back their tears. Instead of saying anything he nods and looks at the ground. He looks up as Bracken speaks again. His words rattle.

"Haley here." He nods in her direction. "She's going to take care of you from now on." He coughs and inhales a sharp breath.

"When did you get bitten?" Huxley asks.

"Back there someplace."

"You don't know for sure that you're going to change, right? It can't kill everybody, can it?"

Bracken smiles. "Everyone's heard the stories, remember? Someone claims they were bitten and didn't turn. Someone has a brother or a cousin or a friend someplace. And maybe. Maybe that's true. I don't know." He glances down then back up. "But that isn't the way this story ends." He coughs into his fist and spits a viscous mouthful to the side. "It's already going to work on me pretty hard." He shakes his head.

They stare at each other. There isn't anything more to say and they both know it. Huxley wants to beg and plead and cry and grab him and hold onto him and not let him go, ever. He wants to curse and scream and fight until, somehow, this isn't happening, until, some way, everything works out in the end. This is what he wants. But he knows that can't happen. He knows that isn't how the world works, and that nothing he can do will change that fact.

Bracken stands. He walks over to Haley and takes off his jacket and the layers underneath it. He bends down and removes his boots. Soon he stands barefoot and naked to the waist. His various scars are bright pink in the sun, almost glowing. He empties his pockets onto the pile at his feet.

"You guys will need all of this at some point."

He pops open the revolver and checks the bullets. "Last one," he says and tucks the gun into his belt at the base of his spine.

He looks at Haley. She stands to one side, arms crossed, eyes wet and red. He nods and walks over to Huxley. He bends down and rests his forehead gently on the top of the boy's head and squeezes the back of his neck reassuringly.

Huxley feels the radiating heat of Bracken's fever through his hair.

Bracken kisses him on the top of the head. "Stay good, kid."

He walks away. Huxley watches him. He doesn't look back. He disappears.

That's when the tears come. They come quietly, but stream down his cheeks and drip off of his chin. Tremors run through his small body and he balls up his fists, digging his fingernails into the palms of his hands. The sharp edges pierce into his flesh and he stares at the last place Bracken was, like he will reappear, like this is all some sort of twisted joke. But he knows it isn't, he knows this is the end. He wipes his face and forces his eyes to stop their crying. There isn't room in his life for tears anymore.

Haley comes over and touches Huxley on the shoulder. He looks at her, nods, and rises without a word.

They collect their supplies and walk away, still heading north.

The echo of the single gunshot carries on the wind and follows.

ACKNOWLEDGEMENTS

I've never done this before and I'm terrified I'll miss someone. Just know that, if I don't mention you by name, you mean nothing to me. Kidding, I love, I love. Here we go.

Melissa Warner for putting up with my constant nonsense, and the Small Dogs for the constant judgment.

My parents and sister for supporting me no matter what idiotic, wholly unprofitable endeavors I embark upon.

Lish McBride for writing times, general encouragement, and occasional, much-appreciated cold slaps of reality related to the publishing industry. Ramon Isao for post-workshop whiskey drinking, general writing nerdery, and enthusiasm.

All my UNO people: Bryan Camp, Nick Mainieri, Danny Goodman, Nathan Feuerberg, Eva Langston, Tawni Waters, Casey Lafante, Eric Parker, Sonja Livingston, Joseph and Amanda Boyden, Matt Roberts, Meredith Allen, David Dykes, and anyone I got drunk and talked writing with in Mexico. There were a bunch of you.

My thesis committee for helping me birth this monster: Jim Grimsley, Steven "Mansas" Church, and Adam Braver.

Lesley Sabga for the insightful editing notes. Olivia Raymond, all the folks at Aurelia Leo, and you for taking a chance on this.

ABOUT THE AUTHOR

 Born and raised in the Pacific Northwest, Brent McKnight is a graduate of the University of New Orleans Low-Residency MFA program. Over the years, he's worked construction, clerked at a convenience store, moved thousands of pounds of pet supplies early in the morning, and cleaned up dog poop professionally. He lives in Seattle with his partner and a pack of judgmental small dogs named after dead action movie stars. Find his film writing at www.thelastthingisee.com.

CPSIA information can be obtained
at www.ICGtesting.com
Printed in the USA
LVHW111448051119
636416LV00005B/53/P

9 781946 024619